A Stranger
in the
Shadows

A Stranger
in the
Shadows

Keith Russell

First paperback edition 2024

ISBN 979-8-218-40354-6 (paperback)

Cover by: Jennifer Meller

Published by Keith Russell

Keith196734@yahoo.com

For you, Kayla. Without your dedication and endless commitment to our family, I would never have been able to chase my dreams.

Chapter One

0 Hours Missing

Kevin's eyes sprang open, a smile stretching across his face as he reached to silence his alarm. He threw off the top sheet he used as a blanket, scooped up the first crumpled shirt he found on the floor, and tugged it on. It was early, early for a thirteen-year-old boy on the first day of summer break, but he had things to do.

He swapped his cotton shorts for jeans and crept toward the door, his ear pressed against the cool hardwood door. Not a sound. Silently, he turned the knob, holding the tension as he pulled the door open, releasing it slowly so it wouldn't click and give him away. He slipped into the hall, each step as light as he could make it. If caught, his mother would no doubt ensnare him in some chore or, worse, saddle him with his little brother, Mike. Kevin had just turned thirteen and finally had the freedom of a teenager. The summer of '79 promised to be the best he'd ever had, and he wasn't about to let Mike ruin it.

Kevin stepped around all the creaky boards until he made it to the carpeted living room. The front door was just within reach when his mother yelled, "Kevin, is that you?" Before he could answer, she said, "You better be home by six for dinner, and take Mike with you."

He stopped dead in his tracks, hanging his head back, groaning. Mike was only eight and had no business hanging out with Danny and him. Kevin could hear him now: I'm hot, when can we eat, I'm thirsty, I wanna go home. Mike would just get under their feet and would certainly blab to their parents about any mischief that Kevin might get up to.

With his head still hanging back, he yelled, "Mom, do I have to?"

"No," a glimmer of relief bubbled up inside of him, only to burst as she said, "you don't have to take him, but you can't leave the house unless you do."

Mike stepped around the corner, his crooked grin begging for a smack. Kevin balled his hands into fists. If he hit his brother, he'd be lucky to ever get out of the house again. That is, if he somehow managed to scrape himself off the floor after his father found out. Visions of a summer spent pulling weeds and doing chores immediately changed his tune. Swallowing his anger, he sighed and said through gritted teeth, "Fine, Mom."

Kevin gripped the doorknob, not quite ready to let go of his irritation. "Let's go, and you better keep up."

What a horrible start to the summer. Kevin peddled his bike faster down the road than he would have if he were alone. Over his shoulder, Mike's baby legs struggled to keep up, but that was his problem.

Kevin was due to meet Danny in, he checked his watch, thirty minutes at the ball field. It was still a few miles away, and he was not about to let his twerp of a brother make him late. Not that Danny would care too much if he was; he'd care more about Mike being there—period.

Danny and Kevin had been best friends since they were four. Technically, they were the same age, but Danny was a few months older and never let Kevin forget it. Until about five years ago, they had lived next door to each other, but Kevin's parents had upped and moved out into the country. But a few miles couldn't keep them apart.

The ball field came into view and Kevin turned off the dirt road down the grassy hill leading to the field. Once on the other side, he hopped off his bike and leaned it against a bench beside the gravel parking lot. The humidity only intensified the scorching heat of the sun, which would only get worse as the day went on. He plopped down, sweat already beading on his brow, and from the heat searing his cheeks, he guessed they were red.

Mike lazily tossed his bike in the grass, one pedal still spinning as he slid onto the bench beside Kevin. Mike huffed like he'd run a marathon. "Got any water?"

Kevin rolled his eyes. "Do I look like I have some water?" He folded his arms, and the pair sat in silence until, a few minutes later, Danny came plowing into the parking lot, his bright-yellow shirt glowing in the sunshine.

Danny slid his bike to a stop, nearly spraying them with gravel. "What's he doing here?"

Kevin shrugged and said, "My mom wouldn't let me leave the house without him."

"Maybe we should take him to the cemetery and let Old Man Cecil have him," Danny said as he dropped his bike and stepped toward Mike. He rustled Mike's hair before shoving his head. Mike whined "Ow," even though it probably hadn't hurt.

"Come on, Danny," Kevin said, getting to his feet. "Leave him alone. I don't need him telling my parents you were picking on him."

"Fine," Danny said as he flopped to the ground and picked at blades of grass. When he looked up, a trace of mischief had replaced his disappointment. "You guys aren't going to believe what happened to me coming here."

Mike, all wide-eyed and eager, said, "What happened?"

Kevin just looked at Danny skeptically and braced himself for one of Danny's overdramatic stories.

"You know how I gotta pass the cemetery to get here?"

Mike nodded.

"Well, Old Man Cecil was out there."

Kevin rolled his eyes, guessing where this was going.

"He tried to kill me!"

Mike gasped, and Kevin scoffed. "You're full of it. He did not."

"I'm telling you," Danny protested, the excitement causing his voice to crack slightly. "I was riding by, and he tried to kill me, and when I got away, poof," he wiggled his fingers, "he just disappeared."

"People don't just disappear. You read too many comics. And if he tried to kill you, why aren't you goin' to the cops?"

Mike fidgeted, looking even more wide-eyed and nervous than before. Danny doubled down. "You know how when you ride by there you kind of coast by as quiet as you can until you get to the gate, and then you put it into hyperdrive?"

Kevin nodded. All the kids did this.

"Well, I was just at the spot where I was ready to kick it into high gear and speed past the gates when Cecil jumped out from behind a tree and stood at the edge of the road, swinging his shovel at me. I blazed by like my backside was on fire, and when I looked over my shoulder, he was gone."

Mike whimpered, "I want to go home."

"You aren't going home," Kevin said to him. "There is nothing to worry about. People don't disappear. He must have hidden or something. Besides, you can't believe a thing Danny says. He once told me he saw Farrah Fawcett at Moss's Stop and Grab. I asked Mr. Moss about it, and he just laughed."

"OK," Danny threw his hands up, "that was a lie, but I'm telling the truth now."

Kevin just shook his head, and although Mike still looked nervous, he didn't ask to go home again, so Kevin quickly changed the subject. "We have to get out to the tree house; I want to finish it this summer."

For the last two summers, Kevin and Danny had been building a tree house out in the woods, but this year, they would finally finish. Since the boys knew nothing of construction, their previous attempts were less than stable. But each year they learned more, and Kevin just knew this time they'd get it right. During the fall and winter months, they had collected boards and nails from junkyards and construction sites and taken them out to the tree house. Now that school was out, they had all the time in the world to work on it.

Danny agreed. "We better get going."

They each picked up their bikes and rode off down the winding country road. A quarter of an hour later, they pulled off the smooth paved road onto a dirt road that cut through a cotton field. Amid the relentless heat, many cotton shoots were already up to their knees. Kevin wanted to let his hand pass through the deep-green sea of leaves as he rode but knew it would be a mistake. It was harder to bike on the dirt road than the paved. Kevin's legs burned with the effort, though he kept up a fast pace, unwilling to be the slowest of the group. Soon, they were jumping off their bikes and running toward the pile of supplies they had amassed.

The old white oak they had selected for the tree house was perfect. Its limbs fountained out, giving them easy places to lay the foundation. The tree was about two miles off Vildo Road, near a cotton field, just far enough into the woods to be hidden, but not far enough that they were likely to get lost.

Mr. Waller owned the cotton fields and most of the land in this area of the county. Two summers ago, Kevin was riding his bike through one of the fields in search of a good spot to build the tree house when Mr.

Waller saw him. It didn't take long before his father received a call about the damaged crops. Kevin had spent three whole weeks helping in the fields to pay for damages. Mr. Waller had asked him why he was out there, and when Kevin told him about the tree house, he said he wouldn't mind them building a tree house on the condition that they didn't wreck any of the crops.

Mismatched boards were piled up against a tree beside a rusted-out toolbox that had been Danny's dad's before he had died.

"Woah!" Mike hopped off his bike, again letting it fall, and rushed to climb up the ladder he and Danny had built.

Kevin had never brought Mike out there, which accounted for their slow progress, since it was hard to leave the house without him. All things considered, they'd been doing a bang-up job. Although it still needed a lot of work. The walls were a patchwork of the best lumber they could scavenge, and some of the boards had fallen during the winter.

"I wouldn't do that if I were you." Danny stopped Mike from climbing by grabbing his shoulder. "I need to fix it first. Some of the boards came loose, and if you put your weight on it, they'll pop right out. And I don't need you dying and haunting our treehouse."

Kevin laughed. "He's right, Mike. You can go up later. Right now, why don't you start pulling nails from those boards and get them straightened out?"

Mike's face crinkled, but one sharp look from Kevin and he silenced his sulk.

After a few hours of working in the hot summer sun, the boys were sweating buckets.

Mike slumped to the ground, all red faced. "I'm hungry. When are we going? I want to eat."

Kevin's stomach was growling, and he'd heard Danny's rumbling too. "Dad has credit over at Moss's; we can get something to eat there."

"Sounds good to me! I am starving." Danny wiped sweat from his brow with the back of his hand, the hammer still in his fist.

They each walked over to their bikes, but before Kevin mounted, he said, "Hey, Mike, why don't you stay here? We're almost out of nails, and if you keep working while we go pick up the food, then we will be able to get more done after lunch."

"No way," shouted Mike. "I am not staying here by myself."

Why couldn't he just shut up and do as he was told?

"You'll be fine," Kevin told him. "Danny and I are faster riders, and you will just slow us down."

"Why can't you go by yourself and Danny stay?"

"Because I need his help to carry the food back."

Mike stomped his foot and threw down his bike. "Fine," he shouted. "I'll stay, but you better hurry."

Kevin and Danny started off through the field toward the highway. Kevin peered over his shoulder at the sight of Mike walking around picking up nails growing smaller until they turned. A few minutes later, the boys parked their bikes beneath the wooden post sign that read Moss's Stop and Grab.

It was a just a run-of-the-mill country store that sold everything from milk and bread to live fish bait. Kevin and Danny tromped onto the porch under the gaze of three older men who always seemed to hang around Moss's store. They never seemed to buy anything, just talking about the weather, telling stories, or reading the paper.

A little bell on the top of the door jingled as they entered. No matter how many times he had been in the store, that bell always startled Kevin. Mr. Moss sat on a stool behind the counter beside the cash register. He folded his paper in half and peered over at them. Kevin reluctantly pulled his eyes from the wall of candy and cigarettes behind the man to greet him.

"Afternoon, Mr. Moss."

The man nodded. "What are you two doing so far from home?" He was hard of hearing and shouted. Kevin winced.

Danny yelled so the old man could hear, "We're working out behind the Waller farm, in the woods behind the cotton field. Been building a tree house out there."

Mr. Moss squinted his eyes and lifted his head. "You boys been out there the past few nights?"

Kevin guessed some teenagers had been out there causing trouble and didn't want to get wrapped up in the blame. "No, sir!"

Danny added, "Today is the first day we have been out this summer."

"Well, there's been a lot of activity out there the last few nights." He scratched at the white stubble on his face. "Lights and sounds coming from that area up till one o'clock in the morning."

Danny shrugged. "Couldn't have been us. We have to be home about dark or our moms will have our heads."

Mr. Moss chuckled and got to his feet. "Well, as long as you young 'uns are staying out of trouble and Mr. Waller knows you're back there."

"Yes, sir," the boys said in unison.

His expression softened, the accusation disappearing from his weathered face. "Alright, then, what can I do for you boys today?"

Mr. Moss's questioning had momentarily dampened Kevin's gnawing hunger pains, but they were swift to return.

"We have been out working all day and forgot our lunches. Think we could get a few sandwiches and drinks on my dad's credit?" Kevin tried to keep his voice even, but it wavered slightly.

Mr. Moss arched his brow. "Does your dad know?"

The lie came easily enough. "Yes, sir."

Truth be told, his dad didn't know, but Kevin was sure he wouldn't even look at the charges. His dad was a machine operator at the Waller Cotton Mill. Shift work was thirsty work. Odds were if he noticed the charge at all, he'd chalk it up to a drunken purchase.

Mr. Moss stepped over to the cooler that held the meats. "What you want?"

Kevin smiled and tried to keep from appearing relieved. "Three ham and cheese sandwiches, all with mustard."

"Three?" Mr. Moss said, looking between Kevin and Danny.

"My little brother Mike is back at the tree house," Kevin said. Then he walked over and grabbed three Cokes from the cooler. The bell above the door chimed, and Kevin looked to see who was coming in, worrying for just a moment it would be his father. Instead, a greasy-haired man was leaving.

Probably one of the field workers.

Danny elbowed him and nodded toward the magazine rack, grinning; peeking out from behind an issue of *Gun and Ammo* was the cover of *Easy Rider*. A sexy blonde was naked from the waist up, except her chest was covered by the thick, tattooed arm of a man. The boys giggled and turned back to the counter as Mr. Moss brought out their sandwiches. A few minutes later, with their sandwiches, chips, and Cokes in paper sacks. They said thank you, ran out of the store, and jumped on their bikes.

It took a few minutes for Kevin to figure out the proper carrying technique. Not having a place to put the bags made it a little difficult to carry everything. Once he had it under control, they were off and racing each other back toward the cotton fields.

The highway bottomed out from the rolling hill to a place that was long and flat. A car meandered down the road, still a ways off from them. Why were they driving so slow? Most people barreled down that flat stretch.

A few seconds later, Kevin locked up his breaks so hard that the bag fell from his hand. Danny had stopped too and whispered, "That's him."

The car was a 1960 Dodge Dart, and at one time it had been white, but now it was mostly eaten up with rust and blanketed with dirt. Kevin scrambled to pick up the contents of his bag off the road.

Danny looked panic-stricken. Maybe some of his story had been true. "What do we do?" His tone betrayed his fear.

Kevin stood up and mounted his bike again. "Nothing we can do. Let's just get back."

Danny nodded; his Adam's apple bobbed with a gulp. Kevin pedaled slowly down the road. As Cecil neared, his car slowed even more. A person could have walked faster than the car was going. His cadaverous face turned and followed them as they rolled by. No smile, not a glimmer of life on his face. Just a cold, hard stare that made the hairs on the back of Kevin's neck stand on end, sending a shiver down his back despite the heat of the day.

In his fear, he had stopped pedaling until his bike nearly tipped over from lack of momentum. Once they were past his taillights, the roar of Cecil's engine filled the air, sending crows flying. Kevin looked over his shoulder as the car disappeared down the highway.

"Man!" Danny yelled. "He is one creepy old man." Kevin agreed and kept looking back to make sure the car wasn't turning around. Good thing he made Mike stay at the tree house. This whole thing would have made him wet his shorts.

"He has to die soon; I heard he was old as dirt when my parents were growing up," Kevin said.

Danny laughed. "I'm telling you, that man is a ghost. Who lives in a graveyard, anyway? How creepy is that?"

Everyone in town knew Cecil, the caretaker at the cemetery, and no one had a good thing to say about him. Kevin wasn't sure that there was anything wrong with him, but something wasn't right.

"My dad says the county has a house for the caretaker downtown, but Cecil prefers to live in the shed at the cemetery."

Danny curled his lips back in disgust and shook his head.

Soon they were turning off the highway and onto the dirt road that cut through the cotton fields to the woods. Danny smirked and yelled, "Race ya!" then put the pedal to the metal. Kevin cursed under his breath and pedaled as fast as he could the final stretch to the tree house. His muscles burned with the effort, but soon they were side by side, sliding their bikes to a stop, throwing dirt in the air.

"Beat ya," Danny gloated.

Kevin rolled his eyes. "Did not, we tied."

Danny just shook his head.

"Hey, Mike," Kevin yelled, "food's here." He rolled his bike over to a nearby tree, letting it lean against it. When he turned around, he realized the pile of boards looked exactly as they had before he left. "Aw come on, Mike. What did you do the whole time we were gone?" He looked around but didn't see him.

Kevin yelled louder, "Mike, get down here!" he shouted. Kevin assumed he had climbed up after they left.

He looked over at Danny, who only shrugged. "Hurry up before I eat your sandwich," Danny jokingly called.

"I knew bringing him was a mistake," Kevin mumbled. He huffed over to the tree and climbed up the ladder. Peering inside, he was surprised to see it was empty.

"He's not here," Kevin said as he climbed down.

"I don't see his bike anywhere. The little shit must have gone home."

"Great, now I'm going to get a lickin' because he couldn't stay put."

"We'll split his food and get to work. We better get as much done as we can today. If you get grounded, it's gonna set us back."

It didn't take long for Kevin and Danny to finish their food.

Danny stood up and walked to a tree to relieve his bladder. Kevin got to his feet to get to work when Danny turned, still zipping up his pants. "Looks like you get to straighten the nails."

Disappointed, Kevin protested, "What? No way."

Danny lifted his arms up as if to say, I didn't make the rules. Instead, he said, "It's the youngest's job, which means you."

Kevin grumbled as he pulled a plank from the pile. Four nails jutted out from one end like fangs. "I don't care what mom says; he's not coming back."

They worked for several more hours. As the heat increased, they took off their shirts and let the hot southern sun soak into their skin. As the day wore on, Kevin's muscles ached, unaccustomed to manual labor, but he'd never let Danny know that.

When the sun dipped behind the trees, Kevin said, "It's time to get going. Mom said I had to be home by six. If I'm late on top of the stunt Mike pulled, I'll be spending all day tomorrow in the garden pulling weeds."

Kevin tugged on his shirt, taking note of the progress they had made.

Danny must have been doing the same. "Not much done today."

"Spent half the day fixin' nails," Kevin replied. "In a few days, we should have the roof and floor patched up."

Headed home, Kevin was too tired to do much talking, but Danny kept going on about Teresa Hatchett. Teresa was in their grade but didn't live in town.

"I'm gonna marry her one day," Danny said dreamily, no doubt thinking about her green eyes and black hair.

Kevin shook his head. Danny had never even spoken to her. "Please, you know she will never go out with you. Besides, I heard she's dating a guy in high school."

Danny seemed unconcerned by this, still looking as happy as a fool. "I bet you by the time summer is over, she will be going out with me." Danny grinned.

Kevin laughed out loud. "Not a chance that will ever happen, but you keep dreaming."

Soon they came to the intersection where Danny would have to go right and Kevin left to get home. They stopped briefly, both of them propping themselves up on one leg.

Kevin asked, "Tomorrow at eight?"

"Yep, as long as I don't oversleep," Danny said with a laugh.

They both pedaled slowly away, Danny yelling, "Later!"

And Kevin answering, "Later!"

The closer Kevin got to his house, the more his worry about what Mike may have told their mom grew. He played over what his mom would say and calculated his defense, but soon gave up. He would just take whatever trouble came his way.

Leaning left, Kevin guided his bike onto his road. In the distance, he could just make out his house. Relief eased some of his worry. His dad's pickup was nowhere in sight. His father, John Franklin, was well known in their little town of Everett for being three things: a hard worker, one hell of a handyman, and a mean drunk. Though his dad could fix just about anything from a broken car to the handmade oil rig in the middle of Mr. Vincent's corn field, he was useless once he'd had a few, and he seldom only had a few. He drank from the time he got off work till he passed out at home. Many times, his dad would come home so drunk that he would bump into the porch with his truck as he pulled in. Then, he would storm inside, sometimes growling about one thing or another, flip the power breaker, and fall into bed, leaving everyone to sit in the dark. No one dared to turn it back on. It was common knowledge that when dad was home, it was best to stay out of sight. Luckily, for Kevin and Mike, their older brother Steve took most of the heat from their dad.

As he pulled up the drive, Kevin rode his bike around the back. There he jumped off the bike, which continued to roll before wobbling and tipping over into the grass. Kevin eyed his watch as he opened the back door, smiling because he had just a minute to spare before six. A hot wall hit him, carrying the smell of fried chicken. It made his mouth water, and his stomach growl.

Kevin walked down the hall toward his bedroom. Rock music blaring from Steve's room as he passed. He better turn that down before dad gets home unless he's looking for a fight. Kevin sighed, annoyed to see his bedroom door opened. He hated when people went into his room when he wasn't home. Inside, the clothes that cluttered his floor that morning were missing. Kevin closed the door and threw himself onto the bed, exhausted from the long hours of hard work in the sun. As he laid there, thinking about all the things he and Danny would need to work on tomorrow, the sound of the washing machine cranking and the water gushing coming from the laundry room lulled him to sleep. How long he'd dozed off for he had no idea, but his mom's supper call was a shriek that could wake the dead.

He hopped out of bed and hurried to the dining room. There was never enough food for seconds, so last to the table got the least. Kevin grinned at the set table surrounded by empty chairs. His mother swept in with a green bowl full of mashed potatoes as he plopped into his seat.

"Where's Mike?" his mom asked as she placed the potholder on the table before setting the bowl down. Kevin grabbed the biggest chicken leg and said, "I don't know, in his room, I guess."

"Well, go get him," she chided, like he should have known this. Grumbling, Kevin finished heaping his plate before getting up. The last thing he wanted was someone, Steve, taking all the food while he was away.

Kevin jogged to Mike's room, the door slightly ajar, the light off. Kevin pushed open the door and shouted, "Hey, get up and come eat!" He flipped the switch, the yellow light pooling in the empty bed. He must be playing in the yard. Kevin shook his head, ready to punch Mike in the arm. First, he leaves the tree house without telling him, and now Kevin had to chase him down before he could eat. Kevin peaked in the only bathroom in the house as he passed. No luck. Then he flung the back door open and hung out, looking around—he wasn't there. Kevin just shrugged and gave up.

Back at the table, Steve was already polishing a chicken bone. Kevin's eyes fell from him to his plate. The large piece he had stashed away had been replaced with a smaller one.

Sonofabitch, Kevin thought, but he wouldn't say anything unless he wanted to get his butt kicked. As he sat back down, his mother looked at him and said, "Well, is he coming?"

Kevin shrugged and picked up the scrawny leg. "He wasn't in his room."

"What do you mean, he wasn't there?"

"He wasn't in there. I checked the bathroom and the backyard too."

A look of concern creased his mother's face. She moved quickly as she called, "Mike? Mike? Honey, it's time to eat."

Steve looked up from his plate and licked his fingers. "Dumbass."

Kevin didn't bother to reply. Any response would land him on the receiving end of a sucker punch.

His mom continued to yell for Mike, her voice growing more and more frantic.

She leaned back into the dining room with eyes wide with worry. "Where did he go when you got home?" she demanded.

"How should I know? He didn't come home with me," Kevin said, just wishing he could eat in peace.

"What do you mean, he didn't come home with you?"

Great, here it comes. She's going to blame him because that little shit didn't follow the rules. Kevin set down his fork and told her about how he and Danny had left Mike at the tree house to get lunch, and when they got back, he was gone.

"I figured he just went home because he was mad at us."

His mom looked at Steve. "Go see if his bike is here." Steve looked up from his food, a look of "huh" written on his face.

"I said go see if Mike's bike is here."

"Can I finish eating?"

In a voice that made them both jump, she shrieked, "Go now!"

Steve groaned and pushed off the table, slamming the back door behind him. A few minutes later, he came back, his irritation replaced with concern. "I don't see his bike anywhere. I checked the front and the back." Kevin's mom pressed her lips like she was biting her tongue before turning to Kevin and asking in a forced calm. "What time did he leave?"

Kevin thought about it. "Sometime around noon, maybe one, I don't know."

A seriousness tightened the air in the room as she nodded silently. "Boys, I want you to go outside and look for him" Kevin looked in the field next to the house while Steve checked the small patch of woods that backed up to the yard. After checking with the neighbors and looking in the shed, behind the pile of junk their dad collected, Kevin went back inside through the front door.

The muffled voice of his mom drifted out from the kitchen. Kevin pushed over the kitchen door in time to hear her say, "Well, if you see John, tell him he needs to come home right away."

Good luck with that. Finding his dad any night of the week was hard. The only thing that was certain was that, wherever he was, he was drinking. She put the phone on the hook but didn't turn to face Kevin yet.

As Steve came in behind Kevin, he moved over to make room.

His mom turned to face them, her eyes damp. "Did you find him?"

They both shook their heads.

"Did you look everywhere? Did you look in the shed?"

"We looked everywhere, Mom," Steve said in a reserved tone that made Kevin nervous. His big brother was always sharp and cocky. Seeing him like this unnerved him.

Their mom didn't seem to accept his words. "Did you look in the woods behind the house?"

Kevin looked up, wringing his hands, unable to keep the waver out of his voice, "Yes . . . Mom, he isn't here.

Chapter Two

7 Hours Missing

Sheriff Frank Krosby sighed and looked at the clock on the wall beside his American and Marine Corps flag. It was almost eight o'clock. He rubbed his eyes and leaned back in his chair, fingers threaded behind his head, resting his eyes for just a moment. He had just finished completing his budget report for the next year. It was hands down the least favorite part of the job, but the world ran on green paper and his office was no exception. It didn't help that the mayor was a hard-ass when it came to taxpayer money, but Krosby supposed it was better than the alternative.

He stood with a stretch, yawning, then adjusted his gun belt. Thirteen hours behind a desk was too much, thirteen hours on a fishing boat—now that was another story. He chuckled to himself as he made for the door to his office, raking his fingers through his ever-thinning gray hair before nestling his Stetson on his head. With the light off, he paused as he closed the door, staring into his dark office. How much longer could he do this job? He was only sixty-two years old, but most days he felt on the far side of seventy.

The job had taken as much of a physical toll as it had mental. Krosby closed the door and turned, heading down the hall toward the front door in the lobby. He never used the back door like the deputies.

As he entered the lobby, Linda Goodson's voice tugged at his ear. "Yes, ma'am, I will let the sheriff know, and we will send someone over." He stopped, sighing. He couldn't leave now.

Mrs. Goodson's momentary silence broke. "Mmm, yes dear, I'm sure everything will be okay, and he will show up soon."

As soon as she replaced the receiver, Krosby asked, "What now?"

Mrs. Goodson's face creased with worry. "Jesse Franklin says her youngest boy hasn't come home, and they've looked all over and can't find him."

Krosby scratched at the stubble on his chin. "How old?"

"Eight."

Krosby didn't like that. If he were a bit older, say twelve or thirteen, he wouldn't have been too worried, but eight was a bit young to be out this late.

"Want me to send Jimmy over there? He's on patrol out near that side of town."

In all likelihood, he was with a friend or got lost. Krosby didn't want to think about any other alternatives. Marcia Trimble came to mind. But that was a few years ago in Nashville, not like the sleepy little old country town of Everett. "Don't bother him with it. I'll head over there after I eat if he's still not home. Now you get out of here and go home."

She flashed him a quick smile. "I will soon. Just need to file one more report." Then she quipped, "There's just too much criminal activity in this county."

Bush County had its share of petty crimes like fights, drugs, or an occasional stolen boat motor, but nothing serious.

"Well, don't work too hard, ya hear? I'm sure that boy will be home before I finish dinner."

She smiled and bid him goodnight. Outside, the night had cooled, but it was still a bit muggy. The sight of his Chevrolet Blazer made him smile. Best thing the state ever doled out, courtesy of a military surplus, and as sheriff, he had the privilege of driving her.

He eased out of the parking lot onto Pope Street and drove past the high school. Ordinarily, he'd breeze by without a second glance at the familiar brick walls. Tonight, though, something made him cast a lingering look, dredging up memories—some sweet, some bitter—of his time within those halls. Back then, he had wanted nothing more than to escape this town. He wasn't part of any cliques; he was just a face in the crowd. No sports, no clubs, just a guy getting by. Sure, he'd had friends and the occasional girlfriend, but most of his days were spent sweating on his uncle's farm, and not drinking and chasing girls like other boys.

The memories dissolved several minutes later as his tires crunched on the grovel lot of the Diner 64. The place was little more than a converted house five miles out of town, but the food couldn't be beat.

Diana Thomas, the owner, greeted him with a smile as he stepped in but didn't say anything. She and her husband, Jack, bought this place fourteen or so years back, and he'd quickly become a regular, dropping in three or four days a week. He walked to his usual booth, nodding, and saying hello to a few other customers as he passed by. Krosby had just removed his hat when the new waitress sauntered up to the table. She chewed gum loudly with a decanter of coffee in hand; without asking, she made to pour him a cup. He placed his hand over the empty mug in front of him. "I'll have a beer, and tell Jack I want the biggest steak he's got."

She snapped her gum as she yanked a pad from her apron pocket.

"And make sure it's cooked. I don't want to see any red in it."

The waitress made an "uh-huh" sound and turned on her tennis shoes and headed for the kitchen. Krosby shook his head. Pretty girl, but she'd need a bit of training—she didn't even introduce herself.

Krosby smacked his lips as he swallowed the last of his second beer when his two-way radio crackled and the voice of Deputy Jimmy Hawkins came through. "Sheriff? Over." He sighed, popping the last bit of what some would call overcooked steak into his mouth before answering. The deputies knew not to contact him after hours unless there was something major going on. There was probably a serious accident somewhere, maybe even a fatality.

"What is it, Jimmy? Over."

Krosby planned to tell them to pass the buck off to the state police. Let them sort it out.

The walkie crackled and hissed again. "A Jesse Franklin called. She was upset that you haven't made it out to her house yet. Said her son has been missing since early this afternoon. Over."

Krosby rubbed his forehead. He had damn near forgotten about the Franklin boy.

"I'll head there now. Over."

He had hoped the boy woulda made his way home by now. He leaned over, pulling his billfold from his back pocket, and dropped a twenty on the table. Once on his feet, he regretted the two beers.

Twenty minutes later, his truck rolled into the Franklins' driveway. He threw the brake as the front door swung open, the silhouette of John Franklin charging toward him, Jesse and two boys in tow.

Krosby swung open his door. "Sorry for the delay, been a busy night," he said, taking in Mrs. Franklin's tear-streaked face illuminated by the yellow light cast by the open door.

John wobbled; his voice slurred. "I bet folks in town don't have to wait so long for help."

Krosby turned to Jesse, ignoring John. "Mrs. Franklin, I'd love a cup of coffee and to sit down so y'all can tell me what's going on?"

He didn't really feel like coffee, but John looked like he could use a cup or two.

She nodded, and they went inside. In the living room John slumped on the sofa, propping himself up on his knees. The two boys cowered in the corner, eyes sheepishly darting around.

"Have a seat," John commanded more than offered, pointing to an armchair across from him.

"Thank you." Krosby sat down, suppressing the groan he felt.

Krosby waited for Mrs. Franklin to bring in the coffee before getting started.

Once everyone settled and the adults had their coffee, he addressed Mrs. Franklin. "Tell me about your son."

She took a deep breath as if to steady herself. "Mike is my youngest son. He left home this morning around eight with his brother and never came home. We've looked everywhere," she began, tears welling up again.

Krosby balanced the coffee in one hand while pulling a small notepad from his chest pocket. "Have you called his friends? Kids usually run off to a friend's house. Most times, the parents don't even know."

"He didn't run away. He's probably out there hurt or dead by now," John interjected, prompting a shrieking cry from Mrs. Franklin.

Sheriff Krosby leaned forward. "Mrs. Franklin, everything will be okay; we'll find him safe and sound. Just walk me through what happened?"

John snorted dismissively, and Krosby was close to throwing cuffs on him and hauling him off to the jail to dry off, but there were no grounds for it.

"Jesse, please call me Jesse," she said before she recounted Mike's morning and when she realized he was missing.

Krosby turned to Kevin. "What all happened before he left?"

Kevin looked to his parents and then to the ground before he sputtered out. "Nothing. We were working on the tree house, and then Mike said he was hungry, so my friend Danny and I went to get lunch. When we got back, he was gone; I thought he just went home."

"Where's the tree house?" he asked, still jotting down details.

"In the woods near the Waller farm, a couple miles off Vildo Road. There's a dirt road there that cuts through the cotton fields."

He nodded. "I think I know about where you're talking. Did y'all check there? See if he went back?"

John slammed his coffee cup on the table, sloshing the black liquid on a stack of magazines. "Of course we did. What do you think we're fools or something?"

Krosby's patience was wearing thin, but he couldn't let a guy like John Franklin get to him.

"Jesse, does he have any friends or family he might go to or look for if he got lost?"

She shook her head. "No. He had a hard time making friends, and we haven't got much family nearby."

"Can you describe him for me? Do you know what he was wearing this morning?"

Blotting her nose with a crumbled tissue, she said, "Blue shorts, white t-shirt, and white tennis shoes." Her voice quivered on the verge of breaking into tears. The older of the two boys spoke up. "Mike is eight; he's got short blond hair. He's about this tall," he said holding his hand in the air. Krosby guessed four, four and a half feet tall.

With a final jot, he closed his notebook and slipped the pen and pad into his pocket. He set his unfinished coffee on the table and rose, knees clicking as he did. "Alright, I think I've got everything I need for now, but if you think of anything else or he shows up, you call the station right away."

Jesse nodded, and John, who appeared more subdued and sleepy, grunted.

"I'm gonna drive around a bit and see if I can find him out in the woods. It's too late to get a group out in the woods tonight, but first thing tomorrow, if he's not home, my men will get Mr. Waller's permission to comb those woods."

Jesse gave him a sad smile and showed him out. Mustering all the sympathy he could, he said, "We are going to find him."

It was going to be a long night. Missing kids were one of the things all law enforcement departments dreaded. Unless they found the kid alive and unharmed, there would be an outcry from the community. If the kid was kidnapped, killed, had an accident, or was just a plain runaway, it was always the sheriff's department's fault for not doing more. Krosby radioed instructing all patrolling officers to be on the lookout for the boy and mind any ditches for any signs of the boy. His biggest fear wasn't an abduction. This was God's country, small-town America, Tennessee. That sort of thing didn't happen here. He was more worried about the boy being struck by a car in a hit-and-run, which left him injured or dead.

The drive out to Waller's cotton farm was slow. Krosby took his time scanning the roads for any sign of the boy. A few times, he stopped to check out something in the ditch. Nothing more than trash bags and dead animals.

The truck rattled as it left the smooth pavement for the dirt road leading through the cotton fields. A light far off in the distance caught his eye. He thought it was strange since there was nothing in that direction other than woods.

Probably just some poachers spotlighting deer. Finally, he reached the clearing where the boys were building their tree house. The headlights splintered through the thin trees beyond the clearing. With very little moonlight under the overcast sky, it was too dark to really see anything. As he got out of his truck, he grabbed his flashlight. Walking the area, he could see bike tracks, several differently sized footprints, and tread marks from what he guessed was John's truck.

He yelled a few times for Mike, not really expecting him to answer.

Back in his truck, he tossed the flashlight in the passenger seat and turned the key.

He reversed slowly, praying that there were no stray nails lurking on the road. He shifted into first, pulling the truck forward, when a metallic glint flickered in his headlights. Narrowing his eyes, he scanned the woods. He pressed the clutch and threw it back in reverse, recreating the pass. There it was again. Parking the truck, but leaving it running, he grabbed the flashlight and hopped out. Shining the light until the metal winked at him again. With careful steps he moved toward the object and his heart stopped for a second as the beam from his flashlight landed on a small boy's bike.

More frantic now, he searched for signs of Mike. His movement was more careful and methodical. But he found nothing more than what looked like bits of field stripped cigarettes and a half-empty can of Schlitz. The cigarette papers and tobacco were dry, and the beer smelled fresh. Suddenly, he was very interested in those lights he had seen in the distance.

Chapter Three

17 Hours Missing

Cecil had trouble sleeping. The damn gophers were at it again, coming in from the woods and tunneling into the cemetery. Their chewing and scratching were loud enough to wake the dead. He shivered, imagining what the gophers did when they encountered a casket. He didn't want to think about it.

He rose with a groan, his bony back creaking like the swaying pines outside. Arthritis plagued worse some mornings, and today each movement shot splinters down his haunches. Rotating his shoulder with a wince, Cecil peered out the smeared window.

A low fog crawled and curled over the graveyard. The air was already muggy; it was going to be another blazing day. At least the small confines of his shed-turned-cabin ensured no long hobbling journeys to begin the daily rituals.

He never did warm to the idea of occupying the house provided by the county. The place was too spacious, too empty somehow despite a decent wood stove and running water. Rattling about in a structure intended for a bustling family only sharpened the persistent ache he'd carried for fifty years since he lost Millie.

He had modified the old tool shed on the grounds of the cemetery instead, filling the narrow room with handmade shelves and a squat writing desk wedged by the tiny camp cot he'd shared season after season with various mice and silverfish occupants.

Skillets and mugs hung neatly above the old ceramic washbasin. On the far end of the room leaned the wheelbarrow below his tools lining the wall. Light pierced through chinks in the weathered planks, making odd patterns on the worn quilt and single nightstand.

Pausing by the table, Cecil reached for the faded photo of his beloved Millie grinning brightly at the autumn harvest fair two years before cruel fate prematurely silenced her laughter. His gnarled thumb caressed the glass above her beloved face, scarcely aged from the beautiful blushing girl he first courted when the world was a better place.

"Morning, dear," Cecil rasped gently. His tired eyes lowered, accepting the new creases lining his own features, clearly no longer those of the shy railroad worker cradling his bride-to-be so proudly back then. Time had a knack for rendering everything unrecognizable if one stared too closely. With a last tender graze and weighted sigh, Cecil replaced the photo carefully parallel to the crooked cot.

He shuffled stiffly toward the percolator waiting atop his single burner wood stove and slowly prepared a pot of coffee. The contraption hissed and groaned as it brewed and Cecil dressed; the gentle movement alleviated some of the stiffness in his body. After downing bitter black coffee without even sugar to sweeten the tin cup's ashy residue, Cecil tucked a handkerchief into his hip pocket and grabbed the shovel propped just outside. Sure enough, several mounds of freshly churned earth marred the otherwise tidy aisles between markers.

Cecil followed the meandering ridges and holes, the earth beneath his boots crunching with each step. The scent of damp soil filled his nose as he shook his head in frustration. After digging down into the tunnels a bit, Cecil gathered small bundles of dried grass and green leaves, their fragrance mingling with the musty odor of the underground passages.

Trading his shovel for his .22 long rifle, Cecil crouched with the gun propped beneath his arm, being certain to keep the barrel out of the dirt. He struck a match and lit the grass in the holes. The grass crackled as ruby embers left blackened blades of grass in their wake. When the leaves caught a thick plume of acrid smoke billowed out. The acrid tang of burning green wafted through the air, mixing with the smell of the damp dirt.

It didn't take long for the pains in the neck to squabble and pop up from other holes twenty odd feet away. The gopher chatter directed him. He pivoted laying his iron sights on one bastard after the other. A few quick pops of the rifle saw three of 'em dead, but several got away.

With a groan, he pushed himself upright, feeling the lingering ache from squatting. The smoke wisped from the ground, and he stamped the holes until he was sure the burning was out.

Three of 'em would have to do for now. Later he'd take a ride down to Hadley's hardware and get some jaw traps.

Cecil stowed the rifle back in the shed, then he headed toward the woods, walking along the edge. He needed to take a piss before he headed to town. The door to his Dodge Dart whined open, and he sank onto the torn bench seat.

"You and me both," Cecil mumbled.

The old engine cranked, protesting every inch of the way.

"Come on now, you old rattletrap. Come on now."

His foot tapped anxiously as the engine sputtered and whined.

"I know, I know."

It finally turned over, a cloud of black smoke pouring from the tail pipe.

"Alright."

He patted the dash and pulled away from the cemetery and started down the road. Cecil rolled down the window, enjoying the feel of the summer breeze and the sound of the birds. The engine hummed, the wind rushed in the open window, and the smell of fresh grass drifted through the cab.

The radio played one of his favorites by Cash, and he tapped his thumb on the steering wheel to the train-like rhythm as he cruised into town.

His car was a rusted pile of junk to some, but it still was his pride and joy. The white paint had yellowed, the tires had seen better days, and the muffler rattled and groaned, but Cecil didn't care.

Downtown Everett, at this time in the morning, usually bustled with activity. Maybe there was some town event going on elsewhere that had taken everyone away. The street held only two cars, and Cecil was able to park right in front of the hardware store. He cut the engine, which wheezed and sputtered, the engine block clattering noisily.

Inside the hardware store, Ellis Hadley, the owner's eldest son, stood behind the counter. The young man couldn't have been more than seventeen or eighteen, his face scarred from the scourge of acne, and he still had that wiry look of boy. Cecil tipped his hat to him, noting the suspicion in his eyes. Cecil ignored it and crossed the room to the pegboard wall where straight hooks offered an array of items from jaw traps to shovels.

"Looking for anything in particular, Mr. Jordan?" Ellis asked, leaning over the counter, a smug grin on his face revealing yellowed teeth that looked too big for his mouth and more apt for a horse. There was a faint hint of distrust and uneasiness in the boy's tone. Cecil was used to folks giving him trouble for no reason other than he was a recluse and had been for nigh on sixty years. No use letting it get under his skin now.

"Just some traps. Gophers are causing trouble out at the cemetery," he said without looking at the boy.

"Not in need of a new shovel and lye, then? Maybe you need to dig a new grave, a boy-sized one?"

There was no point in getting riled up. It would only add fuel to the fire, but Cecil bristled anyway. His brows furrowed as he glared over at the pockmarked face of the punk. "And just what exactly you trying to say, boy?"

Ellis held up his hands. "It's just, with that boy missing, folks are on edge since word broke this morning. Word is the boy went missing near your cemetery and all. . . ."

Dread flooded Cecil's chest. "A boy is missing? Who? Since when?" The image of the boys on bicycles he had spotted near the Waller farm yesterday flashed through his mind. Could it have been one of them?

"Yeah, Sheriff Krosby's got a search party out in the woods near the Waller's place. But most folks reckon they should be out at your place." The kid folded his arms across his puffed up chest, like he was some big man, but in reality he was just a brazen fool.

Cecil scoffed and his mind raced as he walked to the counter and slammed the traps down. Ellis pressed buttons on the cash register, mechanical clacks and chimes rang from the metal box. The boy mumbled the total, and Cecil counted out bills for his purchase.

He clasped the three traps and stormed out, ignoring Ellis's final taunt of, "The whole town is watching you."

Back at the cemetery, Cecil knew it wouldn't be long until the cops or others showed up. But he wasn't gonna give them the satisfaction of waiting around. He had work to do.

Chapter Four

22 Hours Missing

It was mid-morning the next day before Krosby could organize a search party. The morning sun, with its budding heat and high humidity, had him sweating through his shirt even though the search hadn't started yet. Men clustered in the clearing near the half-finished tree house. The air was charged with the kind of excitement that came when men gathered together with a unified purpose. Krosby swatted around his face at the horseflies and mosquitoes which buzzed thickly in the air. He was giving it one more minute for any straggling volunteers to show up, mainly, John Franklin, before they would begin.

Three to four men would walk an arm's length apart, looking for anything unusual. More than a dozen volunteers, along with seven of his deputies, showed up despite the search being hastily organized, but the absence of the missing boy's father was heavily felt.

As he glanced over the faces of each volunteer, he went over the names he could recall. There wasn't a single face he didn't recognize, even if their name escaped him.

The hardened and weathered face of Detective Greg Jones cracked a side smile as he strolled up to Krosby.

"Sheriff," Jones said with a nod.

"Morning, Jones. Thanks for coming."

"It's too damn hot for this; I shoulda stayed in Chicago. But a missing boy is all hands on deck." The way Jones's vowels stretched still sounded foreign to Krosby, even after eight years.

"I'm sure the winters were lovely there," Krosby quipped before redirecting his thoughts to the search. "Have you found anything useful out here?"

Jones looked around the area, and then slapped a mosquito on his arm before answering, "Mostly just footprints and bicycle tracks left by the kids. Bits of shredded cigarettes and the beer can you found aren't much help. We might or might not get some fingerprints off it or the bike, but I won't hold my breath."

Krosby was inclined to agree. "And even if we snag someone, it just proves they were here—doesn't mean they have anything to do with the kid."

"My guess," Jones said, "they were left by a migrant worker taking a break from the field."

If something did happen to that boy, Krosby hoped to God it wasn't one of the workers. They would be damn near impossible to track. The workers moved with the crop, one week in Tennessee, the next they could be in Texas. Not to mention most were illegal—no paper trail. The cigarettes were field stripped, something Krosby had learned to do in the military. The butts were missing, but there were shreds of paper and tobacco. This didn't strike him as something a migrant would do.

"What's your gut telling ya?" Krosby asked. Like Krosby, Jones had been a cop for nearly four decades, most of which he had served working homicide in the Southside of Chicago.

Jones cocked his head from side to side. "Could of just gotten lost, gotten hurt, but—"

"I'm not thrilled that there's a but at all, but I hear you loud and clear." He raised his hands and the chatter of conversation from the men died down. Krosby had given John all the time he could; they needed to get searching.

He instructed the men on the search protocol, and within a few moments they were off into the woods filled with one word, "Mike!"

Hours of searching and they didn't find a thing. As he guzzled down water from his canteen, he saw the one person he had not wanted to see today. Jill Greco, the only reporter for *The Bush County Herald*.

The words, no comment, formed on his tongue as she sidled up to him.

"Sheriff Krosby, it's a find day for a search, ya think?" Her Memphian accent was thicker than tar. "It's hotter than Hell and Tennessee asphalt," she said in a grin a mile wide as she fluffed her pin-straight strawberry-blonde hair to one side.

"Jill, what brings you out here today?"

"Why Sheriff, you know everyone in town is talking about that little Franklin boy. It's a shame what happened to him," she said.

Krosby skewered her with a stare. "And what exactly happened to him, Jill? Do you know something that I don't about the boy?"

"Sheriff, you know what I mean. Just him being missing and all." Her smile faltered for just a moment. "Can I ask you a few questions about the search?"

"No. You know about as much as we do," he said, his patience wearing thin.

"Do you think someone took the boy or did he just get lost?"

She just kept going like he hadn't just shot her down.

"Look Jill, I don't have anything else to say about this. Now if you don't mind, I've got work to do."

"Sheriff, the town is talking about this. Half of the people are curious, and the other half are worried there might be someone out there snatching children like what happened in Nashville. Anything you can add that might help calm their fears would be great."

He wanted to turn and walk away. This case was nothing like Marcia Trimble; what happened to that poor child could never happen here. She was just hoping for a story, something to sink her claws into.

"Right now, it's just a missing person's case. There's nothing to worry about just yet. If we find evidence to suggest otherwise, I will let the public know."

She stared at him a few seconds, her saccharine demeanor faltering for just a moment as she glanced down at her empty notepad, then back to him. "Sheriff, have you had anyone search the old cemetery?"

He shook his head. "Why would we check there? You know something?"

"No, just that folks in town seem to be talkin' bout Cecil Jordan. They seem to think he might have something to do with it."

Krosby rubbed his sweaty brow, no longer hiding his scowl; he'd had enough. "I'm not interested in some backwater witch hunt. Unless you have a witness come forward tying Cecil to the boy, I'm not interested." Krosby climbed back into his truck, slamming the door before she could get another word in. Cecil wouldn't hurt a fly in Krosby's book. Sure he was a bit odd and all the locals thought him strange, but that's 'cause he kept to himself. Folks just didn't like what they didn't understand. The last thing he needed was a mob looking for justice.

Krosby's stomach growled. He'd grab lunch before checking in with the Franklins. As he drove down the dirt road leading to Vildo Road, a car squealed off. At this distance, he could not determine the make or model, just that it was white or a light-colored vehicle.

Krosby stopped radioing over to the deputies. The sooner he ruled Cecil out, the better things would be.

"I want a few deputies sent over to the cemetery so people will not take it upon themselves to go there. Over."

The search was a gamble. As much as it could clear Cecil's name, it could also give the impression that the boy had been taken there.

"This is Deputy Grayson. Deputy Triplett, Hawkins, and myself will head over there. Over."

"Sheriff, it's Triplett. Do you want us to talk to Old Cecil and see if he saw anything? Over."

"If he's there, you can question him. Also, if there are any civilians out there searching, make them leave. I'm going to catch up with the Franklins if you need me. Over."

Krosby needed to regroup. After grabbing a cold sandwich at his desk to avoid public questions, Krosby reviewed case details, trying to prevent feeling utterly defeated by dead ends. John Franklin's absence at the search still nagged at him. He picked up the phone to call Jesse but opted to drop in on them instead.

Jesse sat crumpled on her couch. After one day she somehow looked smaller and more frail. Her voice strained as she spoke. "John's over at the Callahan farm doing a job. He promised me he'd join the search after."

Krosby frowned, simultaneously sympathetic yet bothered John put labor ahead of looking for his own child.

The younger of the two boys he had met the other night lingered shyly at the door to the living room. Impulse made Krosby beckon the boy in. "Kevin, right?"

The boy nodded, his brown curls flopping. He looked more like his father while Mike favored his mother.

Kevin sat down beside his mother, who didn't so much as look at him. It was like she couldn't see anyone in the room except the absence of her son.

"Kevin, I need to ask you something tough, but I want you to be honest. You won't be in trouble. We just need you to tell the truth. Understand?"

He gulped and nodded but said nothing.

"When you guys were out at the tree house, was Mike in an accident or maybe you and your buddy were playing a joke and Mike got hurt? Sometimes accidents happen and folks get scared; they decide to cover it up instead of telling the truth 'cause they don't wanna get in trouble."

Wide-eyed Kevin looked between Krosby and his mother before speaking, his voice low. "You mean like we did something bad to Mike and got scared?"

"I know you'd never hurt him on purpose. But accidents happen sometimes."

Tears filled the boy's eyes. "We didn't do anything. He was there, and then he was gone. I don't know where Mike went. But I wish I did. . . . I really do. I shoulda never left him alone."

"OK, I believe you. I told you I just had to ask. And Mrs.—Jesse, you were here the whole time the boys were out."

She nodded absently, and pain tightened on Kevin's face as he watched his mother.

"And what about John? Where was he when all this went down?"

"You don't think he had something to do with this? How dare you come in here and ask questions like that."

Though her words were bold, her tone was weak, passive like it wasn't really her who had those thoughts, but like they were spoken on the behalf of the absent John.

"I'm not saying he did. I'm just trying to get a lay of the situation."

She picked at a wrinkle in her faded flower sundress. "Work and then Harry's, I suppose. I called Harry's, but he wasn't there yet. But he came home not long after."

Harry's was one of three local watering holes favored by men like John. The beer and liquor was cheap, and Harry let them run tabs up as long as they cashed their check with him.

"But he wasn't there when you called?"

"No, but sometimes he works late. You know how it is with Waller. He buys cheap machines and wonders why they break every five minutes. John often stays late to get the machines ready for the next day."

Krosby made a mental note to verify John's movements but said nothing about it. He didn't want to cause Jesse further distress. "Alright, thank you. And your other son?"

"Steve." She added, "He was home all day with me. I had him

mowing the yard and doing some other odd jobs around the place."

"Well, thank you. I think that's about all I needed. Someone will be in touch soon."

Krosby bid Kevin and Jesse goodbye, the weight of their worry sitting heavily on his own shoulders as he walked to his Blazer. He needed to regroup and reexamine every angle of Mike's disappearance before the trail went completely cold.

Sliding behind the wheel, he spread a map across the dash. What if the boy had wandered out to the river or one of the creeks hoping to cool off?

Krosby traced the nearby terrain with a finger, dense forest giving way to craggy shale outcroppings and a feeder creek off the river as you moved northwest. He tapped the creek nearest the tree house. Water always drew children. If Mike had ventured out there and gotten injured or trapped or . . . he didn't want to think about it. He imagined weak cries for help fading with the sun. There were still searchers out there. With any luck, if there were faint pleas to hear, they would hear them.

Guilt and frustration battled acidly in Krosby's gut. He needed to get back out there and search too. The search for Mike the day before had revealed nothing, but two-thirds of the party had resumed at dawn the next day, and Krosby's new hunch had brought him to the banks of the river. He'd left the volunteers on the outskirts, the terrain too rugged for anyone else. The only sounds were the birds singing in the trees and the buzz of insects as the sun beat down. The smell of damp earth and moss rose up, and his shoes sunk into the mud as he followed the creek.

Krosby had not been this way since his childhood, when he used to fish along the river, about two miles east of where he stood. He followed an offshoot of the river, a creek that kids were known to spend a lot of time at. Even he had spent time in the river during his youth. In the summer, he would come here to fish or swim, but as he'd gotten older, he and his buddies would drink whatever they had managed to steal from their fathers.

After an hour or so, Krosby had gone along the entire bank of the creek without seeing anything. With his stomach rumbling and his legs aching, he headed back toward the clearing. There were some more volunteers out now, but he could hear voices in the distance and decided to head in the direction they were coming from.

"What's going on here?" Krosby asked; his pulse quickened seeing Jones waving insistently from the creek shallows. Striding closer, Krosby realized Jones was pointing toward a small heap of fabric half-submerged. He halted, suddenly making out a small pair of blue shorts and a shredded white t-shirt.

"Found them jammed under some branches downstream there," Jones explained, brow knit anxiously. "Already did a full sweep both directions but no other items turning up yet."

Krosby crouched cautiously, examining the pile while dread curdled his empty stomach. Silt obscured the lettering, but the colors matched Jesse's description. If he had to guess, the sizes aligned awfully well for an eight-year-old too. But she hadn't mentioned anything about lettering on the shirt. His thoughts halted as he took in the speckled traces of maroon peppering one ragged shirtsleeve.

He peeled back the wet layers carefully. "Do you think the clothing is fresh or have they been here a long time?" Please say very long time. . . .

Jones shook his head helplessly. "Hard telling when stuff gets this soaked. Could've been weeks ago or maybe a few hours. Might never know."

Krosby grunted, straightening as he considered his options.

"That looks like blood."

"Not much but," Jones paused, stroking his chin as he thought. "Couldn't have bled out much 'cause ain't no blood on the rocks or dirt here."

"Maybe someone tried cleaning it up then," Krosby offered.

"Possibly, but . . ."

"What is it?"

"There's no drag marks," Jones said.

Krosby rubbed his brow, wishing his headache would ease. "We're gonna have to get men to search the rest of the creek. You organize the men; I'll take these over to the Franklins and see if I can get them to ID the clothes."

"I'll let everyone know," Jones said.

Krosby sighed heavily, dreading the visit to the Franklins'. If the boy had fallen in or had been drowned, he might never be found.

Krosby bagged the clothes. As Jones strode away, he prayed they would not have to tell Jesse Franklin that her son was dead.

Chapter Five

It was a grim task, this business of death, but someone had to do it. And for Cecil, it didn't matter, a job was a job.

After setting and baiting his traps with carrots to lure in the vermin, Cecil set about taking care of odd jobs around the cemetery. Watering flowers, clearing debris, this and that. The whole time he kept looking over his shoulder wondering when the cops would show up. But so far, they'd stayed away.

Once he finished eating, he collected his shovel and set off into the woods to excavate a hole for the creatures he had already taken down. Burying them would keep the coyotes and coy-dogs from coming too close. He had enough on his plate; he didn't need wild dogs terrorizing the cemetery.

With the shovel propped on his shoulder, he collected the bodies of the gophers stacked near the shed. Just as he reached the edge of the woods, the sound of tires crunching on gravel drew his attention. He paused, the shovel balanced on his shoulder, his body tense with anticipation. In a town like Everett, unexpected visitors rarely brought good tidings. It could have easily been someone coming to visit one of their loved ones, but he knew exactly who it would be.

His first instinct was to run, to disappear into the woods and wait for the visitors to leave. But innocent men had nothing to hide, or so the saying went. And yet, in a place where gossip and suspicion ran rampant, the truth was often less important than perception.

No, it was better to face it now head on, come what may.

The cruisers rolled to a stop, kicking up clouds of dust that hung in the still air. Cecil stood his ground, his grip tightening on the shovel handle as he watched the officers emerge.

Then a few moments later a few green-eared deputies made their way up the path. He didn't walk toward them; they could come to him. As they approached, Cecil caught sight of another car parked just beyond the police vehicles. It was a sleek, modern thing, all shiny chrome and tinted windows—a stark contrast to the rusted pickup trucks and battered sedans that populated Everett's streets. And there, behind the wheel, no doubt a notepad in hand, was a woman he recognized all too well.

It was that reporter lady, Jill something or other.

She was one of them big city women complete with big a mouth and bigger attitude. What a woman like her was doing in a town like Everett, he hadn't a clue. He met her gaze briefly before she peeled out of the parking lot. He shook his head.

And people thought he was the strange one.

Three deputies approached Cecil as he leaned casually on his shovel handle, trying not to appear nervous.

The oldest looking one had a nameplate reading Grayson. He removed his hat respectfully. "Morning, Cecil. Hate to trouble you, but we need to ask about that missing Franklin boy. Folks are real worried for him."

Cecil nodded. "Just heard myself. Terrible thing. I'll help any way I can."

The one with a plate reading Triplett gestured back toward the shed. "Would you mind if we take a look in your place there for any signs of him? And search the woods and such? Maybe he just ran away and was hiding out here. Have you seen anything?"

"Be my guest. I ain't seen nothing, and I got nothing to hide."

The youngest of the group, a cocky upstart with Hawkins emblazoned on his name tag, snorted in disbelief. His slick black shoes sank into the soft earth as he eyed Cecil with open disdain. "Yeah, we'll be the judge of that. Best if you don't wander far for the time being either."

Cecil tensed, his grip on the shovel tightening until his knuckles turned white. It took every ounce of self-control not to lash out, to put the arrogant young pup in his place. But he knew better. Men like Hawkins were just looking for an excuse, a reason to bring the full weight of the law down on someone they deemed unworthy.

To Cecil's surprise, Grayson intervened, shooting Hawkins a stern glance. "You're free to go about your day, Cecil," he said, his tone brooking no argument. "Hawkins is just overeager. Ignore his tone." With a tip of his hat, Grayson and Triplett headed toward the shed to begin their search.

Hawkins lingered, blatantly watching Cecil as he carried the dead gophers into the woods. His distrustful glare bore into Cecil's back until he disappeared a good fifty yards down the hill where he had dug a narrow pit between two lightning-split oaks.

Cecil dropped the rodents and began his work, the shovel biting into the earth with a satisfying thunk. The digging was hard, the ground unyielding beneath the blade. But he welcomed the labor, for the chance to burn off his anger through his muscles and in the sweat trickling down his brow.

The ground was as hard as a preacher's heart, but he didn't mind the fight. It was something real, something he could push against, not like the whispers and sideways glances that followed him everywhere he went.

As he dug, his mind wandered to that missing boy, to the pure hell his family must be going through. It was a pain Cecil knew all too well, the kind that left a hole in your soul that never really healed up right.

He'd seen it before, watched as the town ripped itself to shreds when trouble came knocking, like a pack of wild dogs turning on each other when the food ran out. He remembered that hit-and-run, twenty years back or so, the one with the young girl, barely more than a child herself. It had been a drunk driver that did it, but that didn't stop folks from pointing fingers every which way, looking for someone to blame.

And Cecil, well, he was an easy target, what with his keeping to himself and his morbid occupation.

He could still feel their eyes on him, the whispers that dogged his every step. It didn't matter that he had an alibi, that he'd been right here tending to the graves like he always was. In the minds of the good people of Everett, he was as guilty as sin until proven otherwise—and even then, the stink of it never really washed off.

The shovel hit something hard, jarring Cecil out of his thoughts. He looked down and saw the twisted root of an old oak, its gnarled fingers reaching up like it was begging for mercy. He let out a bitter laugh as he yanked the blade free. Here he was, burying the varmints that plagued his cemetery, while the real monsters walked free, hiding behind their fancy titles and the goodwill of the town.

He thought of Krosby, the one man who'd seen through all the lies and the backstabbing, who'd chased the truth like a hound on a scent. In the end, he'd caught the real killer, had dragged the dirty laundry of the town's golden boy out into the light for all to see. But it was a hollow victory, the damage already done, the wounds too deep to ever really heal.

If Krosby hadn't given them someone else, Cecil would have bet good money that the town would have probably formed a mob and delivered their own justice. They had it in them. Killer instincts. The world was a mean place, a hard and unforgiving land where the strong ate the weak. And if he'd learned anything in his time on this earth, it's that anyone can become a killer, they just need a reason and opportunity.

Deep in his bones, Cecil knew that the same fate was waiting for him. The town had already made up its mind, had already cast him as the villain in their little morality play. No matter what he did, no matter how hard he tried to clear his name, the doubt would always be there, festering just under the skin like a poison waiting to take hold.

With one last heave, he tossed the last of the dirt onto the grave, them gophers buried deep where they belonged. He stepped back, leaning on the shovel as he looked at his handiwork, his chest heaving with the effort and the weight of his thoughts.

When he looked up, Hawkins's eyes were on him, chest puffed out, thumbs hooked in his belt loop. Men like him should never be given authority. Cecil guessed the thug in police clothing suspected he was disposing of evidence or even remains. But let him think what he wanted; Cecil refused to hurry or cower because numskulls like him couldn't see past their own damn noses.

"Whatcha got there?" the man called. Cecil repressed the urge to scoff. Ridiculous or not, the man was an officer of the law.

"The same gophers you saw me come in here with."

"Why bury 'em? Why not just burn 'em or leave 'em to rot?"

What was this man playing at?

"Burning 'em takes too long," Cecil said as he huffed his way back up the hill. "And leaving 'em above ground can attract all sorts of animals I have no interest in dealing with."

Cecil stepped from the shaded woods back into the hazy afternoon light, sweat beading his forehead. Deputy Hawkins still stood, arms crossed, brow lowered as his probing stare swept Cecil up and down.

"You buried them critters deep?" He nodded back toward the trees. "Six feet down maybe? I bet you know that from experience."

Cecil bristled, gripping the shovel handle tighter. "And just what exactly is that supposed to mean, Deputy?"

Hawkins stepped closer, his hand no doubt deliberately resting on the revolver at his hip.

"It means blood has a way of seeping to the surface eventually, no matter how deep one tries to bury it." He tapped the gun butt, eyes narrowed. "Mighty curious how that missing kid up and disappears near your stalking grounds."

Cecil's pulse raced, but he forced himself to hold steady. "The only thing curious is you seeing fit to harass an innocent man on a fool's errand when there's a child needing finding." He pointed the spade's tip at Hawkins' chest, glaring back. "I'd mind that loose tongue."

Just then, Grayson emerged from the shed, shaking his head. Clearly, their search found nothing incriminating. But Hawkins's sly wink sent an ominous promise that Cecil hadn't seen the last of him.

<u>Chapter Six</u>

24 Hours Missing

Jill Greco hopped in her car, not content to cool her heels when one of the most interesting things to happen in Bush County since she moved here five years ago was playing out. Maybe her peak journalistic career years weren't over, maybe this would be a story to put her back into the world she had walked away from. She paused and thought back to her former life in Memphis.

She had always wanted to be an investigative journalist. Someone that sorted through various stories and facts to get a definitive answer.. She had often thought of the world in black and white then, that when someone used the term 'gray' to describe their actions or the situations, it was a cop out and a desire to resist facing consequences and acknowledging the truth of the matter.

Jason, Jill's now ex husband, had changed all of that. She met him two years into her journalistic career. She had caught the eye of top editors with the response readers had to her articles. She wrote facts, but had a way of humanizing the people while still weaving in the evidence to support her article's primary point. It was 1968 and she had managed to work her way up to covering the city protests of workers asking for livable wages and better working conditions, a topic that had captivated and impacted all of Memphis. So much so that one of the most notable civil rights activists of the time planned a trip to publicly support the cause.

When Martin Luther King Jr. had come to Memphis to lend his support to these protesters, both Jack and Jason were assigned from their respective papers. She was waiting at the Mason Temple beside the stage when a tall man sidled up to her. She saw him out of her peripherals, but had planned to ignore the man unless she had to engage.

"I have admired your work," the man said, "what angle do you think you are going to take with the events of today?"

Since her original plan to ignore the man was dashed, she turned towards him to provide a retort, but faltered for a second as she recognized him. Jason Blevins' work often was written with a lens very opposite of the ones she chose when she wrote. He left ambiguity and openness for reader interpretation and she had never fully been able to decide if she liked the style or not. She wrote with passion and to win an argument, he wrote with something she likened to indifference that was meant to prompt the reader to draw their own conclusions.

"Well, if I told you that you might snag it for yourself to try and win over some readers to your articles." She quipped back with a comically sweet smile. She had always been quick witted and always read for a challenge. She locked eyes with him as she waited to see the usual male ego flare up and treat her as though she was a child who knew nothing, or a woman who didn't understand her place and therefore a challenge to break. However, he only chuckled.

"I don't think I could steal your fan base. Your work moves people. You draw hard lines and boundaries. People like rules and a world of metaphorical, and sometimes literal, black and white. I often compare how you write about something with how I write about something, and I mean it when I say, I admire your writing." He held her gaze the entire time he spoke, and she felt a sense of genuineness that she wasn't accustomed to.

"Well, thank you. I haven't spent much time reading your articles," a semi-lie but it was best not to inflate men's ego unless working an angle she had found, "but I'll be sure to read over what you write about Mr. King in your next article."

Before she could continue reminiscing on the past, a cluster of deputies buzzed on their hand-helds not far away, drawing her back to the present. Shortly after, they divided into two cruisers and sped off. Jill's focus quickly shifted from her walk down memory lane to the present and the story that she was covering. Watching the cruisers speed off, a touch of adrenaline kicked in. She wasn't a betting woman, but she'd stake odds they were following a lead on the Franklin boy.

***

"Alright, boys, let's see what you've got," she said, starting her car and rolling out after them.

It didn't take long for her to figure out where their little parade was headed. The cruisers braked as the cemetery came into view, then turned onto the gravel driveway. It looked like the seed she'd planted about Cecil was bearing more fruit than the sheriff had let on. Jill guessed they would be searching the grounds and maybe talking to Cecil. That conversation was the scoop she needed.

The deputies moseyed out of their cruisers as she pulled into the parking lot. They each turned to look at her as she got out of her car. She wanted to snap: Ain't your mamas ever teach you it's not polite to stare? But she needed them sweet.

One of the deputies, a young man who looked barely old enough to shave let alone be a deputy, marched up to her. "Ma'am, you can't be here while we are searching the property."

She pulled off her sunglasses and batted her lashes, mustering the prettiest smile she could. She may be closer to fifty than forty, but she could still turn a few heads, especially in Bush County.

"Deputy Triplett," she said, looking from his nameplate and back to his goofy face. "This is public property, and you can't stop me from walking around. Unless this is an active crime scene?" He squirmed slightly in the silence, and she pressed on. "You know the Sheriff would not appreciate you restricting me from doing my job."

Triplett collected himself, adjusting his belt. "Ma'am, with all due respect, I also have a job to do. There is a missing child, and we can't have you, or anyone else, walking around here until we have looked it over. I am sure you understand."

She was just about to up her protest when Deputy Grayson approached. He was older than the rest, maybe closer to her age. His face was practically plastered with a sign reading Mr. No-Nonsense.

"Ms. Greco, you have to leave, now," Deputy Grayson stated, not asked.

She bit her lip, not wanting them to tattle to Krosby. She wanted to keep her lines of inquiry open, and Sheriff Krosby may be more willing to give her a statement later if she didn't step on his shoes now.

"Fine, I'll get out of your hair. But if you guys catch wind of anything, I would appreciate you leaving a message for me at the *Herald*." She winked and turned to climb back into her car.

Her mind already making a list of new leads. Top of the list, Jesse Franklin. With any bit of luck, John Franklin wouldn't be home.

While she didn't know either of them personally, John's reputation was well known throughout town. As she turned the key and her engine roared to life, she caught sight of Cecil standing near the trees at the edge of the cemetery, just outside the shed he was alleged to live in. His eyes seemed trained on the deputies strolling toward him before his gaze met Jill's. It sent a shiver down her spine despite the heat. Creepy bastard. He held something in his hands that hoisted up and rested on his shoulder like an old soldier would hold a rifle while he shook hands with the deputies. She squinted. It was a shovel. She shook her head and drove off.

Jill left the cemetery and headed over to Moss's Stop and Grab. The parking lot was empty except for Mr. Moss's beat-up old truck. She shoved her hand in her purse, combing for nickels or dimes. Her heels crunched in the gravel as she made her way to the smudgy phone box. The bi-fold door jammed on its track as she forced it opened and shut. Her shoulder held the receiver to her ear as she fed in her coins. The muffled tone changed to a full dial tone as her nickels clinked in.

The line rang three times before the familiar voice of Shirley Murphy picked up. *"Bush County Herald*, this is Shirley speaking. How may I help you?"

"Hey, Shirl, it's Jill. I was wondering if you could find me the address for Jesse and John Franklin?"

"Oh, the missing boy's house. So sad, any word on him yet?"

"Nothing new. So about that address?"

There was a rustling on the other end of the line. "I'm looking it up now."

Pages in what Jill guessed were the phone book flicked. "OK, I got it." Shirley rattled off the address, and Jill made a quick goodbye before she needed to feed the box another ten cents.

The cotton fields sprawled with rows of green shoots. Her eyes flitted from the road to the fields in ditches as she imagined spotting something that didn't belong, something that looked like the body of a boy. It wasn't that she wanted the boy to be hurt; it's just that her mind couldn't help but slip to the more macabre side of things. She wondered how many others were doing the same thing. It would be a good anchor point for her story.

When Jill's divorce sent her looking for a fresh start, Bush County had seemed like the perfect place. Idyllic to outsiders, dead end to those who were born here. She always felt the truth was somewhere in between. As she continued to drive, she went over some of the questions she planned to ask. It would take a soft touch to get the information she was after. Jill had no children of her own and couldn't fathom what the poor family was going through.

Jill pulled into the driveway of a small white ranch. The paint was cracked and peeling off in many places. A small brown dog scampered through the yard, likely a stray that had wandered in one day and never left. An old yellow Ford Falcon parked in the driveway, she assumed it was Jesse's and that John would drive a truck, like most men in the county. As she cut the engine, the afternoon heat hit her like a brick. The air conditioning in her car only worth its salt while it blew.

Steadying her nerves, Jill knocked and waited. Jesse opened the door, her blonde hair slightly disheveled and face red and puffy from crying.

"Hi, Mrs. Franklin. You may not know me, but I'm Jill Greco. I'm a reporter with the *Herald*."

Jesse gave her a glazed looked before saying, "I know who you are."

"I thought you might like help getting the word out about your son. All I need is for you to answer a few questions and maybe give me a picture of your boy?"

"Mike, his name is Mike."

Jill hadn't meant to offend her and hoped this wouldn't put her off answering her questions. Born and raised in the city, she was polite but direct. Even after half a decade, Everett had yet to mold her city instincts to fit its small-town sensibilities.

"Yes, Mike. Mrs. Franklin, I just want to help."

Jesse nodded and stepped back, motioning her inside. "Please have a seat, and Jesse is fine," Jesse said leading Jill to the couch.

"Thank you for taking the time to speak with me. I know this is a difficult time for you."

Jill settled onto the worn couch, her eyes tracing the patterns of the outdated wallpaper that adorned the living room. Observing the tidiness of the house, Jill couldn't help but imagine Jesse keeping herself busy today by cleaning. Just sitting and worrying would drive a person crazy. Jill pulled her notepad and pen out of her purse. Jesse's eyes fixed on the paper. "I hope you don't mind if I take notes."

Jesse shook her head. "It's fine, it's just—" she paused, covering her mouth with a trembling hand. Tears thickened her voice as she finished, "you never imagine yourself in this place. My son is missing and there is a reporter in my living room." She held her face in her hand and sobbed for a moment. Jill sat quietly and let the woman get her grief out.

Dabbing her eyes with crumpled tissues, Jesse said, "I'm sorry,"

"Oh dear, you cry all you need. You love your boy, ain't nothing wrong with that. Now why don't you tell me about him? What's he like?"

"He's my baby," she said holding back more tears "He has a big heart. Sweeter than other boys his age. Always helping me with things around the house or asking to help cook dinner." She smiled a little while wiping away tears.

Jesse's voice trembled as she continued, each word weighed down with the kind of pain only a mother can know. Some minutes later, Jesse was in such a state she excused herself and Jill thought it best to split soon. Not only because she did not want to be there when John got home but she didn't want distress Jesse further.

While Jill waited for Jesse to return, the creak of the front door caught her attention. A young boy entered, his eyes locking onto her. "Who are you?"

Jill smiled. "Well, hello there. I'm Jill Greco. You must be Mike's brother. I work for the paper and just dropped by to talk to your mama."

The boy narrowed his eyes. "My dad won't be happy if he sees you here."

"I understand, and I don't want to cause trouble. I'm just here to help get the word out about your brother."

His brows furrowed skeptically, but he said nothing else.

"What's your name?"

He leaned against the door frame. "Kevin."

"You were the last person to see Mike before he went missing, right?"

A glint of irritation flickered in Kevin's expression. "Yes, ma'am."

The poor kid was probably blaming himself. She hoped to set him at ease. "I know you must be upset, and you're probably blaming yourself. But this isn't your fault, you hear me?"

Some of the tension in his face relaxed. "No one has come out and actually said it's my fault. But I know they're all thinking it."

"I'm sure no one thinks that. It might feel that way, but at the end of the day, everyone just wants to find your brother."

He swallowed hard and nodded.

"Do you remember anything about that day that seemed out of place, or did you see anyone hanging around that you didn't usually see?" she asked on the off chance he'd remember something now that he was a bit calmer. Kevin seemed to roll her question around in his mind. "No, ma'am." But as soon as the words left his mouth, his expression twisted.

Jill urged him to speak. "What is it? Do you remember something?"

"Cecil," he whispered. "My friend Danny and I were riding back from Moss's and he came driving past. He was acting strange, cruising all slow from the direction of the tree house—where we left Mike. Once he passed us, he took off real fast."

That was an interesting tidbit. But she knew well enough that the cemetery wasn't too far from there. It could have been a coincidence.

Kevin launched into another story. "Danny said that Cecil chased him with a shovel earlier when he was riding his bike past the cemetery that morning."

She blinked, trying to sort the facts of his story from fiction. "You said your friend Danny was chased by Cecil with a shovel?" The image of Cecil slinging the shovel over his shoulder before she came there replayed in her head, adding credibility to the kid's story. At least he saw Cecil at the cemetery the day before.

"Yeah, well that's what Danny said, but he's always exaggerating stuff."

She nodded. "Could you give me Danny's last name and his phone number? I would like to talk to him."

But before Kevin could answer, the sound of a truck roaring into the driveway and screeching to a stop drew both of their eyes.

Her heart raced, not wanting a confrontation with a hulking drunk man. "I should get going." Kevin nodded urgently and rushed out of the room. Jesse turned the corner, panic in her big brown eyes as John nearly ripped the door from the hinges. He staggered in, swaying a little as he stopped and eyed Jill.

"Who are you? And why are you in my house?"

"Hello, Mr. Franklin," she said, hoping her cheery tone would disarm him. "My name is Jill Greco; I write for the *Herald*. I—"

He swiped a massive calloused hand through the air. "Get out. We have nothing to say to your kind." The words came out in a slippery growl as Jesse shook beneath the intensity of his gaze.

Jill hoped to redirect his anger at her. She hated the thought of what would happen when she left. Jesse had to live with this. "Mr. Franklin, I think it would help if the folks around here knew a little more about your son, Mike, and might help bring forward information."

"The only thing that will help is for the police to get off their lazy asses and do their damn job."

Jill pressed her lips, biting back her comment. John Franklin had been conspicuously absent from the morning's search, but she wouldn't provoke him.

Jill turned and took Jesse's hand, offering a gentle squeeze. "Thank you for your time."

As she passed John Franklin, he grabbed her arm. His thick fingers dug deep into her muscle. "I better not see any story in your paper about my boy. You hear? If there is, there'll be hell to pay."

Jill looked down to where he was holding her arm, her face a mask of defiance as she jerked away. "And if you ever put your hands on me again, you'll have hell to pay."

Shock gave him a glazed-over dumbfounded looked that bought her enough time to slip out of the front door. She doubted anyone ever stood up to that bully of a man. She just hoped Jesse wasn't paying for Jill's antics.

Jill considered driving back by the cemetery, curious to see if the deputies were still on site. What the Franklin boy had said about seeing Cecil played over in her mind. Did he have anything to do with the boy being missing?

Torn between conducting her own little investigation and passing on what she learned to Sheriff Krosby, she headed to her office. Perhaps she could do both.

Chapter Seven

26 Hours Missing

Arm hanging out the window, he pulled into the lot of Moss's Stop and Grab, cigarette nearly smoked to the butt. Bits of smoldering tobacco and paper rained down from his hand as he rolled out the cherry. He flatted the filter between his index finger and thumb before dropping it into the chest pocket of his shirt. Not much had stuck with him from his Army days but knowing you don't drop a cigarette butt on the ground was one of them. Just one butt on the ground would have a platoon cleaning for hours. Few things stuck with him following his discharge from the army, but that had. He eyed himself in the rearview mirror. His long greasy hair, sunken gray eyes, leathered skin from too much sun, and the weight loss made him look homeless. Not that he gave a shit what other people thought. It was better they thought he was a drifter and not the ex-soldier who was dishonorably discharged for sexually assaulting a female soldier. Or the disgraced Vietnam veteran who molested a teenage boy, only to become the ex-con on parole. People had labeled him many things in his life, but here in the middle of nowhere Bush County he blended in with the poor farm community, and that suited him just fine.

He never liked to stay anywhere too long, he'd only been stuck in Everett this long because he hadn't done anything to send him running, until now. Mr. Waller rented him a small trailer, nestled way out in the woods. The trailer was once used as a hunting retreat, but now it was just a rundown tin box located near the bank of the Hatchet River.

He grinned thinking about the police calling for the boy in the woods that morning. Only three miles or so as the crow flies from his home. He had driven past the cotton fields a few times to watch the police activity. Too curious for his own damn good. The last time he drove past, he stopped at the edge of the road that led into the tree house. Foolish, but the feeling coursing through his veins was better than any drug. And he'd done his share. He sat watching the police activity. He watched them walk around like headless chickens for several minutes. Suddenly, he noticed the sheriff looking in his direction. After laying eyes on the Sherrif's truck leaving and headed in his direction, he'd peeled clean out of there.

He hadn't planned to take the boy. Though he'd seen a couple from time to time cutting through the fields off Vildo Road, he had resisted the urge to follow them. But yesterday, the universe threw him a line, and he took it. It wasn't his fault that those snot-nosed bastards were blabbing away to Mr. Moss about their tree house and the fact that the younger one had stayed behind alone.

His lips curled in a Cheshire grin. Oh the luck he'd had.

The urges were strong, but he had not planned it. Too many things could go wrong. What if someone saw him driving over there? He had known it was too risky, but it sweetened the thrill. He almost walked away once he spooked the boy. A taste he thought was better than nothing, but as hard as he fought against it, the pull inside him to take the boy was too strong. His head hurt and he couldn't think straight. He had to take him; it was the only way to make the pain go away.

Pulling himself to the present, he pushed open his car door and tromped into Moss's Shop to pick up his usual pack of Schlitz, cigarettes, and a few cans of tuna and potted meat. Last minute, after setting his usual goods down, he grabbed a few bags of chips, Cokes, and candy bars.

Mr. Moss looked between him and his items and said with a grin, "What's with all the candy and Coke? Never seen you buy junk food before."

His heart raced and the urge to run came. Idiot! This was a mistake. The missing boy was the talk of the town, and he was suspiciously buying stuff kids eat.

His mind sputtered like an engine that wouldn't turn over, but finally it caught. "It's just some extra food for the field workers," he said. "I like to give the hard-working ones a little treat every now and again."

Two older men he hadn't noticed before laughed at him. He glared at them but knew better than to say anything. One mistake was too many, and he didn't need to make any more. The bell chimed overhead as he left, more laughter rising behind him.

Shit, shit, shit!

By the time he pulled up the windy dirt path leading to his home, he'd calmed down. He parked on the side of the trailer in the grass, grabbed the paper bags from Moss's, and went inside. After dropping the bags on the table, he toed off his dirt-caked boots and peeled off his socks. He scooped up the box of beers and dragged himself over to the TV, flipping the dial before flopping down.

He ripped open the box and freed a beer. With the top popped, he took a long pull. It was piss warm, but he didn't care. The local news churned out some garbage about proxy wars and the Soviets. Stuff he didn't care about and damn sure didn't want to watch.

In the kitchen with a fresh beer, downing it, he fumbled in his kitchen throwing together two tuna sandwiches. Leaving one sandwich on the counter, he returned to the news. Nothing about the missing boy—yet. That would change soon enough. The beer can clattered on the floor as he tossed it away and brushed the bread crumbs from his chest. On his feet, he switched off the TV and put his boots on. Grabbing the other sandwich and some of the goodies he had picked up earlier, he slipped out of the back door and headed toward the woods.

***

Mike woke and cried as he breathed in the musty smell of the damp dark building. It wasn't a dream; it wasn't a dream. He must have cried himself to sleep, convincing himself that the vision of his bedroom with his mother by his side, gently stroking his forehead, had been real. Without thinking he sat up and pulled his legs to his chest, but the chain fastened to his ankle caught and he screamed. It was too tight and cut into his skin. Warm blood streamed down his foot and pooled on the floor.

His face ached from crying; his eyes as dry as his cotton mouth. How long had he been here? The fear had dulled slightly, though his body was still on edge. Mike thought back to Kevin and Danny leaving the tree house to go get food. While they were gone, he had collected boards and started removing the nails like they said. Not long after they left, a car cruised slowly down the dirt road, kicking up dust. He had been a little bit scared, but looking back, he should have been more frightened. He was sure he was going to get yelled at for being out there when it should have been Kevin getting yelled at.

The man stepped out of the car, and as he stepped toward him, Mike couldn't help but stare at the dirt and grease covering his hands. In one hand he held a can of beer, the other a cigarette. The man rounded the front of the car and perched on the hood. Nervously, Mike put his hands in his pockets as the man looked all around before saying, "What are you doing out here?"

Eyes on his feet, Mike answered. "I came with my brother. We were pulling nails out of old boards to build a tree house."

Immediately, the man replied, "Where is your brother now? He left you all alone?"

"He and Danny went to get us lunch," Mike said, his heart racing. The man continued to draw near him causing Mike to back up and trip over a board he had been working with.

As Mike regained his footing, the man demanded, "You will have to come with me. You can't be out here; this is private property. I have to take you to Mr. Waller's house and find out if he wants to let you stay out here."

Mike couldn't keep the tears in anymore and he gushed, "My brother will be back soon, and you can ask him. He asked Mr. Waller already, and he said it was okay."

The dirty man shook his head, the greasy locks of his hair swinging like vines. "You still need to come with me. If you don't, then I will have to call the sheriff and have him come out here."

Mike was scared and didn't know what to do. He didn't want to get in trouble, and he certainly didn't want the sheriff coming to get him. If he got arrested, his dad would tan his hide. So he decided to beg. "Please, mister, just wait for my brother and his friend."

The man looked over his shoulder, "We don't have time. Get in the car, and we will be right back. This won't take long."

Out of options, Mike climbed in the back of the white car. He had to move greasy fast-food wrappers and beer cans off the seat and onto the floor, which was already cluttered. Mike looked up to see the man awkwardly carrying his bike while still holding his cigarette and beer can. Why was he taking his bike? Mike watched as the man carried his bike to the edge of the woods and threw it as far as he could into the trees. He threw it so hard that the beer fell out of his hand. The man stood there for a few minutes; it looked to Mike as if he was talking to himself. He appeared upset. Then he took the cigarette from his mouth and dropped it onto the ground. After a bit, the man returned and opened the car door.

"What did you do to my bike?"

"I moved it so no one would steal it." The man grunted as he slammed the door.

Alarm bells rang in Mike's gut. He needed to get the heck out of there. Grabbing the door handle and pushing, he found it wouldn't open. Panic set in, and he screamed for help, frantically yanking the lever, but the door wouldn't budge.

The man moved calmly in front of him, leaning forward and pulling something from the glove box. Suddenly, the man turned around holding up a bowie knife, spit flying as he screamed, "SIT DOWN AND SHUT UP!"

Mike sobbed in barely a whisper, "Please, let me go, mister; I won't tell."

Through clenched teeth the man said, "If you say another damn word, I will cut that little tongue right out of your mouth. Am I clear?"

Mike cried, covering his mouth to dampen the sound and nodded his head.

Now, he lay chained to a pole, shackles around his wrists and ankles.   He was convinced he would not get out of this alive. The door rattled and more chains clinked. Mike crawled closer to the pole near the back wall and tried to make himself as small as he could. He shook as the dim light outside filtered in around the man as he entered, and Mike guessed it was evening. The man placed a few items down on top of an old bucket.

Mike didn't want to look at him for fear of making him angry, so he covered his face until he turned and left without speaking. After the door closed, the chains rubbed and clinked before the lock clicked shut. Terrified from head to toe, Mike's whole body shook so much that for the first time in as long as he could remember, he wet himself.

Chapter Eight

27 Hours Missing

The afternoon with Jill had swallowed everything, and Kevin just sat in his room, lost in his thoughts long after she left. His dad's loud grumbles had disappeared after his dad's truck peeled out of the driveway. But he could still hear his mom quietly crying sitting in Mike's bedroom.

Kevin itched to hit the streets and search for any sign of Mike. The need to find clues gnawed at him, but there was no way his mom would let him out of the house now. Kevin was lying on his bed staring at the ceiling when the plan hit him. After his mother disappeared into her room, Kevin sneaked into the kitchen and snatched the phone from its wall mount, yanking the long, overstretched cord with him into the bathroom around the corner. Dialing Danny's number, he held his breath waiting for someone to pick up.

A few rings later, Danny's older brother Ricky murmured, "Hello."

"Hey, Ricky, is Danny home?" Kevin said quickly, hoping Ricky would get on with his usual taunting so Kevin and Danny could get down to business, but to his surprise, Ricky didn't tease him.

"Any word on Mike?" There was something in his tone of voice that made Kevin want to squirm. The teasing would have been better than whatever this was.

"Nah, police haven't found anything yet."

Ricky snapped his tongue. "I'm not surprised; those guys couldn't find a titty in a whorehouse."

Kevin laughed and the line when quiet, then Ricky yelled, "Hey, Danny, get your ass in here; Kevin's on the phone." Kevin pulled the receiver away from his ear and then put it back in time to catch him saying, "Tell Steve to give me a call. A few of us are going out to the river this weekend."

"Sure, will." Kevin promised. There were some slapping sounds on the other end of the line, and Kevin could see the brother's slap boxing in his mind before Danny's out-of-breath voice came on. "Hey, Kevin, what's up?"

"Your mom working the next few days?" Kevin didn't bother with greetings; Danny wouldn't care.

"Yeah, she works every day. Why?"

"I want to go out looking for Mike or at least see if I can find something. I think Cecil had something to do with it, and I want to look around his place." Kevin waited for Danny to agree to help.

"OK, but what does that have to do with my mom working?"

"I doubt my mom will let me leave the house, except to go to your house. But I need you to call me back in like half an hour to see if I can stay over tonight and tomorrow. If my parents think I'm with you, they won't know what we're really getting up to."

"OK, I'll call, but do you really think your parents will let you come over? I mean, aren't they freaked out with Mike being missing?"

Kevin shrugged, even though Danny couldn't see. "Of course, they're freaked out. But my dad's out, probably at the bar, and Mom is just crying all the time. Trust me, they won't care."

"Alright, I'll call you soon, later." Danny clicked off as Kevin echoed, "Later."

An hour trickled by and the phone finally rang. Kevin made a show of yelling, "I got it," while running from his bedroom to the kitchen.

"Hello?" Kevin answered.

Danny said, "Sorry, lost track of time."

"Man, you really suck, but hold on. Let me go ask my mom." As he went to peer down the hall, his mother's puffy, tear-streaked face looked hopefully at him as she stepped out of her room. Kevin hadn't thought about the fact that the ringing phone might have given his mother hope.

He whispered, holding the phone to his chest, "Hey, Mom. It's Danny; can I stay at his house for a couple nights?"

Her arms dropped, and she turned back toward Mike's room. "As long as his mother doesn't mind, and you stay there. I don't need to lose you too."

Her words hurt, but he swallowed it.

When she was back behind the closed door. Kevin was back on the line. "She said it was OK as long as your mom didn't care."

"I haven't asked because she's working, but you know she won't care."

"Doesn't matter to me. I'll ride over soon. See you in, like, an hour."

"Hey, I can meet you out by the funeral home. That's about halfway. Then we can ride out to the tree house and see what the cops are doing."

Kevin smiled, glad Danny was so willing to help. "Yeah, OK. I'll see you soon then." Kevin hung up and ran to his room, hastily stuffing a duffel with whatever clean clothes he laid his hands on, before thundering outside and onto his bike, pedaling toward the funeral home.

The sun was low, barely peaking over the trees, as Kevin pedaled as fast as he could. The road that led to the funeral home parking lot dipped down, and Kevin let up on the pedals, coasting down until he spotted Danny, already there and lounging on the grass beneath a tree. Kevin pulled up, stopping hard on the grass so that the handlebars jabbed him in the gut. Danny stood up. "What took you so long?"

"What do you mean? It's a thirty-minute ride from my house."

Danny smirked. "I could do it in twenty."

Kevin rolled his eyes. "No way. You'd be lucky to make it in forty." He laughed. "You'd get distracted by everything you pass."

Danny laughed too and shrugged as if to say, what can you do?

Danny mounted his bike, one foot ready on the pedal. "Where do you want to go first, the cemetery or tree house?"

Kevin looked out to the road and the disappearing sun. "Let's head out to the cemetery first and see what we can find out there. The deputies might still be out at the tree house, anyway."

"OK, but if Cecil is out there with that shovel, I am not staying," Danny said.

Kevin laughed nervously and agreed.

They biked off slower than they usually did in silence until Kevin broke it. "There was a reporter at my house earlier. She wants to talk to you about your run-in with Cecil the other day."

Danny's eyebrows shot up and disappeared beneath his shaggy brown hair. "How does she know about that?"

"She was asking me questions about what we saw and stuff. I told her what you said about him chasing you with a shovel. She asked for your name and number."

"What!" Danny yelled, cupping his forehead. "Why would you tell her that? Did you give her my phone number—I don't want Cecil coming after me."

Kevin shook his head. Of course, Danny would make a mountain out of a molehill. "Relax, I didn't give it to her. Dad came home and chased her off. I doubt she'll be back."

Danny calmed down a little. "Good," he said. "Your dad could scare a mama bear away from her cubs with his beer breath."

The cemetery wasn't far, and as they neared, Kevin furrowed his brow at the sight of a single police cruiser parked in front of the cemetery.

"What do you think the cops are doing there?" Danny whispered as they both slowed to a stop.

"Not sure," Kevin answered. "But the sheriff's car isn't there. He would be there if they found something. Guess they just wanted to talk to Cecil. Maybe ask if he saw anything."

Danny's lips tightened. "I don't know. I think something's up."

Kevin thought for a minute. They couldn't ride over with the cops there. At best they would be told to leave; at worst, their parents would be told what they were up to.

"Let's take the old dirt road that goes to the river. We can walk through the woods and come in the back side of the cemetery without being seen."

"Yeah, sounds great. Let's just walk through the woods into Old Cecil's pit of doom. I'm sure it will be fun to find him walking in those woods with his shovel."

Kevin was turning on his bike when he said, "Stop being a baby and come on."

About ten minutes later, they were riding around the county barriers that discouraged people from driving back there. The ride was rough, but they managed it. As they got to the hill where the road dead-ended they dropped their bikes in the grass. Danny looked uneasy as they climbed the hill into the woods. Neither boy said anything for a few minutes. Kevin bet Danny's thoughts weren't far off from his own. The woods were creepier when there was a chance someone or something might reach out from the shadows and make a kid disappear. Kevin had never been afraid of the woods until then.

Kevin's eyes scanned the ground, trying not to picture his brother's body among the fallen leaves and pine needles. The eerie shadows danced behind every tree; it was more than enough to keep him on his toes. Danny stopped to pick up a thick stick, about three feet long, which he used to poke into brush spots. After poking a few times, he would move on to the next spot, like the detectives did on TV. After twenty or so minutes of walking around, they found themselves on the back side of the cemetery. Kevin put out his arm to stop Danny from leaving the tree line. Cecil's shed wasn't far from where they stood.

"Do you think he's in there?" Danny asked.

"Who? Mike or Cecil?"

"I meant Cecil, but, since you mentioned it, Mike could be in there."

Both boys stared at the shed for a few minutes. Kevin didn't know what to do next. Searching the woods was easy, but breaking into Cecil's shed? That seemed impossible. What if he was a killer? He would kill them if he found them. But if Mike was in there, and still alive, they could save him.

As they stood, trying to decide what to do, Danny grabbed Kevin's arm and whispered, "He's coming."

Kevin followed Danny's gaze to where Cecil was dragging an old feed sack behind him.

Danny whispered, his voice strangled, high pitched, "There's something heavy in the sack."

Cecil disappeared into the shed, and Kevin let out the breath he hadn't realized he'd been holding.

Danny began to panic. "What do we do, what do we do?"

Kevin tried to calm him. "Shh, look, we don't know what's in the bag."

"A body, Kev, a body is in that bag."

Kevin pressed his hand to Danny's mouth. "We don't know that. Besides, there's a cop out front. No way he'd be moving around a body now."

Danny's breathing evened out as he seemed to accept the logic. The shed door flung back open, and the boys clung to one another, then dropped down as Cecil emerged. This time there was nothing in his hands. As he closed the door, he turned and stared in their direction.

Both boys froze. "Do you think he can see us?" whispered Danny in a quivering voice.

"Be quiet," Kevin scolded under his breath. Cecil kept looking in their direction for a few more seconds. Then, he turned and walked toward the front of the cemetery.

"Whew, I thought we were dead for sure," Danny said, getting to his feet and brushing the dirt from his knees.

"Why is he out here and not talking to the police?" Kevin asked, but Danny only shrugged.

Kevin wanted more than ever to get a look inside the shed now. But he had no clue how to do that with Cecil out walking around. As they sat, just looking at the shed, there was a snap of a twig behind them. Kevin whirled around a silent scream in his throat. Cecil stood less than twenty feet away from them.

"What are you boys doing out here?" His gravelly voice was weaker than Kevin had imagined it would be.

Kevin considered running, but fear fixed him to the spot.

"Answer me! What are you doing snooping around?" he demanded.

Kevin found his voice before Danny and he stammered, "My brother, Mike, is missing. We were just out looking for him."

Danny blurted, "We didn't mean to cause any problems; we just wanted to see if he got lost out here and maybe got hurt."

Kevin nodded; glad Danny made it sound like they didn't suspect Cecil.

"Your brother isn't out here; just ask the cops. They have looked over the whole place and found nothing."

Kevin, in a rush of bravery or stupidity, said, "What's in that feed sack you put in the shed?"

Danny gave him a wide-eyed look, no doubt wondering where he'd gotten this unexpected courage.

Danny added, "What he means is it looked heavy. Too heavy to be just some feed."

"So you were spying on me?" Cecil said, brow raise, his crooked and stained teeth bared.

"N-n-no, it's not like that. We aren't watching you. We just happened to walk up when you were carrying the sack inside," Danny said with his arms out as if to ward off a charging dog.

Cecil straightened, folding his arms across his chest. "Not that it's any of your business, but it was a few gophers I trapped. I'm tired of folks always coming out here and accusing me every time something goes wrong. What have I ever done to anyone in the town? Huh! What? I'll tell you what—nothing. I have done nothing to harm anyone. Still, everyone wants to blame me."

He stopped, and Kevin let his gaze fall to his shoes. Guilt. He hadn't expected to feel guilt. When the boys didn't say anything, Cecil continued, his voice softer as he crouched down and put a hand on Kevin's shoulder. "I am sorry your brother is missing. But there is no reason to go telling people I had something to do with it."

Kevin nodded. "Yes, sir. Sorry, sir." Cecil let go of his shoulder but stayed crouched down.

"Do your parents know you are both out here? There might be

someone out there taking young kids; you ought not be in the woods."

"Mr. Cecil, I'm so sorry I got you wrapped up in this. I didn't mean to tell that reporter lady we saw you. I didn't know she'd tell the cops. I was just scared."

Cecil's brows furrowed like Kevin had surprised him.

Danny spoke next, "We had to go looking. We were the last ones with him, can't expect us to just sit home and do nothing."

Then Kevin quietly breathed, "It's my fault. I shouldn't have left him alone."

Cecil looked at him for a few seconds and said, "It's not your fault. Don't blame yourself. Guilt will eat you up inside. I'm sure the cops will find him soon."

All the emotions Kevin had kept a lid on escaped at once in hot tears rolling down his cheek.

Chapter Nine

41 Hours Missing

Sheriff Krosby's alarm went off, and all the stress and unanswered questions flooded back to him. Today marked the third day since the Franklin boy had gone missing, and he had nothing. No clues, no suspects. Detective Jones and some of the deputies had questioned the landowners and many of the field workers. Nothing.

Lacing his boots, Krosby's phone rang, quickening his heart. He stood, his untied laces clacking on the linoleum as he went to answer it. "Krosby speaking."

"Morning, Sheriff. It's Jill."

He sighed; she was the last person he wanted to be talking to. "What can I do for you Jill?"

"I wanted to ask you about Cecil Jordan. Kevin, the other Franklin boy, said he and his friend Danny saw him come from near the tree house when they were going back."

Krosby rubbed his brow; he didn't need this woman stirring up drama over nothing. "Look, this is an ongoing investigation. At this time, we have no suspects or persons of interest. And I don't appreciate you harassing the Franklins."

His words didn't seem to affect her. She pressed on. "Then why the search of the cemetery? Why was there a cruiser parked out front there all night?"

Krosby's frustration boiled over. "Because of this and people like you. Every time something happens people blame Cecil. We searched the grounds so that folks 'round here would leave him in peace and not take to searching themselves. That officer was there all night to keep Cecil safe in case a mob showed up."

Jill stayed silent for a moment. "Well, you got anything else for me?"

"No!" he bellowed and slammed the phone onto the receiver. He'd feel bad about bein' rude later. Right now, it felt too good to let out a little steam.

Approaching the station, a few news vans lurked in the parking lot like carrion birds. They had likely picked up the story from local news outlets. Ever since the Trimble case, reporters were always chomping at the bit hoping to break the next big story. It was disgusting to capitalize on the grief of others. As Krosby scanned the vans, he was relieved there were no stations from Memphis. Walking into the police station, he was greeted by Mrs. Goodson. A few moments later, she was in his office with a cup of coffee for him and handed him a stack of phone messages.

He skimmed them, mostly from reporters and several from the mayor. They could wait.

"We have reporters from Jackson wanting to brief about the Franklin boy." Linda said as he sipped the coffee.

Krosby leaned back in his chair, spreading the blinds to glance at the reporters outside. "Tell them we have no comment at this time."

She nodded, clasping her hands in front of her. "You know that line never works."

Krosby sighed and said, "Just get them out of here. I will not have them tearing our town apart because they think it will make a good story."

She offered him a sad smile and turned to leave. "Thanks for the coffee," he called after her. That was the second woman he'd been rude to this morning.

Walking through the hallway, past his office and the break room, he second-guessed himself. Had they missed something? Was there evidence they overlooked? Lost in thought, he bumped into a deputy. He looked over his shoulder in the eyes of Deputy Eric Pritchard.

"Sorry, Sheriff," Pritchard said in his Alabama drawl.

"No, that was my fault, sorry about that." Krosby offered a half smile and continued toward the small room now used as the war room for the Franklin case. Detective Jones was on the phone at one of the desks.

Standing in the doorway, Krosby examined the pictures on the wall—a map of the area and a smiling school photo of Mike. Not much.

Jones looked up, still talking on the phone. "OK, thank you—Yeah, you too."

When he hung up, Krosby addressed him, "Please tell me you have a lead."

Jones shook his head, looking disappointed. "Sheriff, we have found no physical evidence, no witness, no clues whatsoever. All we have is the boy's bike. We dusted for prints, but we don't have the boy's prints or other family members on file to eliminate."

He glanced at Sheriff Krosby with an exhausted, almost defeated look. "The cemetery grounds were a bust. The deputies didn't check any of the buildings though. I think we need to get a warrant and go back. Take a good, long look."

Krosby let out a long breath. "Greg, you know we have no grounds to get a warrant. I'm sure I could get Judge Mills to grant just on Cecil's reputation, but if we don't find anything that will not stop the people in this town from crucifying him. Plus, if we do find something, and we didn't have good grounds for that warrant, any attorney would get that evidence thrown out of court."

Jones sat on the edge of the desk. "Sheriff, we got nothing else."

"I don't think going after Cecil on the account that folks don't like him is a good habit to get in. If we spend all our time on Cecil while the real perp is out there, we might be inviting another kidnapping. I say, until we have solid evidence linking Cecil to the scene, we leave him out of this."

Krosby intentionally omitted what Jill had mentioned that morning. He wasn't in the habit of passing off hearsay as evidence. He'd pay a visit to Danny Gaston and Kevin Franklin later. Their story needed a second going over.

"But what do we do now?" Jones asked when Krosby had stayed silent.

"I want at least one deputy to patrol the area around the cemetery, 24/7. I'll follow up with the brother and his friend, see if there is anything they forgot to mention. After that I'll head over to Moss's store to see if Mr. Moss or any of the old timers who hang out there have anything to add."

Jones nodded along, seeming to approve of his plan. "What do you want me to do?"

"First off, get those damn vans out of our lot. I don't care what you do, just get them the hell out of here. Then, you and a couple of deputies should check back in with the farmers, see if anything changed from yesterday."

"Alright, sounds good."

Krosby nodded and turned away to leave, but Jones stopped him. "Wait, you think we should set up a tip line."

"Fine. That might draw the state and feds in on this, but it's worth it, if we find him."

It was a bit early, but he wasn't willing for this case to grow cold. The picture of that pretty little Marcia Trimble popped into his mind. She was missing for just over a month before they found her body, and the state's heart broke when they found out what that young man had done to her.

Krosby squealed his tires as he pulled out of the lot, leaving the news crews in a cloud of dust. He chuckled at the sight of them coughing and running to protect their equipment in his rearview.

At the Franklin's Krosby wasn't surprised to see John's truck absent. Before he could get out of his truck, Jesse stood in the door looking like a ghost without a home to haunt.

"Sheriff, any news?"

He stood and shook his head. "I'm afraid we've got nothing. But we'll find him, I promise." Krosby wasn't the type to make promises he couldn't keep, but the anguish in the woman's face twisted his heart. She needed hope, and even if she hated him later, it was a mercy to give her hope now.

She flashed him a sad smile.

"I'm actually here to speak with Kevin."

"He's not home, um—" she paused, wiping her eyes and nose, "he's staying at his friend Danny Gaston's for a couple days. I thought it might help him keep his mind off things."

Krosby nodded. "Not a bad idea." He wished he could do or say more. "Well, I'll head on over there. I wanted to speak with Danny as well. Nothing bad, of course," he added when concern raised her brows. "I just want to go back over their stories, see if they remembered anything they may have forgotten to mention yesterday."

The drive to Danny's house was a bit longer. His tires crunched on the gravel drive. Bikes lay scattered across the yard, but he didn't see the boys around. The front porch creaked underfoot as Krosby strained to listen for any sign that someone was home, but he heard nothing. He knocked on the front door, and when there was no answer, he tried the handle. The door was unlocked, and Krosby cautiously stepped inside.

"Hello?" Krosby called out, the word lingering in the stillness.

A figure turned a corner, a boy in his late teens, curling dumbbells in gym shorts with no shirt. "Uh, hi, Sheriff," the boy said, stopping mid-curl and tossing the weights with a clatter onto the carpeted floor of the adjoining room.

"Is your mom home?" he asked, knowing the boy's father was long dead.

He shook his head. "No, she's got a double today."

"Is Danny home?"

"I haven't seen him today. He and Kevin were here last night though."

Krosby didn't like that one bit. "What's your name, son?"

"Richard," he stammered, "Ricky."

"Alright, Ricky, do you know where your brother and Kevin might have gone off to?"

He just shrugged.

And Krosby repressed a sigh. "OK, well if they come home and say they haven't spoken to me, have them call my office. Understand?"

He nodded. "Yes, sir."

Worry gnawed at Krosby as he backed out. He didn't need two more missing boys on his plate.

The first place he could think of was the tree house. Sure enough, as he cruised down the dirt road, a pair of bikes gleamed in the midday sun. Relief eased the tension in his chest as the boys too came into view.

They squirmed beneath his gaze the way Ricky had. Kids were always scared of cops, like they were going to get arrested if they looked at a cop wrong.

Krosby got out of his truck and leaned against the grill. "Boys, what are you doing out here?"

Kevin gulped. "We wanted to see if Mike came back."

Krosby had to work to keep the concern from showing on his face. "Well, that's mighty kind of you, but I don't think you should be coming out here. Not until we figure out where your brother is. Think about your parents? Do they know you're out here?"

Kevin looked down. "No, sir."

The honesty was refreshing. "I've been looking for you boys, wanted to go over your stories from the day Mike went missing."

The boys looked at each other and Danny gulped. "We don't think it was Cecil anymore."

Krosby furrowed his brow. "What made you say that?"

Kevin put a hand up to keep Danny from talking. "We searched the woods by the cemetery yesterday. You see, we saw Cecil driving down the highway toward Moss's the day Mike went missing. He was driving kinda funny. Real slow. I forgot when I talked to you, but then I remembered later. I'm sorry."

Scratching his chin, Krosby tried to keep his temper under control. They were just boys.

"Look, boys, I know you're trying to help, but if you get hurt, it's going to make our job finding Mike harder. Leave the searching to the grownups."

"I'm sorry, sir. We're just trying to help."

Krosby crossed his arms. "I know, I know. Now, take me back for a minute. Tell me about what happened with Cecil that day?"

Danny spoke up, "We were just riding, and he was going real slow, and then once we passed him, he sped off."

"But you didn't see Mike in the car?"

Both boys shook their heads.

"So why did you think it was him?"

Danny shrugged. "Well, it's Cecil, you know?"

Kevin shook his head. "I guess we didn't think about it too well. I mean he could have been in the trunk or something. Besides, we talked to him last night; we think he's innocent."

Krosby pushed himself forward. "Anything else you forgot?"

They both shook their heads, and Kevin said, "We've been talking about everything that happened a lot and neither of us can remember anything else."

"OK, well I want you boys to get on your bikes and head home. I'm going to run over to Moss's, and when I come back this way, I don't want to find you still here."

The boys nodded and jumped to their feet.

Kevin and Danny may have ruled out Cecil, but for the first time since Mike went missing, Krosby had some questions for the old man.

<u>Chapter Ten</u>

38 Hours Missing

He woke with a start, sweat pouring down his face, heart racing. Chest heaving, he sat up, catching his breath, and then looked at the clock.

3:05 a.m.

Fuck.

He ran his fingers through his hair, his hand coming away damp.

A dream, it was just a stupid, damn dream.

There were cops chasing him as he crashed blindly through a blackened underbrush, lungs burning and pulse raging as loud as the baying dogs. They had found him before he'd had a chance to kill the boy. The darkening woods swallowed him whole while dogs gnashed at his heels. But he'd woken up before they'd had the chance to sink their fetid fangs into him.

A dream, he reminded himself over and over as his body twitched and ached with the tension, as if it had really happened.

But it hadn't.

He was too smart to get caught, but he needed to get rid of the boy soon or else—or else the dream may become a reality.

The faces of the others blurred in his mind. The thrill of killing them, the sound of it, remained a pleasant memory, though it did little to cheer him beyond a fleeting smile of remembrance.

He swung his feet out of the bed, the wood floor sticky and gritty beneath the soles of his bare feet. Fumbling in the dark, he felt around for a shirt and tugged it on. Then, without turning on the light, he shuffled across the hall, opening the door. His heart pounded so hard it felt like it would explode. Memories swirled in his head, and he wanted to claw at them, to quiet them, but only one thing would.

The trailer door whined open, and he patted his pocket to make sure he had the key he needed. His hand pressed the hard metal into his skin and some of the tension in his body eased. As he tromped outside, a gush of humid air descended on him like a wet blanket. He wasn't sure if it was worse inside or out. Cicadas and crickets sang along with the glugging of the river while an owl hooted somewhere nearby. Good, he thought, it meant no one would be around to hear what was about to happen.

The path to the shed was easy enough to get to in the dark, especially with the silvery trail of moonlight. People always think the universe is on their side. Rooting for the good guys. Little did they know, the universe didn't give a shit about good or bad. Sometimes it just gets bored, and if you're lucky—it makes things easy for you.

Like the day it gifted him the boy and now the way it illuminated his path.

It was all too easy.

He slipped the key into the padlock; it opened with a satisfying click before he freed it from the hook. The uneven door swung out with a creak, but it didn't wake the boy.

Mike's slow, measured breaths purred into the night. Excitement swelled inside him then. He shuffled closer and squatted down. Slowly, he extended his arm, grazing the boy's cheek and then running a finger along his lips.

Mike stirred.

"It's play time," he whispered, grabbing the boy by the arm and dragging him out of bed.

Mike screamed, but it didn't matter, the gag muffled it. He couldn't handle screamers.

"Shut up," he growled as he flipped Mike over onto the mattress. But ghosts from his past flooded his senses.

The sound of his father's uneven scuffing steps as he made his way down the hall. His hot Johnnie Walker breath on his neck. But he wasn't the little boy anymore.

"Be a good boy, my special boy," he said, echoing his father.

Mike bucked and squirmed. The thrill of that alone should have been enough to get him hard but nothing. He was flatter than roadkill.

"Don't struggle," he hissed.

Mike didn't listen. He kicked, thrashing his legs and wriggling like a worm on a hook.

He grabbed the boy's pants and pulled them down, his drawers going with them.

No, no, no. Why wasn't this working?

"You're gonna like this, boy."

Tears poured from Mike's eyes, leaving damp spots made silvery on the mattress by the moonlight seeping in through the holes in the roof.

"Shut up," he screamed either to himself or to Mike; he didn't know for sure.

With every scream, with every sob, with every tear, he found himself wanting to stop, but then the pictures flashed in his mind, goading him to continue.

"No! Be a good boy."

He took a deep breath, he couldn't afford for his concentration to waver.

The boy continued to struggle, kicking his legs and throwing his arms.

"You'll like it. It'll feel good. Just relax." He tried to ease him, but it wasn't working. He was going about this all wrong.

He reached into his own pants, anger and disgust at himself surging. He got up pacing as he cupped and stroked himself, his dick hanging there like a piece of rotten meat. He needed to calm down, if this was going to work.

Mike's crying wasn't helping. "Shut up!" he screamed, running a shaking hand through his hair. Up and down, he worked in his pants, the desire and rage mixing together. But it was limp, still fucking limp. So he gripped it, pulling it and squeezed. The pain made him wince.

"It's going to feel so good, Mike."

But nothing happened. He was a goddamn failure.

All the while Mike screamed.

"Don't be a damn baby," he muttered to himself, trying to find courage.

He couldn't do it. He quit, removing his hands from his pants, then went to Mike, who winced with his touch. He yanked up the kid's shorts.

It was not going to happen now.

He let go of Mike's arm, a sob escaping his throat. Mike's legs gave out and he slid down, his head banging against the wall, his ass hitting the floor.

Then the tears came. More tears. The man stood there watching the boy cry as memories of the others flashed through his mind, the way they screamed, the way they cried, the way their blood felt on his skin. He had no problem getting it up after killing, but he wanted a live one.

Later, later he would have him and kill him.

But not now. Not yet.

He stormed out, locking the shed behind him. Of course after having a dream like he had, he couldn't get in the mood. Who could?

After work, he'd get the boy to relax with more Coke and candy. Then they'd play.

It was just past four when he returned. He couldn't decide whether it was better to stay up or try to sleep the remaining hour. He didn't want any more dreams. But against his will he fell back asleep, this time dreaming of all the things he would do to that boy.

His alarm rang at 5:30, and he stumbled out of bed. He finished off what was left in a stale can of beer down with his oatmeal and was off to the cotton fields for the day.

It was a hot morning, and by the time the sun was up, he'd sweated through his shirt and had taken off his work gloves to cool off.

He couldn't help but glance up at the woods that surrounded the fields. What was going on in the shed, just beyond his line of sight?

***

The room got hotter as the sun moved overhead, trickling in from different angles through cracks and holes in the shed. Mike tried not to think about what had happened with the man. Nothing about it made sense, and it turned his stomach sour. His mind would go blank like nothing happened until he remembered again and cried.

Being good, whatever that meant, was all Mike could think to do. Otherwise, what? The man said he would hurt him if he wasn't good. And if what he'd done already wasn't hurting him, Mike didn't want to find out what he meant by hurting him.

The scratchy cloth in his mouth made it hard to breathe. Maybe if he was good, the man would stop being so mad.

But he was scared and wanted to go home. He tried to think of something else. He missed his mom and even his stupid brothers.

Tears pricked the back of his eyes and his stomach hurt. He needed to use the bathroom, but no matter how many times he tried, he couldn't make himself go in the bucket unless it was a number one.

A bird cooed nearby. Through a crack in the wall, he could just make out the mourning dove as it fluttered down, landing just outside the shed. It pecked at the dirt, and Mike scooted as close as the chain would allow. The bird took a few more pecks at the ground, then flew away. He wished he could fly away.

Mike's clothes stuck to his body, and the air was heavy. He closed his eyes, trying to will himself to fall asleep, but his mind wouldn't stop. The man's words rang in his ears,

"You'll like it, boy. I'll show you a good time."

His stomach rolled, and he bent over as his body tried to throw up.

He cried, and his mouth watered around the gag as he retched, but there wasn't anything in his stomach. Finally, his body stopped heaving, and his throat burned. He sat back, the world spinning, and his vision went black.

He was in his bedroom. The light was on and the closet door open. It was empty except for his clothes hanging up. His eyes were on the bed. A small figure laid out, a knife sticking out from its chest. Blood, red and thick, oozed out. His mouth dropped open and he screamed.

Then his mother's arms were around him.

"Shh, Mike, it's okay," she soothed, her hand rubbing his back.

"But the blood," he whimpered, the sight still fresh in his mind.

"There's no blood, Michael. It was just a bad dream. It wasn't real."

He looked back, and she was right; it was all gone. "Are you sure, Mama?"

"Of course, I'm sure. Now, it's late; you should go back to sleep."

She pulled him into her chest, and he listened to her heart beating, the sound a comfort.

"Don't let the boogeyman get you," he said as sleep pulled at his eye lids.

She chuckled and her breath was warm on his head.

"The boogeyman isn't real."

"He is too; I've seen him."

"You had a nightmare. None of it was real. You're safe."

"I don't think it was a dream." He pouted, heart beginning to race as tears raced down his cheeks.

She sighed, rubbing her hand along his back.

"Don't you worry about all of that. I'll stay right here until you fall asleep; how about that?"

He nodded. She hugged him tight, and he relaxed, snuggling against her. It wasn't long before she was breathing deep. The steady rhythm and warmth of her calmed him, the way it always did.

"Goodnight, Michael."

A sleepy smile curled on his lips. "Goodnight, Mama."

Mikes eyes shot open, the comfort of the dream evaporating as his surroundings filled his eyes. His face was wet, the salty tears drying. The sky had changed, the bright blue gone, and a grey had settled in.

It was hotter than ever. The sweat making his skin sticky and uncomfortable. The gag made his tongue dry and thick. He imagined what it would feel like to plunge into the river. To just sink below the icy water. But that was impossible.

The door creaked open, and he winced, not wanting to look. From the way he came and went, he guessed the man worked.

"Look at you, all sweaty." The way the words rolled off the man's tongue felt wrong, but he couldn't explain why. The man stepped inside and closed the door. Mike's muscles clenched and his hands became slick. He wanted to scream, but he had nothing left.

***

53 Hours Missing

He set the plate of Vienna sausages and baked beans on the pail by the boy. "Here ya go, Mike. Got some grub for ya," he said, trying to sound cheerful.

But the ungrateful boy just cried all balled up, hugging his knees. His big blue eyes full of fear peered out from beneath his mop of hay-colored hair.

Damn it. Mike had no idea just how bad things could be. He stopped himself from ruffling the boy's hair and sat down on a bench, leaving some space between them.

"I'll unchain your wrists and cut your gag if you promise you're gonna be a good boy. You wouldn't want to do anything that would make me angry would you?"

Fresh tears wet Mike's eyes,, and he shook his head no.

"That's what I thought. You and I are gonna get on just fine then." He shoved his hand into his pocket. The longing and anticipation of touching the boy made his hand shake, but it was too soon; the boy didn't trust him just yet. But like a wild animal, all he needed was to be patient and give him food, and he'd be putty in his hand.

The metal of the knife was hot from his skin, the weight of it familiar and comfortable in his hand. He could kill the boy now, watch the life leave his rabbit-like eyes. But where would the fun in that be? He had more needs than just the thrill of the kill.

He cut the gag, sliding the back of the blade against the boy's round cheek. The momentary contact made his cock pulse with longing, but not much else. Don't think about it. He gripped the boy's chin tightly as he pumped the knife until the blade worked through the fabric. Then he folded the knife and rummaged in his pocket for the key to the shackles he had filched from a cattle farm he'd worked out west. They'd come in handy over the years. With the boy's mouth and hands free, he stepped back, not wanting to push his luck.

"Go on and eat up now, ya hear? Beats a tuna sandwich, don't it?" The boy kept eyeballing him like he was some three-headed mule. He sighed, trying to hold his temper. "Just eat, I won't bite, Mikey."

Showing the boy that he hadn't poisoned the food, he picked up a link of sausage, shoving the whole thing in his mouth. A few minutes passed before the boy's hunger won out, and he started eating. When the boy finished, he licked the last remnants of food from his fingers and wiped his hands on his shorts.

"Now, that wasn't so bad, was it? We're gonna be friends, you and me."

"Where am I? Can I go home now?"

"Now, Mikey, don't be giving me a hard time. I brought ya here to show ya a good time, and that's what we're gonna do. Now, I'll tell ya, when the time comes, but for now, just know this is the best place for ya."

The boy's eyes watered, and he began to cry again.

"Now, none of that," the man scolded. "I didn't bring you here to have you bawling. Ya know, I didn't want to have to do this, but you give me no choice."

The boy's eyes went wide, and his lips trembled as he tried not to cry.

"Please, mister, can't I go home? I miss my mom. I'm sure she's worried sick."

He smiled. The boy was so damn cute. He reached his hand to pat his cheek. Mike flinched, but his hand landed gently on the soft skin of the boy's cheek. He didn't resist as he ran his hand over his shoulder, then down the soft skin of his arm.

Mike pulled away and wrapped his arms around himself, trying to cover his exposed flesh.

"Don't be shy, boy. You've got nothing to worry about."

The boy scooted farther away, and he lost his cool. "Fine. I'm done being nice."

His hand shot out, and he gripped Mike's forearm, pulling the boy against his chest. Mike's breath caught in his throat, and he could feel his heart beating out of his chest. He grabbed the boy's hand, forcing it against the bulge in his pants.

"Don't you see, boy? You do that to me. Just touching you like that gets me all hard. It's natural, and if you're a good boy, I'll let you touch me whenever you want. You just gotta be a good boy and listen."

Tears streamed down Mike's face. "Please, mister, let me go."

The words made him angry. How dare this kid deny him?

"Now, I won't ask you again. You're gonna do what I say, and maybe, I'll let you see the sunshine."

Mike whimpered a little, not saying anything. "That's a good boy."

Mike turned his head, and he caught the side of the boy's mouth with his finger. The touch was electric, sending a current to his cock. He moaned. "I think I want to kiss you. Would you like that, Mikey? If I kissed you?"

Mike was still as a mouse and didn't reply.

He sighed. "If you don't talk, how will I know what you want?"

Mike was quiet, so he pressed his lips against the boy's soft cheek. "You like that, don't you?"

The boy whimpered.

"Tell me you like it."

"I like it; please, mister, I wanna go home."

The words stung, and he wanted to strangle the kid.

"What did I say about being a good boy?" he asked through clenched teeth.

Mike nodded.

He pressed his lips against Mike's cheek. He tasted salty from his tears. But it was too late, as he had already gone limp. Rage filled him then, and he pulled his hand back, slapping the boy across the jaw. Mike fell back onto the bench.

He was breathing hard, and he wanted to hit him again, but instead he walked away, locking the door behind him.

The voices came then as he sprinted through the woods back to his trailer. He thundered up the steps and slammed the door behind him, sinking to the floor, crying as the images of the monster under the bed came back to him. The arm that could always reach him, the gravelly voice that always told him it was okay to do bad things, things the others said were wrong because he was his father's special boy.

A fresh wave of tears washed over him and his whole body ached with the memory of his touch, the feel of the belt biting his skin, the burning scent of the alcohol in his nose. He heard the voices screaming in his head. Challenging him to let them take over.

"You're no better than him."

He covered his ears, trying to block out the voices.

"I'm not," he said, his voice thick.

"Then prove it."

"I can't, not right now. It's not safe, not yet."

"Coward."

He didn't answer; there was nothing left to say.

<u>Chapter Eleven</u>

112 Hours Missing

Krosby stepped out of his Chevy squinting in the late afternoon sunlight, his boots crunching on the gravel as he made his way into Moss's store The bell overhead tinkled as he stepped in, the men chatting away stopping as the door closed behind him.

"Evening, Sheriff," the men called in unison.

"Gentlemen," he said, tipping his hat, taking in Sal Whitman and Cletus Ball. Two retirees with nothing better to do than hang out here and chew the fat.

Moss peeked out from around the corner, broom in hand. "Sheriff," he said with a nod.

"You got a minute, Moss?"

"This about that Franklin boy?" he said with one gray brow arched.

"Afraid so." Krosby kept his tone neutral, not wanting to give Moss or any of the other ears in the room any space to read into things. These men were harmless but terrible gossips, and he didn't need the gossip mill muddying the case.

"You found him?"

"Not yet." Krosby step closer to him and rested his hip against the counter.

Moss leaned the broom against the wall and folded his arms across his apron clad chest.

"So what can I do for ya?"

"Tell me about the day Mike Franklin went missing. I've been told that his brother came here that day?"

"Not much to say, really. He and one of the Gaston boys came in here, buying lunch on John Franklin's credit. They talked about the tree house they was buildin'. They ordered three sandwiches, and that was when they told me that the little 'un was still out there. Nothing else worth mentioning; they took their stuff and left."

"That's it? Anyone else in here 'round then?"

"Well . . ." Mr. Moss looked away and sighed. "Not long after the boys left Cecil showed up. He bought a couple of Cokes and some candy."

"Is that unusual?" Krosby asked, trying to restrain the irritation he felt at the mention of Cecil. Couldn't people just let that man be?

Moss shrugged. "Not really, but he did buy two Cokes, instead of one."

"I see," he said in an exhale.

"He coulda had that boy in the trunk of his car, and we didn't even know," Cletus offered.

Krosby masked his frustration with a smile like a kindergarten teacher at the end of her rope, explaining something for the eighteenth time. "Let's not jump to conclusions. Everybody always wants to blame Cecil every time something goes wrong, and he's yet to do a damn thing."

Cletus and Sal just shrugged, looking at him like he was the dumb one in the room.

"Look, I'm following all leads, but right now, I don't think it was Cecil, and I don't want you guys gettin' folk all riled up about it. The last thing we need is a manhunt when we should all be looking for this boy. Am I clear?"

All the men grunted and nodded their heads, but it didn't sit well with Krosby. If things weren't handled carefully, Cecil could be in danger. It wasn't a crime to buy two Cokes, especially on a day as hot as that, but he had to follow it up.

If anything, it would give him a chance to warn Cecil.

"Thanks, gentlemen, I'll be in touch if I have any more questions."

The men mumbled their goodbyes, and he tipped his hat, letting the door slam behind him.

He climbed in his Blazer, the leather seat burning his ass even through his uniform. If it was this hot in June, what the hell would it be like come August when the heat really set in?

He chucked his hat on the passenger seat. "Damn it," he hissed as he put the key in the ignition and turned it over. The truck rumbled to life. He flipped the A/C and cranked the vents toward him, letting the balmy, not-quite-yet-cool air blow over him. Something was better than nothing.

The engine hummed as he reached over and pulled open the glove box. Inside sat the case file. He scanned the thin notes, wishing something useful had added itself in his absence. No luck.

There was nothing he hadn't already seen, but there was something about it gnawing at him. It had been forty-eight hours, and the longer they went without a lead, the worse it was going to be.

While a Coke purchase was circumstantial at best, he was in the area at the time the abduction occurred. The men were right; Cecil had the opportunity, and at the end of the day, opportunity mattered more than motive.

Motive seldom made sense to anyone outside of the perpetrator's head. Here he had to focus on opportunity, even though his gut told him Cecil was in the clear.

Krosby pulled the shifter in to drive and sprayed gravel as he backed up and lurched out onto the road, headed toward the cemetery.

The Chevy bucked and bounced along the one-lane highway leading toward town. He pressed the gas pedal to the floor, the engine roaring as he flew past the turnoff to the tree house. His fingers tightened around the steering wheel, the leather squeaking as his sweaty palms rubbed against it.

"Just hold on, Mike," he pleaded through a clenched jaw. "I'm gonna find you; I just need you to hold on."

As he approached the turnoff to the cemetery, he eased off the gas and the truck slowed to a crawl. The suspension whined as the truck coasted through the open wrought-iron gate and down the dirt road to the gravel parking lot. He parked in a patch of shade near the entrance and killed the engine, the cabin suddenly quiet.

His door opened with a creak, and he climbed out and then ducked back in to retrieve his hat. Krosby's heart hammered in his chest. Cemeteries were never his favorite place to be. The idea of bodies in boxes six feet below made him uneasy. He would take a living thug over a dead saint any day.

Krosby's mouth suddenly went dry, but he straightened his hat and strode up the hill toward Cecil's shed. He had only made it a few yards when he stopped short, glimpsing a figure hunched over a crooked headstone, tending to the flowers at its base.

"Afternoon, Cecil," Krosby called out, ambling over.

Great, they were going to have this talk in the thick of bodies.

Cecil looked up, squinting against the glare. "What do you want?"

Krosby gave a thin smile. "I'm not here to hassle you. I just needed to ask you a few questions about the other day."

"Oh lordy, what now?" Cecil groused, while wiping his hands on his overalls, leaving streaks of dirt.

"Just routine inquiries." Krosby tried a more sincere tone to put the man at ease, but it did little. Anger wrinkled the lines between Cecil's brow, and his mouth hung open slightly, revealing a tremor. He seemed so weak and fragile. Could he really have overpowered the boy?

One glimpse at the tough biceps bulging off of stick-thin arms argued he could have. Caring for the cemetery was manual labor. He may be lean, but he was probably still strong.

Krosby tucked these observations away and kept going. "Moss said you came into the store a couple days back, bought two Cokes instead of one. Any reason for that?"

Cecil snorted. "Shoot, you drove all the way out here to ask me about why I bought a drink?"

Saying it out loud did make Krosby feel ridiculous, but it was a reasonable enough line of inquiry when the alternative line was a big fat blank. "It's not just that. Other witnesses say you were seen near the area where the Franklin boy went missing shortly before his brother discovered he was missing."

Cecil snapped, kicking a clump of dirt. "So a man goes out to buy a drink and suddenly he's accused of kid snatching." He shook his head. "I've already been searched from pillar to post, I got nothing to hide, so either arrest me or let me get back to work."

Krosby held up a placating hand. "Nobody's aiming to arrest anyone. But a kid's gone missing so I gotta follow every lead." He paused. "You didn't happen to see anything strange the past few days, did ya? Anyone lurking about?"

Cecil shook his head. "Ain't seen nothing. But I'll be sure to alert you if I spot any shady-looking Coke drinkers." He grinned mockingly through anger still darkening his eyes.

Krosby touched the brim of his hat. "Appreciate the help, Cecil." Krosby almost apologized. It wasn't the man's fault that the folk in this town didn't like him. Again, his instincts buzzed in his gut, telling him Cecil wasn't his man, but instincts weren't admissible in court.

He sighed. He was grasping at straws and there wasn't anything here. "Alright, well, I'll be off. You take care now, you hear?"

"Yes, sir," Cecil called.

As he opened the driver's-side door and sat down, something on his boot caught his eye. Strands of paper clung to the grooves of his boot sole. Frowning, he lifted his foot up and plucked one off. It was a strip of cigarette paper like those he'd seen near the tree house.

He scraped a fingernail along the crevices, pulling up shreds of tobacco mixed with dirt.

Strange, he didn't remember stepping on any cigarettes by the truck.

Krosby glanced back over his shoulder, a sinking feeling in his chest. Not two hundred feet away, Cecil struck a match and lifted it to the cigarette perched in his lips, then shook the flame out. Krosby's breath caught in his throat as Cecil's cheeks hollowed with the inhalation.

He rested his head against the steering wheel as the slight breeze carried the scent of the smoke his way. He hadn't known Cecil smoked, and though he wanted to believe the old man was harmless, the investigator in him couldn't ignore what seemed to be mounting evidence.

Still, Cecil deserved to be innocent until proven guilty, same as anyone else. Krosby could only follow the evidence, wherever it led. . . .

With a heavy sigh, he raised his head and turned the key.

Twenty minutes later, Krosby pulled into the station parking lot, his stomach in knots. Several more station wagons plastered with different logos now accompanied the news vans parked haphazardly near the entrance, antennas pointing skyward.

The gaggle of press swarmed him as he cut a path through them to the front door of the station. They peppered him with questions about Mike Franklin. Krosby quickened his pace and met them with a gruff "No comment" before slamming the door on their microphones.

Inside, the station bustled with a tense energy. Phones rang constantly. Deputies shuffled back and forth, conferring on notes. Mrs. Goodson, with the phone receiver pressed to her ear, waved him over, worry lines creasing her face.

"It's a madhouse, Sheriff! The tip line hasn't stopped ringing since the news report ran. I've got a stack of messages with people claiming they saw a creepy guy and a boy out by the cemetery. And there's been three calls saying Cecil has the kid locked in a cellar or—" she paused glancing down at her hastily scribbled note, "a cave."

Krosby dragged a hand down his stubbled chin. "Christ . . . OK, thank you. I'll take those."

"There's more. Mrs. Whitiker swears—"

He cut her off. "Swears she saw the devil himself with glowing red eyes and horns hiding in Cecil's shed?"

Mrs. Goodson gave an exasperated snort. "More or less. There are a lot of rumors going around that he did it."

"Emphasis on the rumors part," he said picking up the tip-line messages and skimming through them.

"Well, he doesn't exactly put people at ease," she said, and Krosby shook his head.

"Why is it his job to do that? Last time I checked, it's ours."

The phone rang, and she answered it. Krosby walked away, not wishing to say something he'd regret. Mrs. Goodson was nice enough, but it didn't take much for folks around there to pick a side and die before they changed their minds.

Krosby shook his head, anger building as he reached his office. The door slamming behind him made the flag peel down in one corner. He shoved the tack back into place and plopped in his chair.

Krosby let out a heavy sigh and loosened his tie. He eyed the overflowing inbox and messages stacked atop folders and reports. Outside his office, phones continued ringing as more tips poured in.

A knock at the door came seconds before it opened. Deputy

Hawkins stepped in, Jones at his heels.

"Got anything worth my time?" Krosby barked before either man could speak.

Hawkins gazed at the pad of paper in hand, then looked up. "A few people claim seeing the kid alone over by the bakery downtown."

"Anything else?"

Jones answered this time. "Mostly just complaints about Cecil."

"Let me guess, mostly anonymous?"

"Yup. Unless you count Mrs. Whitiker's devil sighting."

"I want all the bakery sightings checked out. Send Jenkins and Hayes. The anonymous ones about Cecil . . . we'll keep tabs. I'm sure more will roll in. As for the widow's devil tale," he raised a dubious eyebrow, "tell Mrs. Whitiker to lay off the sherry before noontime."

Following procedure meant checking out every story, no matter how ludicrous or obviously cooked up out of spite. He didn't have the time or manpower to chase these horseshit leads.

A sharp rap at his door drew all of their gazes. Mrs. Goodson entered, holding out a written phone message, her mouth pressed thin. "Just took this one, Sheriff. I think you ought to handle it personally."

Frowning, Krosby accepted the note. His eyes scanned the scratchy writing and his fist unconsciously clenched, nearly tearing the paper. Hot anger coursed through him as he read the detailed threat promising to "string that baby killer Cecil up good."

Krosby crumpled the page, tossing it forcefully toward the waste basket. "Son of a bitch!"

He paced behind his desk, chest heaving. This was exactly what he feared. Wild rumors fueling some idiot with a vendetta, itching for vigilante violence, whether Cecil was guilty or not.

Krosby jabbed an angry finger at the phone. "Get me Cecil on the line, now! And tell Deputy Hayes to haul his ass over to Cecil's place. Guard detail until further notice."

Mrs. Goodson nodded, hurrying out with the other two to follow orders as Krosby sank heavily back into his chair. He kneaded the tension in his neck, staring at the aging Marines flag on the dingy walls. He had to get a handle on this circus before things got uglier. Baseless gossip and old grudges wouldn't sway his duty. Just the facts would guide him, no matter what anybody said or who they wanted to blame.

Krosby leaned forward, cradling his head in his hands. The nagging ache behind his eyes throbbed relentlessly. He pressed the heels of his palms against his eyelids until bursting lights appeared.

Dropping his hands, he blinked hard in the dim office, the shadowed corners swirling like living things. Or shadows of all the faceless suspects his gut told him held the answers. It could have been anyone, or even someone just passing through.

He shoved away from his desk to pace, loose change and keys rattling across the chipped surface. He could feel the hands of the clock boring into his back, like eyes accusing, questioning. One thing was clear—time was ticking away for that missing boy.

The public wanted a face for their fear and outrage. They pointed fingers at Cecil, but Krosby knew that the truth was much more elusive. His suspect was without form or name. Just a black, hulking question mark.

The clues seemed to change shape– misshapen and disjointed no matter how he tried forcing them to align. Soda bottles. Cigarette butts. Shadowy forms hovering at the fringes of the crime scene. It all swirled together with his frustration, never coalescing into anything substantial he could grasp onto.

Krosby slowly turned, gaze leveled at the window behind his desk. He drew closer, his own haggard reflection materializing as if summoned from his agitated mind. The bags under his eyes held mute accusation.

You're running out of time and luck, Sheriff. . . . Tick-tock.

Then he yelled, "Mrs. Goodson—get the mayor on the phone."

Chapter Twelve

117 Hours Missing

Jill tucked an errant hair behind her ear as she scanned the sea of tense faces packing the stuffy town hall. The propped-open doors did little to ease the heat. Krosby and his men had alerted the paper, and the Appalachian telegraph, a.k.a. the gossip mill, that an emergency town meeting was being held that night to address community concerns about the disappearance of Mike Franklin.

Mayor Andy Lewis tugged at his shirt collar as sweat beaded on his forehead. No doubt trying to wrap his small-town sensibilities around something this unpleasant was getting to him.

"Alright, folks, settle down . . ." he began, and the rush of voices dulled until the room was dead silent.

"People in the rest of the country don't understand what it means to be from a small town like Everett. People like us work hard through good times and bad; we're a tough people, and we will get through this the way we always do, by staying strong as a community."

His typical canned lines about "staying strong as a community" rang hollow. This wasn't a drought, with farmers worrying about their cotton crop; this was a missing boy. Fear and frustration rolled off the impatient crowd. Lewis knew these people wanted decisive action, not platitudes.

"Mayor, I've got kids afraid to go to sleep!" a woman's shrill voice cut through the din.

"Now, I'm just as upset about this terrible incident as the rest of y'all."

Jill suppressed an eye roll, watching the mayor flounder while voices in the crowd hissed their judgment to their neighbors. Jill shifted in her seat, trying to tune out the noise. The heat of so many bodies pressed in around her. She tugged at her own shirt collar, a rivulet of sweat running down her back, all while Lewis continued to spew his usual B.S. that he trotted out at every town ceremony while avoiding specifics on the investigation.

"What are we gonna do to find that poor child?" a voice called from the opposite side of the room answered by another. "Cecil is the creep that did this! If the cops won't get 'im, we should."

Mayor Lewis's eyes burst wide as he stammered, "P-p-please, I need your help here, folks. We gotta stay calm and organized, or we'll be no better than wild dogs."

The mayor tried unsuccessfully to gain control. A large, angry man rose and started shouting.

"Mayor, this ain't no joke! My four kids came crying to me saying Cecil was outside their window. My girl is terrified that he's coming for her. I don't wanna be woken up at midnight to find some pervert snatched my baby. You need to do something, or we will!"

Murmurs of agreement rippled through the townspeople as Krosby took the podium. Jill readied her pen, curious if he had any new information that could possibly appease this crowd.

Krosby raised a hand, unsuccessfully quieting the crowd before he shoved two fingers in his mouth and let out an ear-shattering whistle. Jill winced and cupped her ears with her hands. When she let go, the room was silent.

"That's enough! Mayor, I'm gonna take this from here. Y'all sit tight while I lay out where we stand. Then I'll answer questions. But I want to reassure y'all that we're following every lead until we find the boy."

Despite his assurance that they had leads, he remained frustratingly tight-lipped. Maybe they had nothing. As far as she knew there was no evidence. It was as if Mike had disappeared into thin air.

"While you waste time covering your ass, Mike could be dead!" John Franklin bellowed. Jill had not seen him in her previous surveys of the room, and she guessed he'd only just arrived. Behind him in the darkened doorway Jill could just make out Jesse, Kevin, and another boy, a later teen maybe.

She bit her lip. John Franklin oozed violence, and she bet he stank of beer or liquor. Beer, if she was guessing. It was strange the way a man could be so well liked by others in his community when sober, but the moment he drank, he turned into something unrecognizable. A mountain of a man who left a trail of fear in his wake.

John walked deeper into the room, his family slinking in behind him. Jesse led the boys to the right, where they lined up against the wall, but John walked down the aisle between the rows of folding metal chairs, his gaze never wavering from Krosby.

"We've got every man out beating the bushes, searching every nook and cranny. We're doing everything in our power to bring your boy home safe."

"Well, then why is Cecil still free?" The room erupted into a cacophony of shouts and waving fists. Jill watched Sheriff Krosby try in vain to reassure the riled mob, his voice strained. But John's wild accusations only whipped the crowd into more of a frenzy.

"Why are you protecting Cecil? He's the one you should be after!"

Jill frowned, shaking her head. She wanted Cecil to be investigated, but this group was ready to see him executed, without evidence. Unless they knew things she didn't, and she doubted that.

Sheriff Krosby tried to respond, but John cut him off. "Why haven't you arrested him? He's probably out there right now, snatching up more kids!" John's words came out slippery with streaks of angry spit flying through the air.

"We don't have anything solid to bring him in. If we arrest someone on a whim, we're no better than the criminals we're chasing.

We gotta do this right."

"The hell with your useless rules, I want my boy!" Franklin erupted. His mammoth frame seemed to fill half the aisle as he lurched unsteadily forward. Before anyone could react, he charged the front like an enraged bull.

Jill watched in horror as Franklin plowed into Krosby full-force. The sheriff had no time to brace himself as the two men toppled backward in a tangle of limbs. The sharp crack of Krosby's head hitting the wooden floor reverberated like a gunshot, followed swiftly by the sickening thud of Franklin's meaty fists finding their mark.

Chaos exploded. Deputies swarmed to intervene, but Franklin was a mountain of frenzied muscle. His blows came relentlessly despite two men clinging to each bulging arm. Blood arced through the air with every furious swing.

"I'll kill you!" he roared as Krosby desperately tried deflecting the blows. "Worthless pig!" The sheriff's face was a pulpy mess, shirt stained dark crimson.

Finally Deputy Tripplett intervened, eyes blazing and pistol drawn. He jammed the barrel under Franklin's ear. "Get off him, goddamn it! Now!!"

Panting, face twitching with rage, Franklin slowly unclenched his bloody fists. As deputies hauled him off the battered sheriff, Jill spotted deep gouges torn across Franklin's neck and forearms—defensive wounds courtesy of Krosby's fingernails. She shuddered, considering how much worse it might have been.

The sheriff, face covered in blood, stood, his lip swelling. He dabbed the back of his hand to his split lip. "Listen up! You want your boy found, I'm the best chance you got. Now I'm gonna ask you to trust me, and I'll get the sonofabitch that did this."

He turned, nodding to his deputy.

"Tripplett, lock him up for now."

"How dare you lock me up while Cecil goes free? What about my son?" John struggled in the officer's grip.

"We're doing the best we can."

John shook his head, his eyes bloodshot. "Not good enough."

Krosby nodded at the deputies. "Take him."

As they hauled the struggling man away, Jill caught the look exchanged between the two officers. It wasn't encouraging. She bit her lip, the tension in her neck and shoulders increasing.

Once the man was out of sight, the Sheriff turned back to the restless crowd who seemed to be on the side of John Franklin.

They began shouting, "Arrest Cecil."

"Hang the bastard!"

Jill shook her head in disgust. How could people behave this way? They had no idea who had done this or even if Cecil had a connection. It made her sick to her stomach.

The frenzied mob pressed toward the exit, the mood turning uglier by the minute.

"Let's go ask Cecil ourselves," one potbellied man whispered to another. Soon the plan spread like wildfire through the crowd. And a convoy of trucks departed. Jill ran inside to where Sheriff Krosby sat being patched up by Dr. McGregor. Blood still dripped from a nasty gash above his eye, the white of his left socket a burst crimson starburst.

Jill waited until the doctor was finished, a cold sweat trickling down her back. She had no desire to get in the way, but this was a huge story, and she would not pass it up.

Krosby caught her gaze and scowled.

"I'm not in the mood, Miss Greco?"

Jill nodded, shifting from one foot to the other. "You need to send everyone you can out to the cemetery."

"What are you talking about?"

"I overheard some of the men, just now. They're all going out there. . . ."

Sheriff Krosby cursed and got to his feet, unholstering his two-way. "All units, this is Krosby, I need all available men to get out to the cemetery. Copy?"

The radio crackled, but no replies came. Jill and the sheriff stared at each other.

"I've got a bad feeling about this," she said.

"Since when do you care? You're the one helping to fan the flames against him."

The hairs on the back of her neck stood up as anger roiled in her gut. "Look, we are on the same side. All I did was pass along information to you that Kevin Franklin told me. I didn't spread it around. Think what you want of me, but I have integrity, and while you sit here, throwing darts at me, Cecil may be in danger."

He nodded but said nothing else, simply strolled out of the building. She followed, but not after Krosby; she hopped in her car and high-tailed it out to the cemetery. A story was a story, and she was going to see it through.

The dirt road leading into the cemetery was crowded with vehicles. Jill pulled off the side and hopped the fence. As she walked toward the commotion, she noticed that many of the cars were unoccupied, though their engines idled and headlights lit up the sea of men around the shack.

Her heart hammered as she crept closer, the scene before her playing out like a nightmare.

Men poured into the shed where everyone knew Cecil lived, shouting, "Come out you creep," or some similar phrase, but she did not see Cecil. Where was he? It was gone eight. He hadn't been at the town meeting, so where was he?

Her brows furrowed slightly. It was good he wasn't here, but at the same time, it didn't look good for him.

"He's not here." One of the men yelled, "Burn it down."

Suddenly a shotgun blast went off, and Jill nearly dropped to the ground uncertain of where the sound had come from

"Get away from here," Krosby's voice barked. She searched the scurrying crowd but didn't see him.

In the chaos of the mob breaking apart, the sudden swoosh of flames seemed unreal, dreamlike. Flames crawled across one wall of the shed, greedily lapping at the wood until, in mere seconds, the entire makeshift home was aflame.

She stared transfixed by the growing flames. She should go, but something held her rooted to the spot, eyes darting over the faces in the crowd.

A movement, almost imperceptible, caught her attention. A dark figure crouched behind a tree, not too far from the shack. She squinted, straining her eyes as the figure slipped away. She couldn't see any defining features, and yet, something about it was familiar.

"Hey!"

Jill jumped and whirled around. Her pulse was racing, and the world seemed to tilt and swirl. She took a step back, suddenly lightheaded, but it was just Krosby, shotgun still in hand. "I can't reach anyone on the radio. I need you to go to the firehouse and tell them I said to get their asses out here, or they will have me to answer to."

Still in shock, Jill nodded and retreated to her car. She drove too fast, the images played out in her head on a loop. The men, the shotgun, the burning building. Her hands trembled as she gripped the steering wheel. It was startling just how quickly ordinary people could become monsters.

The firehouse was dark when she arrived. She cupped her hands on the glass of the door to the garage bay. The firetruck was inside. She rang the buzzer on the door to the attached living quarters. Holding it for longer than necessary to ensure anyone inside knew this was serious. Lights flickered on inside the main firehouse as footsteps shuffled to the door.

The chief, a plump, friendly, and mustachioed man with a permanent smile etched on his face, unlocked the door.

"Jill, what's going on?"

"A mob set fire to Cecil's shack."

The chief's face morphed from friendly and open to shock and dismay.

"I'll get my men on it."

With that, Jill ran back to her car. The adrenaline had faded, and she felt her energy ebbing, the long night finally taking a toll. But there was more work to bed done.

Twenty minutes later, she sat at her desk, hands poised over the keys. She rolled the platen knob, lining up the paper, and began tapping the keys:

> Last night, a mob of angry townspeople set fire to the home of Cecil Jordan. Sheriff Krosby arrived on the scene and intervened, causing the crowd to disperse. Mr. Jordan was not at home during the attack, which leaves the question unanswered as to why the town reacted so harshly.

Although no connection has been made between Mr. Jordan and the disappearance of eight-year-old Mike Franklin, who has been missing for nearly three days. To this reporter's knowledge Mr. Jordan has no criminal record.

Jill frowned and reread her last few sentences. Her words seemed hollow, but it was the truth. She could not report more than what she knew.

She pulled the paper from the machine and readied the next sheet. She rewrote her description of the mob setting flame to Cecil's shed while police, except Krosby, turned a blind eye. She slid the carriage return with a resounding ding, paused to gather her thoughts, then continued relating the details circling back to the important element the mob seemed to have forgotten.

The town is still searching for answers, and hopefully the return of the missing boy.

Until then, the only thing that can be done is wait, and continue the search.

She hammered the final period key fiercely and leaned back. Jill scanned over the copy, making sure the ribbon ink had not faded too much. Her hands trembled and chest felt tight, but she refused to self-censor, though one thing still gave her pause, a nagging thought prodding her conscience.

There was a possibility that Cecil had taken the boy. And yet, as much as she tried, she couldn't quite make herself believe it. She hoped for the sake of Mike Franklin she was wrong.

With a sigh, Jill stood, stretching her aching limbs. Jill gathered up the typed pages and neatly stacked them before clipping them together. She swiftly folded the papers in thirds and tucked them in a folder. Grabbing her handbag, she headed out the door into the darkness of the night.

It was twenty to midnight and the town was asleep, save for the workers at the newspaper office. She drove along the quiet, dark street, passing closed shops and the darkened diner. A lone streetlamp illuminated the alley separating the barber shop and hardware store.

She pulled up behind the single-story brick building that held *The Bush County Herald*. Jill hurried inside, making a beeline past the empty receptionist's desk for the production room in the back. The smell of fresh ink filled the air as the printing press whirred, spitting out the latest edition.

Jill spotted her editor Hank gruffly overseeing the final printing. "Hank, I've got something that needs to run in tomorrow's paper."

The bulldog-like man arched a bushy eyebrow. "Oh you do, eh? This have anything to do with that mess down at the town hall tonight?"

At Jill's solemn nod, the editor gestured to his office door. "Well c'mon then, let's take a look."

Jill exhaled in relief as she followed him inside. Hank could be cantankerous and often left Jill feeling uncertain of where she stood with him. Almost like he would disagree with her just to humor himself. As he scanned the first few paragraphs, his frown deepened, but resolve glinted in his eyes when they met Jill's.

He pointed his hand at her words and said, "I can't run this."

Jill's face fell. "What? Why not?"

"Listen, if this is true—" she cut him off.

"It is true; I witnessed it myself!"

"This is gonna make a lot of people angry, and we need those people to enjoy our paper. If half of the town thinks we don't support their view," he tsked his tongue, "then we're toast, sweetheart."

She sat straighter and smacked the desk. "But it's the truth. The whole town is too busy looking at Cecil; they could be making it easy on whoever really did this."

He shrugged and dropped the paper. "You're right."

Hank folded his hands across his suspendered belly. "Maybe we'll just tweak it a bit."

"That's censorship!"

"It's smart. Look, stop acting like this is the USSR. I'll add a couple lines asking the questions people want to know, like where was Cecil during the meeting at the town hall, and then we circle back to the tragedy."

Jill's face twisted, disgusted. "That's a bunch of horse crap."

Hank's eyebrows raised. "It's the only way it's getting in."

"Then don't run it. Run mine, and let them know exactly how the town is behaving. You won't have to worry about subscribers because you won't have any."

He leaned forward, eyes narrowed. "You're awfully fired up for a small-town newspaper reporter."

Jill crossed her arms and leaned back. "Just tell me, are you running the article, or not?"

Hank shook his head, a hint of amusement in his eyes. "I'll run it."

Jill smiled. "Thank you."

She stood and turned to leave the office. She could feel his gaze boring into her back.

Jill awoke early the next morning, anticipation making her restless. She had barely slept wondering about the town's reaction to her words. Practically jumping out of bed, she hurried outside in her robe to check the newspaper delivery box by the front gate.

Her hands trembled slightly as she pulled out the new edition, heart quickening as she unfolded it, expecting to see her headline emblazoned across the front page. Instead, it read, "TOWN SEEKS JUSTICE FOR FRANKLIN BOY."

Confused and angry, she stormed back inside to call Hank, nearly ripping the phone cord from the wall. His gruff voice answered on the second ring.

"Hank! What the hell happened? Where's my article?"

"Now don't get your panties in a twist. I thought about what you said and decided to run it with the tweaks I mentioned."

She scanned the article as he spoke. "Tweaks? You sensationalized the whole damn thing! This is barely the story that I wrote."

"I gave it more pizazz, added some more flair."

"No, you took the whole thing and made it about Cecil and not Mike Franklin. Where are the questions? Where is the information about the missing child?"

"Now listen, Miss Priss. It's not all about you and your opinions. We are trying to sell papers. I didn't think it would be so difficult for you to understand."

Jill felt heat rising up her neck, anger coiling in her gut. But before she could say anything, he said, "If we have a problem, I think tomorrow's paper is going to have an ad for a new journalist in it."

She tightened her jaw. "Understood." Then she hung up.

Chapter Thirteen

120 Hours Missing

He tore through the darkened forest, heart racing, hoping no snarled root or other unseen thing would trip him up. The fucking bitch reporter had seen him. But it didn't matter. It was dark; he was pretty forgettable in daylight, let alone at night. Besides, what did it matter? No one knew him, and he wasn't the one committing a crime, at least not there.

And that felt pretty damn good. Still, he couldn't be too careful. Better to shit n' get than be gotten.

Filtered moonlight cut between the trees as his boots pounded the uneven ground. No other sounds except his wheezing breaths came as the roar of the mob died away. Since he'd been out of jail he'd let himself go. Not like some of the fat fucks down at the bar, with their pig bellies rolling over their belts. He was wasting away. That's what happens when you drink more than you eat.

Maybe, after the boy, when he moved on to another place, he'd take better care of himself. Farm work ensured he stayed strong, sure, but running was a whole different thing. He remembered running during basic. The way the drill sergeant got off on seeing scrawny men floundering in the heat, shivering in the rain, while he demanded they run faster and harder.

He'd kill that man if he ever got the chance to. Simply because he deserved it.

He stopped running, slowing as he got to his car, still parked where he'd left it at Waller's farm. A grin spread across his sallow face as he savored the electric atmosphere in that stuffy town hall.

Everyone who was anyone had gone to the town meeting. It would look strange if he hadn't. So he'd jumped in a truckload of the other pickers who'd headed over to the town hall.

All those self-righteous blowhards, usually too busy minding everyone else's business, were now turning on each other as rumors flew about that caretaker and devil worship.

As he slid into his car, a cackle escaped him thinking of the way that drunkard Franklin went apeshit attacking the sheriff.

When it'd happened, he'd had to clamp a hand over his mouth to keep from cackling out loud at seeing the Everett's little provincial world unravel. Served them right for being so quick to blame Cecil with no proof except their own ignorance, but it suited him just fine.

Best of all had been shouting along with those men by the door about grabbing Cecil up for "real justice." In the past, his kills had been swift and planned. By the time a search party was gathered, he was long gone. This was the first time he'd stayed around long enough to see the effects of his actions, and he had to admit he liked it.

Too bad for them that they were chasing the wrong man, or they might've saved the cop some legwork. Those bunch of hicks couldn't find their own assholes with a hunting dog and a flashlight.

The drive back to his trailer was clear and quiet. No car had been within sight. His rotten-planked trailer finally emerged, windows dark as pitch. But he didn't go to his trailer. Instead, he grabbed a flashlight from his car and cut onto the path to his shed. He fumbled with the key in the stubborn lock while his ears strained to detect any sounds within.

Hinges squealed loudly in the eerie silence. He wedged himself through the narrow opening. A frightened rustling met his entrance as Mike Franklin recoiled deeper into the shadows from the beam of his light.

The reek of stale urine burned the man's nostrils, and he curled his lip. A plan had come to him just then. Stepping closer, Mike cowered as he dragged him to his feet. He didn't cry; that was a pleasant change. The townies could go on blaming each other to their hearts' content.

"I'm gonna free your hands, and I want you to take your shirt off." He tried to keep his tone stern but not threatening. The boy still didn't cry, simply extended his arms. Maybe he was learning after all.

He undid the restraints and prepared for Mike to attack, but he did nothing but remove his shirt and hand it to him.

"Good boy. " After re-securing his hands, he undid the chain around his ankle. Mike winced and sucked in air with the pain. His ankle was bruised and bloodied. Serves him right for thrashing about and probably trying to pull his leg out.

"Remove your shorts, but you can keep your drawers on," he said, but when Mike shimmied out of his shorts the piss stain in his underwear set him off.

Cursing silently beneath gritted teeth, "Ah shit, you filthy animal. You're supposed to use the bucket."

Mike said nothing and handed him the shorts.

"Take those off too. I'll get you something else to wear."

Mike's hesitation was the first hint of communication, but he didn't protest, just went along with it, peeling off the filthy garment.

"Good, now sit down and don't move."

Mike did as instructed, keeping his gaze averted. It wasn't like he could go anywhere if he wanted to.

He stepped out and went into the small closet at the end of the trailer. He kept spare clothes in a box. He found a pair of pajama pants and a t-shirt and took them back to the shed.

He removed the chains from his wrist again.

"Stand up and raise your arms." Just then he realized the boy had not been chained at the ankle and hadn't tried anything. He could have tried to run now, but he didn't.

Mike continued to obey, standing awkwardly in the middle of the floor while he pulled the shirt over the boy's head, letting his fingertips graze over the boy's nipples.

Mike shuddered slightly, but otherwise remained still.

"Put the pants on."

Once Mike was dressed, he returned the chain to Mike's wrists and hesitated at the ankle.

"I'm going to leave that off; don't make me regret it. And if you try anything funny . . . I know where your family lives. It would be a shame if I killed them all because you couldn't behave, wouldn't it?"

Mike's eyes widened, his lower lip quivering.

"Don't give me that face; just behave, and they will live."

He grabbed the kid and shoved him back down on the pallet.

"I'll get you some dinner."

He locked up the shed and went back into the house. He opened another can of pork and beans and dumped it into a bowl. They tasted fine straight out of the can, no need to trouble himself with heating it up.

He trudged back to the shed feeling fed up with the work of keeping the kid alive. The thought made him cackle.

Back in the shed, Mike was sitting cross-legged on the pallet, his hands clasped together and his head down. He hadn't cried today. Which was a good sign—he was almost ready then.

"Here's your dinner." He set the bowl on the pallet, and Mike took it with an appreciative nod and began the awkward task of eating with his hands bound. He was too tired to try anything with the boy tonight. As he left, he glanced back at Mike and thought, Tomorrow, we will play tomorrow.

The next morning, before the sky had barely lightened, he rose, got ready, and went to work. He had to show his face among the sleepy-eyed early shift pickers as they headed to the fields. None would mark his absence today as he slipped away to pay a visit to the cemetery.

He planned to plant the clothes somewhere on the grounds near that shed Cecil shacked up in. He parked his car on the dirt road that wound down below the cemetery. He hiked through the woods hoping Cecil was still hiding out somewhere else after last night's attack.

Among the musty dirt smell of the woods mingled the smell of wood smoke. It was heavy in the hazy, muggy morning. Someone must have had a good fire. Gnats swarmed his sweat-soaked neck, but he dared not slap them away for fear of making a sound. He clutched the bundle tightly to his pounding chest.

He was a few feet away from the clearing when he saw the charred remains of the little shack. Those men must have gotten more out of control than he realized.

This was just perfect; he could just roll the clothes in the ashes and make it look like the clothes had always been there.

He crept up to the shack, the bundle of Mike's clothes tucked under his arm. As he got closer, he kept eyes peeled for Cecil but saw and heard nothing. He approached the burned-out shell, the remains of the shack still warm. A thick layer of soot and ash covered the ground and walls.

He kneeled and rolled the clothing around in the ashes. After a few minutes, he stood up and brushed the dust from his knees. Satisfied, he started walking back toward the forest.

"Hey, what the hell are you doing?"

His heart seized as he whirled toward the angry shout. Oh shit! Cecil stood there regarding him warily. How had he not heard the old man approach?

"What are you doing?" Cecil barked, but he was already running back into the woods. Cecil shouted curses at him, struggling to keep up, but he was too fast for the old man.

His mind raced through plausible excuses, but none quite added up. Panic flooded his veins, but he didn't look behind him; he just sprinted blindly through the woods. He crashed through briars and low branches, Cecil's shouting growing fainter. After an eternity, pine scrub opened up to reveal his battered car.

Gulping air, he sped from the cemetery with a silent prayer. What were the odds Cecil could identify him later? Or that anyone would believe that kook's wild story anyway? He swallowed hard. Only one loose end now remained before vanishing for good.

He reached the car and tore down the dirt road back onto the main road. Heart racing, he gripped the wheel and focused on slowing his breathing. It was fine. Who would believe the man they all thought was guilty? It sounded ridiculous even to him that a man would just show up with clothes belonging to a missing boy. Cecil was as good as damned, and if he knew what was good for him, he'd stay quiet if he found the clothes.

He grinned. He liked his chances. But he couldn't afford anymore close calls. Better to deal with the boy tonight and skip town.

***

While using the god forsaken bucket to do his business, an idea struck him. The key to the shackles around his wrists was little more than a pin. If he could get something metal and thin enough, he could pop it open. The handle on the pail looked to be about the perfect size. It had taken hours in his weakened state to bend the metal until it broke. He was so exhausted and hot, but without the ankle chains and gag, he was feeling better than the day before.

Mike's wrist cramped as he tried to angle them to line up the keyhole with the broken bucket handle. It took a while, but he got it, and he cried when the latch clicked open.

He made circles with his wrist and rubbed them, wincing with the pain that was somehow relieving despite the discomfort of it all. Then he ran to the door and threw his body into it. But it didn't budge. Mike clawed at the corner of a rotten and cracked board until it gave way, and he fell backward. He hit the bucket of his own filth, spilling the contents but not caring. He thundered back to his feet, freedom so close. He ripped at another board, this time stabilizing himself so it gave when he stood his ground.

The opening now was just wide enough that he could slip through, and with all his might, he took off running. Crashing into the dense woods, Mike glanced back at the sound of an enraged yell. The man charged from his car, which must have just pulled up to the trailer. He couldn't be certain, but he wasn't usually back this early.

Panic rocketed through his weakened body, forcing his limbs to pump harder. Veering into dense underbrush, he hoped his small size would give him an advantage. Low branches clawed his face raw, and the man was still gaining on him.

"You get back here, boy!" the man bellowed from close behind.

Gasping through agonized sobs, Mike drove himself faster as the need to survive overrode physical exhaustion. He splashed into a frigid river, hoping water might throw the man off trail. It had felt as good as he imagined.

Risking a glimpse backward, Mike looked just in time to see the man barrel into the water. A menacing grin revealed the man's gray teeth as he drew nearer.

Mike's next panicked step caused him to stumble, and with a shrill cry, he tumbled down into the water. Agony screamed from his left leg, the already bruised ankle twisted. Mike tried crawling forward, but it was impossible in the water. It was over. He couldn't escape.

Water sprayed, covering him as the man pounded closer. "Thought you could get away, huh, boy? I told you what would happen if you tried any funny business!"

With one hand fisted cruelly in Mike's hair, he dragged him dazed through water. Rocks pelted against him until everything went black from fear, pain, or exhaustion.

***

With a ragged whimper, Mike opened his mind, ticking over his surroundings. The smell of exhaust, the rumble of the engine. He was in the trunk of the car. His wrists and ankles were bound again, but this time with something like rope. The car slowed and then came to a stop. Mike's stomach lurched as the engine sputtered off. Moments later, he felt the car rock as the man exited. A few seconds after hearing the car door slam, the trunk lid opened. The man looked down at him, then grabbed his wrists and hauled him out of the trunk.

"I got a new place for us; what do ya think?"

He nodded toward a cabin that looked almost as busted up as the shed he had him in before, just bigger. The river roared and foamy white and brown water rushed by just through the thin tree line.

The man dragged him across the dirt. Mike dug his heels into the ground, but it didn't help. The man was much stronger than him.

"Old Man Waller told me about this place. It was his father's, but he had no use for it and said he left it to rot."

At least someone knew about this place, knew it existed. Maybe even teenagers like Steve would come out here, looking to party. They would find him, save him.

Hope swelled in him until it popped when the man opened the front door and shoved him inside. The cabin had an old woodstove, a small kitchen, and a large bed. A thick layer of dust coated everything in his flashlight beam, and the old, musty smell made Mike wrinkle his nose and want to sneeze. There was no sign of teens partying here. No one would find him. He would have cried if he had anything left to give, but he just couldn't do it.

"This will do just fine," the man said, dragging him further into the cabin.

"Now let's get those chains on you."

The man grabbed the all-too-familiar shackles and chained his ankles together and his wrists, attaching the chains to a ring on the floor.

"Since you've proven you can't be trusted, now you don't even get a bucket, and I think I'll leave the ropes too, for good measure," he said with a wink, and all the fight in Mike went out.

He didn't even have the energy to beg or fight.

The man left, and the only sounds in the room were his own ragged breaths and the gushing river. The sun had gone down, and the room grew even darker as evening faded to night.

Mike's stomach growled, reminding him that he hadn't eaten since yesterday. He lay down on the dusty floor and stared at the ceiling.

He didn't know what to do. He couldn't escape. He was stuck here.

"God, please help me," he whispered. "Please."

But there was no answer.

Hours had gone by, and the darkness had truly set in. The room was eerily quiet, and Mike's mind raced. What if the man never came back? What if he left him here to die?

His stomach growled, and his throat was parched. The air in the cabin was heavy and thick.

He couldn't sit still anymore. Mike sat up and tried to pull the chains from the ring. They didn't budge.

"Oh, come on," he groaned. That's when something broke inside of him, and he knew that even if he made it out of here, whether someone saved him or Mike saved himself, he would never be the same. He thought of all the things that used to be so great. The way it felt on Christmas morning, seeing the gifts beneath the multicolored bulbs. Or even the bad things, like the way his dad stormed around at night. None of it seemed to matter anymore compared to this.

But he couldn't give up, couldn't sink into the emptiness that was filling up his insides. So he kept pulling, his wrists and ankles burning, until his body collapsed onto the floor, every part of him aching—still the chain would not give. So he rolled onto his side and closed his eyes.

Chapter Fourteen

130 Hours Missing

Sheriff Krosby slammed his office door shut, wincing. Damn, he hurt all over and shame wracked him over what had happened. On top of chasing leads about the Franklin boy, he needed to have a word with his men. What they allowed to happen last night was a grave miscarriage of justice. And he'd be damned if they let that happen in his precinct.

Krosby sat at his desk, nursing his first cup of coffee and reviewing notes on the missing boy. His head was pounding, courtesy of John Franklin's fists.

He closed his swollen eyes, trying to put together pieces he didn't have. In the corner of his mind, the shadow he felt lurking over the case peered out, and he willed it to give him a face or clue that would bust the case wide open.

It had only been days, and the case was wearing on him. There was no denying it now; he was too old for this. Too old to be chasing shadows and way too old to be on the receiving end of fists. Worse, he'd been scared. The pure rage in John's eyes said he would have killed Krosby had no one intervened.

Aging was not for the faint of heart. It just sneaks up on you, stealing your body and your mind. He shook his head, then winced with the pain of it.

Raised voices came from out in the hall. "Mr. Jordan, you can't just go back there."

Then his door flung open. Cecil stood with a paper sac cradled in his arms the way a mother holds an infant after something terrifying has happened—all wide-eyed with fear and worry.

Krosby was on his feet immediately, coffee slopping over the brim. "Cecil? What's happened?"

But as the man opened his mouth, Mrs. Goodson protested, "Sheriff, I told him he couldn't just barge in here."

Almost as soon as Cecil walked in, Officer Jones and Tripplett filled the doorframe behind them and commanded Cecil to put his hands up.

Jesus, this place was a damn circus.

The three men began to argue, along with Mrs. Goodson throwing in a terse comment every chance she could.

He'd had enough.

Krosby pounded his fist on the desk, sloshing his coffee again, but not caring.

"Enough. Tripplett, Jones, stand down."

"Yes," they both murmured.

"We'll be down the hall if you need anything."

Krosby raised his brow, hoping they got the message. Jones just smiled and nodded while Triplett looked like boy called to the principal's office. They disappeared out of the doorframe, and only Cecil and Mrs. Goodson stood there. Cecil still looked fearful, while Mrs. Goodson's face flushed, indignant still by the man's intrusion.

"Cecil, please come in. Mrs. Goodson, get Cecil a coffee, would ya."

Cecil nodded appreciatively, and Mrs. Goodson looked offended. Her lips pursed, and she straightened her blouse and then her glasses. "Yes, sir."

She'd be giving him curt greetings for a week, but oh well.

Krosby gestured to the seat in front of his desk. Cecil eased into the seat, the sack now resting in his lap. Krosby took a deep breath and tried to relax, but something told him this wasn't going to be pleasant.

"Let me clean this up, and we'll get down to it." Cecil looked more uneasy somehow, and he kneaded the bag, the crinkling paper sounding loud in the uncomfortable silence. Krosby pulled out his handkerchief and blotted up the coffee and sank back in his seat.

"What's in the bag, Cecil?"

The older man's hands shook, and he seemed to be wrestling with something internally. Right before he opened the bag, Mrs. Goodson entered with two coffees. He'd only asked for the one for Cecil, but after spilling most of his, he could do with a fresh cup. She set them down with a strained smile, then collected his old cup and soiled hanky. Then in a military-like fashion, she about-faced and left without another word.

Cecil kept one hand on the bag and reached for his coffee, hand shaking. He took a sip but didn't wince even though steam plumed upward from the mug.

Then he opened the bag and handed it over to Krosby. The smell hit him first, something foul like unwashed body and other horrible things he didn't want to think about. Next, he caught a glimpse of fabric, and Krosby's stomach flipped. He took the bag and looked inside, already certain he knew what he was looking at. The clothes Mike Franklin was last seen wearing. He'd need Jesse or Kevin to confirm it for the record, but he knew.

"Where did you get these?"

"Some man was near my shack this morning. I don't know who it was, but I seen him hiding it."

"So you're telling me that someone showed up and handed you the clothes of a missing boy?"

"So they are his?" The fear and concern in Cecil's eyes pulled at Krosby's conscience.

"I can't confirm; the family will need to, but I think so." Krosby scratched at the stubble that was slowly becoming a beard. "I'm sorry about everything that happened last night. Things should have never gotten that far. We let you down."

Cecil nodded and sighed, looking defeated. "You can't keep people from believing the worst. That's just the way people are."

Krosby was not sure that was entirely true but didn't push it. "I'm going to give it to you straight. I believe you. But this doesn't look good."

"I know."

"Do you have any idea who it was?"

"No. Just some man. Greasy looking, maybe he's a picker or something. I had just gotten to the cemetery. Wasn't sure what to expect, you know. I didn't want to park too close in case the fire was still going. So I parked on the road and walked up. He was there, hiding them in the rubble."

Krosby furrowed his brow and took a sip of his coffee, considering. This was huge. The first piece of hard evidence and an eyewitness. But if word got out that Cecil found the clothes, his life could be in danger.

"And then what happened?"

He shrugged and picked up his coffee. Krosby closed the bag, unable to take the smell anymore. It conjured too many repulsive images.

"I hollered, and he ran off. That's all."

"And you didn't get a look at the car?"

Cecil shook his head. "I chased him into the woods. He was on foot. No car, by the time my old bag of bones made it down to the road through the woods, he was gone, just a cloud of dust."

"And then what happened?"

"After I caught my breath, I hiked back up to the shack, and that's when I found those."

Krosby rubbed the back of his neck and stared at the bag.

"Cecil, I need you to keep this to yourself. This guy knows you've seen him; you could be in danger, not to mention if the rest of the town finds out. I think you should stay here."

He shook his head. "I'm not gonna hide. I've done nothing wrong."

"That doesn't matter. I'm not gonna let them butcher you like some scapegoat. It's just safer if I know where you are."

Cecil frowned, staring at the bag. "No." He got to his feet, his old knees cracking with the movement. "If I'm not under arrest, I think I'll leave. I got things that need taking care of."

Krosby sighed. "Okay. Just please be careful. And promise me you'll keep this between us. No one needs to know, okay?"

Cecil nodded. "You have my word."

"Good."

He rose and shook the older man's hand, feeling just how bony they were. "Thank you. If you see anything else, call me right away."

"Yes, sir."

With that he was gone, and Krosby was left with the bag. He scooped it up and went to brief the others.

"You've got to be shitting me."

Jones's mouth dropped open. "Holy fuck. I can't believe it. I mean . . ."

Krosby glared at him.

"Sorry, sir."

Krosby cleared his throat.

"Well, this is a big deal. The first real break we've had."

Jones nodded.

"And it's the most important thing we've had. The key is making sure no one else knows about this."

Triplett and Hayes exchanged confused glances.

"Sir, how can you be sure he's telling the truth?"

Anger flared Krosby's nostrils, and the rage and disappointment he felt at the cemetery bubbled up.

"Are you questioning my judgment?"

"Uh . . . no, sir."

"I don't want one damn word breathed to a soul outside of this office that Cecil was the one to turn in the clothes. News is gonna spread fast, but no one better hear about the clothes. Am I understood?"

They nodded. "Yes, sir." Hayes added.

"Good. I've spoken with Cecil, and he's not going to say a word. I tried to get him to stay here in protective custody, but he wouldn't hear it. I'm going to head out to question Waller on something that's been bugging me and following up on the description Cecil gave me. But first, I'll stop by the Franklins' and get the official ID on the clothes."

"You want me to go with you?" Jones offered, but Krosby shook his head no.

"You keep everyone else in check. You have the description, start canvasing, asking questions. It's not much, but it's something. Head out to some of the other farms and maybe the factories. See what you can come up with."

"You got it."

"Triplett, you stick close by. Make sure nothing happens around here."

"Yes sir."

"Hayes, you're on Cecil. Stay a good distance behind, but don't lose sight of him."

"Yes, sir."

Krosby turned and walked to the door, pausing. "Be careful, boys. Don't take any unnecessary chances. Cecil may have spooked this guy, and we don't know what he's capable of."

They exchanged grim glances.

"You heard the man. Get moving. Let's find Mike Franklin and bring him home."

Jones pumped his fist. "We're gonna get him. I know it."

Krosby drove to the Franklin's, his heart heavy. He was dreading the conversation ahead. But there was no use putting it off.

He pulled up to the house, noting the dark circles under Jesse's eyes.

"Morning. Can we talk?"

"Of course. Is this about John? When will he be home?" Jesse said, opening the door wider.

"No, actually. It's not. I believe he's still drying out." He hesitated and Jesse frowned, a crease forming in her brow.

"Come in," she said eying the brown back under his arm that suddenly felt like ton of bricks. She led him into the kitchen, and he braced himself.

"Would you like something to drink?"

"No, thanks." He took a deep breath and held out the bag. "This morning we had a development. A man was seen ditching these clothing items, and I wondered if you could take a look at 'em. Tell me if they are Mike's."

Jesse's eyes narrowed as she looked at the bag, and the color drained from her face. Krosby curled his hand around the rolled down bag and paused.

"I must warn you; the odor isn't pleasant."

Tears wet her eyes, and she nodded, chin quivering. Krosby unfurled the sack and opened it, then handed her the bag. A sob wracked her body, and she covered her mouth with one hand as she clutched the bag to her chest with the other.

"They're his."

Krosby watched helplessly. His mind whirred for something comforting to say, but it was just silence.

"We've got some solid leads now. And I will do everything in my power to get your son home safe."

She sniffled and wiped her eyes.

"How do you know he's . . ." Her words trailed off, but her meaning filled the silence.

"Whoever left these was sending a message. There's no reason to start going down that road."

She nodded.

He wanted to say more, do more, but here in this kitchen, he couldn't. The oldest son, Steve, walked in and immediately rushed to his mother's side.

"What happened?" he demanded as he folded his mother into his chest. Krosby was glad she had someone to comfort her.

"They found his clothes." Jesse's voice came out in a strangled cry.

Steve's jaw tensed and his eyes darkened. "What? Where?"

Krosby tightened his lips. "I'm afraid I can't release that information just yet."

Steve's lip curled and a sneer formed.

"This is bullshit. You're doing nothing. Nothing. You can't even tell us where they found them."

Jesse pleaded. "Son, please. Don't start."

"No. Mom, he's doing nothing, and he won't tell us anything. How are we supposed to help when he's keeping things from us? Was it Cecil? I bet it was Cecil. Why are you protecting him?"

Krosby's eyes burned, and his nostrils flared. "Listen here, boy. Your mother is right; watch your tone. And you're not going to start spouting nonsense. It doesn't help anyone. Not one person. What's more is your brother could be in a lot of danger, and that's why I'm doing everything in my power to find him." He stood quickly, the chair scuffing backward with the jarring movement. He reached out and grabbed the bag of clothes.

"Now I'm going to go find him."

He stormed from the kitchen, slamming the front door and stomping to his car. His hand gripped the handle, but he paused as the throaty growl of engines made him glance over his shoulder.

His pulse spiked at the sight of a small convoy of news vans barreling down the road straight for him—damn reporters!

Word must already be leaking out.

Cameramen leaned from the passenger doors to film his retreat as the small brigade braked in a chaos of dust clouds and swinging side doors. Reporters and photographers poured out, microphones shoved forward.

"Sheriff Krosby! Sheriff! Sources say local man Cecil Jordan delivered key evidence in the Franklin case. Can you confirm or deny? Why isn't this man in custody?"

Krosby threw up a hand. "No comment," he growled. But the barrage only intensified.

"Sheriff, is it true the clothes of missing Mike Franklin were discovered at Cecil's property? Why are you protecting this person of interest?"

Just then the screen door slammed open. Jesse burst into tears seeing the media horde as the reporters swarmed her. Steve stormed out yelling for them to get back.

"This has gone too far!" Steve exploded, pointing at Krosby. He ushered the weeping Jesse inside, reporters shouting thoughtless questions at their backs. Krosby rubbed his temple in frustration. This situation was deteriorating fast. He had to find Cecil before things got uglier . . . if they weren't already too late.

Ignoring the questions still raining down, he jumped in the cruiser. Gravel spewed as he reversed course hard for town, hoping Cecil was safely out of harm's way after his good deed was already being twisted against him. It would have been all too easy for Cecil to cover up that evidence. Make it disappear, but he turned it in knowing how bad it made him look.

Krosby shook his head as he pulled into the parking lot of the police station and parked. He sat for a moment, staring at the building, and considered his next steps.

A knock on the window made him jump. He scowled and rolled down the window. Mrs. Goodson held a stack of paper, fidgeting nervously. She must have seen him pull in and come running.

"Sheriff, there's a reporter from Nashville calling about the Franklin case. Wants to set up an interview."

Krosby rolled the window back up and unlocked the door.

"Not interested. Please, don't let any more of them in."

She nodded and rushed off. He got out and stormed into the station. Jones and Triplett were waiting, eyes wide and anxious.

Inside, the place was chaos. People, mostly reporters, milled about the lobby, the desk was stacked with message slips, and Mrs. Goodson was already taking more calls. Krobsy breezed by and into the incident room where a few men were gathered around.

"Where's Hayes?"

Jones shook his head. "We have no idea. We can't get him on the radio."

Krosby's stomach dropped. "Have you heard anything from him since he went to watch Cecil?"

"Nothing yet."

He ran a hand through his hair. "Dammit."

Jones stepped forward. "We're trying to raise him. But . . ."

"It's not good," Triplett chimed in.

Krosby shook his head. "How many men do you have out canvassing?"

"Five, no new leads."

Krosby sighed. It wouldn't be enough.

The frustrated patter of Mrs. Goodson's heels pattered down the carpeted hall, and before he turned around, she said, "Line one, Sheriff. It's the mayor."

"Get him on hold."

"I'm trying, sir."

"Get him on hold!"

Her eyes widened and her lips pursed. Then she returned again, "There's a Special Agent Henry Crawley on line two."

A wrinkle above her lip pleaded with him not to turn the call away.

"I'll take it in my office. Tell Andy I'll call him back."

She nodded, her relief apparent.

Krosby retreated to his office, slamming the door and sinking into his chair, and picking up the receiver.

"Sheriff Krosby. What can I do for you, Agent Crawley?"

"Good morning, Sheriff. How are you holding up?"

"Well, the whole town is about to riot, and there's a madman on the loose, so not bad, all things considered."

"I'm sure." He chuckled.

"Well, TBI got wind of your case, and we're going to be taking over. Got a few agents who will be on their way out there tomorrow. This is just a courtesy call."

Krosby sat back.

"And how exactly does taking over help my people?"

"It's not personal. This story is about to hit national news, and police are already getting enough bad press. We need this case buttoned up."

Krosby pinched the bridge of his nose. "Fine. But I've already got leads. I'd like to be involved in the investigation."

"That's not the way this works, Sheriff. Our hands are tied. We will keep you informed, but we're in charge now."

Krosby gripped the receiver tightly. "Understood."

"Thank you."

He hung up, the cord whipping back. He had just started making progress, and now the state cronies were on their way, threatening to derail everything.

He got to his feet and stormed out.

Jones was in the hall, leaning against the wall.

"Hey. Any news from Hayes?"

Jones shook his head. "What was that about?" He nodded toward the phone, which was already ringing again.

Krosby rubbed his face, which was aching worse than ever. "Look, the TBI is taking over. I'm afraid they're going to come in here, arrest Cecil, and move on without ever doing a thing to find that boy. They want to look good, and that's all. Which means we have to get a move on or that boy will never get justice."

"What do you want us to do?"

"Follow the leads. Anything. Even if you have to follow up on a hunch. I've got a bad feeling about Hayes, and I'm gonna go check on Cecil. He's the closest thing we've got to a suspect, and if that's not who's behind this, he could still be in danger."

Krosby added as Jones went to speak, "Any thoughts on who leaked it to the press?"

Jones craned his neck and looked around Krosby. "My money is on Mrs. Goodson."

Krosby agreed. "Alright. I'll radio you if I hear anything."

They parted ways. Krosby got in the car and made a beeline for the cemetery, but neither Cecil nor Hayes were anywhere to be found.

Chapter Fifteen

130 Hours Missing

At Danny's kitchen table, Kevin poked at the few remaining cornflakes in his bowl, lost in thought. The past couple of days had been a blur, and nothing felt real. The memory of his father attacking Sheriff Krosby replayed in his mind, whether or not he wanted it to.

Everyone in town knew his father's habits, but for the first time, Kevin had felt ashamed.

Kevin aimlessly chased the last cornflakes around his bowl, unable to think of anything else. Suddenly, the kitchen door flung open, and both Kevin and Danny dropped their spoons at the sound of Ricky yelling.

"Danny! Kevin! You ain't gonna believe this," Ricky panted, bending over to catch his breath. Which wasn't surprising because he had just been out for a run, but his eyes were wide with an excitement that made Kevin uneasy.

Kevin's pulse quickened. Was there news about Mike? Had the cops finally tracked down who really took him? He couldn't really handle any more shocking news unless it was good. After his father's arrest and the fact the Mike was still missing, Kevin wasn't sure he could take much more.

Danny sat up straighter. "What's going on, Ricky?"

Ricky swept aside his overgrown bangs, which stuck in darker clumps to his sweaty forehead.

"That freak Cecil gave clothes to the cops, all covered in mud and blood and stuff!"

Kevin froze, his tongue suddenly sandpaper grinding on the roof of his mouth. No way. Cecil?

He shot Danny an anxious look, but his friend's eyes were glued to Ricky.

"Were they . . . Were they Mike's clothes?" Danny asked, a tightness in his voice that made him sound more like a little kid.

Ricky nodded eagerly. "That's what everybody is squawking about! They say Cecil dragged in Mike's shredded shirt and shorts all nasty and demanded to talk to Krosby. Trying to cut some deal, maybe. But get this—" he leaned in closer, "Sheriff didn't arrest the creep! Just let him walk out free as a bird afterwards!"

Kevin was on his feet, fists balled. "You're lying! Cecil would never do something so messed up!"

Ricky glared back. "I'm just telling you what I heard. Whole town is flipping their lid over it. I heard they've even been talking about it on TV."

An icy dread flooded Kevin's veins. Something wasn't adding up, but either way, he couldn't believe Cecil did it. And poor Mike—if those were his clothes—no, he couldn't jump to the worst thoughts. Not yet. He had to talk to Cecil!

"Come on, Danny, we've got to go."

Danny groaned. "Go where?"

Kevin looked from his friend to Ricky and back again. "The tree house."

Danny brightened, and for a moment, Kevin felt guilty. He had no plans to return to the tree house today.

"Okay. Let's go."

"Don't do anything stupid," Ricky yelled as the boys flew out the door and hopped on their bikes.

Kevin didn't answer, and Danny didn't seem to have heard him.

"So what do you think happened?" Danny shouted, the wind whipping his shaggy hair back as he struggled to keep pace.

Kevin's eyes narrowed. He couldn't let his mind go down that path.

"I don't know. But I bet he'll tell us."

They raced down the drive, gravel spewing from their wheels as they hit the dirt road and skidded into the main street. The road was busier than usual and several cars slowed or stopped to stare as they passed. Kevin raced straight for downtown, nearly clipping Mr. Garvey's bumper as they flew through intersection after intersection.

"Where are we going? The tree house isn't this way," Danny whined.

"I want to see if Ricky is telling the truth."

Kevin barely heard Danny over the blood roaring in his ears.

The police station finally came into view. Kevin squeezed the brakes hard, fishtailing to a stop. He threw down his bike and ran inside, Danny on his heels.

Kevin hesitated just inside the glass doors, nose wrinkling at the strange mix of bitter coffee and cigarette smoke in the air. He'd expected the police station to look more like they do on TV.

But the lobby looked almost boring enough to be a doctor's office waiting room. Rows of wooden chairs with tattered upholstery lined one wall opposite a high receptionist counter. Cheap landscape paintings and community notices dotted the off-white walls along with a rack of old magazines.

An older woman with spectacles on a beaded chain eyed Kevin and Danny over her bifocals as they approached the counter. Her pursed lips at their sweaty, grass-stained state made a bad impression. Kevin straightened his shoulders, trying to look extra responsible and mature.

With adults, you needed to act a certain way for them to take you seriously. But whatever cool act he was trying to put on melted when she said, "Can I help you?"

"I need to talk to the sheriff now!" Kevin blurted to the startled receptionist. Before she could respond, Deputy Jones poked his head out of the back offices, looking confused.

"Kevin? Danny? Everything okay, boys?"

Mrs. Goodson pursed her lips. "These young ruffians just barged in here demanding to see the sheriff. As if he isn't busy enough! Besides, he's not even here."

Detective Jones seemed to study their flushed faces and raised his hands calmingly. "Whoa, easy guys, Sheriff isn't in right now. But why don't you come back to my office and you tell me what's going on?"

Kevin nodded, and Detective Jones gently guided them through a door and down a long, carpeted hall toward a room of empty desks.

Kevin's words tumbled out in breathless spurts, demanding answers about Cecil supposedly bringing in bloody clothes.

Jones raised his eyebrows, but his face gave away nothing. "I understand you must have questions. But for now, let's just say a lot of what people are gossiping is blown out of proportion. We're still investigating."

Kevin slammed his fist down. "But Cecil didn't do it! You have to leave him alone. And while you guys go after him, the real guy is out there." Hot tears suddenly flooded his vision.

Jones gripped Kevin's shoulder. "The truth will shake out, son. I know this is real scary too. But we ain't accusing nobody yet. And the sheriff is working hard to keep everyone protected. Okay?"

His warm smile made Kevin nod, sniffling back sobs. For a second he believed everything would work out somehow. At least he prayed that it would.

"Alright. Why don't y'all head home and try not to worry too much."

Kevin thanked him, and they headed out.

As they crossed the parking lot, Kevin knew they weren't going home. Danny met his gaze. "What are you thinking?"

"We gotta find Cecil."

Danny sighed but didn't argue.

They climbed on their bikes and pedaled back out to the cemetery.

Kevin had no idea if Cecil would be there after everything that had happened, but he didn't know where his real house was or where else he would go.

Twenty minutes later they rode up, the air still and silent. Kevin's pulse picked up, and he jumped off his bike and rushed up to the burnt remains of Cecil's shed. For so long he, like all the other kids, had lived in fear of this place and of Cecil. But they had been so wrong.

Danny followed, peering nervously over his shoulder.

"You really think he'd come back here?"

"I didn't know where else to look," Kevin said toeing at a piece of charred wood. The hollow scraping sound it made sent a shiver down his back.

"Maybe he left town," Danny offered.

Kevin shot him a glare.

"Or not. Hey look, he's not here, and that detective said they weren't gonna lock him up. I think he's fine." Danny crossed his arms, looking bored. "Can we forget about Cecil now and just go work on our tree house?" Danny complained.

Kevin wanted to be mad at him. But he had a point. There was nothing they could do. They were just a couple of stupid kids, and it wasn't like they had any clues or ideas about where Cecil was.

"Alright," Kevin grumbled. "Let's go."

Though the ride to the cemetery had been longer, the short ride to the tree house felt twice as long.

Kevin pedaled lazily, even though Danny sped down the dusty farm road. The late afternoon sun beat down mercilessly, seeming to bake the rows of corn and cotton lining the road. Their leafy green stalks looked wrinkly and thirsty.

Was Mike thirsty? Wherever he was.

Kevin blinked against the threat of tears as Mike's crooked grin flashed in his memory from the morning he had disappeared. He had wanted to punch him then for ruining his first day of summer break, but now he'd give anything to see his smug smile again. His stomach churned with fear, imagining some creepy stranger snatching someone so small. Kevin wanted to scream, but he swallowed it as they turned down the road through the cotton fields.

Danny leaned his bike against the tree, glancing uncertainly at Kevin. "You alright?"

Kevin just shook his head, not trusting his voice. He coasted closer to the tree and hopped off, letting the bike roll a couple of feet before it fell over. He picked up a bowed board, anger and helplessness welling up in his chest.

Blinking fiercely against tears, Kevin flipped open the lid of the toolbox they'd left out there and grabbed a saw. He balanced the board on a rock and sawed violently. He had to channel his feelings into completing the tree house. If they hurried up, then maybe when the cops brought Mike home it would be done. Mike deserved to use it just as much as he and Danny did.

Hammering away, the sun shifted lower than their pile of bent nails and off-cuts shrank. Kevin was about to suggest a break when a voice made them both freeze.

"You're doing a good job."

They whipped around, staring up at the dark figure leaning against the tree.

Cecil smiled sheepishly. "I'm sorry to sneak up on you."

"You scared me half to death!" Danny scolded, gripping his hammer defensively.

"I didn't mean to." Cecil's shoulders hunched, and he took a step back.

Kevin stepped forward, a rush of gladness at the sight of him.

"Mr. Jordan. Did you come here to tell us what happened? Because we heard."

A sad smile crossed Cecil's face, and a sadness flickered in his eyes.

"No. I came out here looking for Mike."

"Oh," Kevin said, feeling a rush of emotion that he couldn't quite wrap his mind around. His own father hadn't even joined the search party the cops had organized. And here, this man who didn't owe them or the town a damn thing, was out here, looking for Mike.

Kevin found his voice. "How can you still wanna help after everything folks said 'bout you?"

Cecil shook his head. "None of that matters. A boy is missing, and that's enough. You boys ought not to be out here. It might not be safe."

Danny piped up, "We can handle ourselves."

Cecil gave them a doubtful look. "That's not what I meant."

"Look. If you're out here to look for Mike, then we're coming with you," Kevin said, dropping his hammer and wiping his sweaty hands on his shorts.

"No, no." Cecil said shaking his head. "That ain't a good idea. Leave it with me. Your parents will be wanting you home. It's nearing supper. Go home, boys."

Kevin and Danny exchanged glances. But neither spoke further; there was no point in arguing.

Cecil was right.

They packed up and got on their bikes.

The evening was quiet but not yet dark, and as they neared the edge of town, the shadows grew larger and longer. The sky was still orange, and a warm breeze rustled the trees.

Kevin pedaled slowly as they approached the road where they would need to turn left to go to Danny's or right to go to his house. He thought of the way his mother had cried and not left her room the last time he was home. A bolt of guilt struck his stomach. He should go home and see how she was doing. With his dad in jail and Mike gone, she was probably alone, unless Steve had stayed around, which he doubted.

"Hey Danny," he said finally reaching a conclusion. "I think I should go on home tonight. I should check on my mom. I'll come by tomorrow and get my stuff."

Danny gave a mock salute. "You got it. How about I come by tomorrow instead? I'll bring your stuff."

Kevin nodded, and they parted ways.

He leaned his bike to one side, easing around the last corner, the road stretched out toward his house. The sight eased some of the anxious coil in his chest. Part of him had worried the angry mob would come here and burn their home down too.

Rounding the mailbox with its faded Franklin name, he hopped off his bike and reached to prop it up when the screen door slammed open. Steve stormed out, face mottled and jaw set. He had the same look as when he was about to get into a fight.

Alarm bells rang in Kevin's head. "Steve! What's going on?"

Steve strode right past him, fury wafting off him. "Going to join the real men of this town and demand the sheriff quit dicking around. We all know Cecil's guilty as shit. It's time he paid."

Kevin grabbed Steve's arm in some idiotic burst of courage before he could open the truck door. "Cecil didn't do anything wrong, and folks stirring things up only makes it worse while the man who took Mike is still out there."

Steve ripped his arm free, nostrils flaring. "Quit your bawling. Cecil knows something, and I aim to beat it out of the freak."

He turned back to the truck before Kevin leaped and seized his shirt. "I can't let you hurt him!"

With a roar, Steve spun and backhanded Kevin hard across the face. Pain exploded in his cheek and nose as he crashed into the dirt.

As if that wasn't enough, Steve hawked a loogie that splattered the blood-soaked dust an inch from Kevin's face. Then he stormed off without a backward glance.

Stunned, Kevin gingerly touched his gushing nose and winced. Blood dripped steadily from his chin. He pulled his shirt over his head and used it to stop the blood. It was already shot anyway.

Kevin wanted to cry, wanted to break something. But the tears won out, and he went inside. His mother peeked around the corner. Eyes puffy and nose red raw. Everything he'd been feeling, Mike, his father, Cecil, it all came out in a gush of tears, his body shaking. She said nothing, just crossed the room and folded him into her arms.

Chapter Sixteen

133 Hours Missing

Kevin and Danny rode away, and Cecil was glad.

It was a damn shame that kids had to worry about things like this instead of just being able to roam freely. He remembered being a skinny, barefoot boy in a town much like this one. Back when summer days seemed to last forever. A series of sun-drenched days chasing grasshoppers and hiding treasures under the porch with his brothers. Sneaking muscadines off Old Miss Ellie's vines or heading down to the river to cool off or fish once his chores were done.

Even now, sixty odd years later, he could still remember the way the grapes burst sticky on his tongue. Or how the cool river felt after a long day toiling in the sun. If he thought long enough about it, he could see his Millie the day when he first laid eyes on her. They were just kids, about the same age as those boys are now. It was that age when girls became a bit more interesting rather than nuisances.

He slipped between the trees, leaning against the trunk of an old oak tree, and peered back down the overgrown trail, listening past the metallic drone of cicadas. But there was nothing doing.

From his pocket, he pulled a slightly squashed pack of cigarettes and placed one between his lips, striking a match, coaxing the end alight. The relieving first inhale filled his lungs, and he relaxed.

The past few days, hell, the past few decades, had not gone as planned. People around here talked about him like he was a monster or a myth, and the kids were afraid of him. A time or two he'd been hollered at by parent's whose little 'uns made up stories about how he had chased them or attacked them.

The truth was, Cecil kept to himself, and some folks just didn't understand why a man would want to be alone. There was a time when it was all different. He had a good life and a beautiful young wife at one time. They had the same hopes and dreams of every young couple in love.

Back then he was working for the railroad company. The days were hard and long, but going home to Millie made every ounce of backbreaking labor worth it. She worked as a secretary at the local elementary school not far from the house they rented.

She loved children, and they were planning on having some of their own once they bought a house. But that all ended when she died in a car accident only three years after they were married.

Part of him died that day too. Hearing the news that she had died was crushing. The foreman on the job had run up to him, his wool cap clutched in his hand as he broke the news. Nothing was right after that.

Food didn't taste right; sleep didn't make him feel rested. She was his everything, and without her, he was lost.

He spent years in the bottle trying to find solace in the liquor. However, no matter how hard he tried or how much he drank, he couldn't find peace. That was fifty years ago, and he loved her just as much now as he did back then. Up until the night before, her picture still sat in an old frame on his nightstand. But thanks to those rabble-rousers, it was gone.

Lost to fire and stupidity.

Now he had nothing left of her.

In the decades he'd lived in Everett, he learned quickly that this town was a dead end. Everyone struggled, and those who didn't left. What remained were threadbare lives woven 'round each turn of season, predictable as worn flannel. Most of the men drank too much, and there was nothing they loved more than talking about other people's lives.

Cecil dropped his cigarette butt to the ground, grinding it into the earth with his boot. He gripped his walking staff and continued pushing through the brambles toward the fields. The image of the man with the missing boy's clothes flashed in his head. There was something dark or twisted in his sunken eyes.

Something that made him shudder.

As he stepped out of the trees into a field of cotton, a man in a straw hat spotted him and pointed. Others turned, and one by one, men and women stopped work, watching him with hostile, distrusting faces.

The silence was suffocating. These people didn't know a damn thing about him, and yet they looked like they wanted to skin him. Cecil stood his ground, searching the weather-beaten faces until his eyes fell on a man wearing a green baseball cap, searching his features, but he wasn't the right man.

Cecil lowered the brim of his hat against the accusing stares and continued on. He figured he'd caused enough of a stir and decided to loop back into the woods. The tree line was cooler, and he was less likely to bump into anyone.

As he picked his way among the shaded trees, he tried to put himself back into the mind of the man dropping off the clothes. If it were him, where would he go? Surely not back to town.

If anything, he could stake out at Moss's, wait for the man to show up there. He looked like a man with every kind of vice. But if the man was smart—and he was sure the guy had some sense, just not the good kind—he would have headed somewhere far from here.

He continued his trek until he saw a large oak tree, its thick trunk wide enough for him to take a rest. He settled his back against the rough bark and fished out his last cigarette, placing it between his lips. The match flared, and he inhaled deeply. The smoke seared his throat, and his head spun a bit.

A noise in the distance had him tensing, and he dropped his smoke. Cursing, he fished for it among the forest debris. Another noise, and he spotted movement in the shadows. He leaned forward, squinting. A shape moved closer, and Cecil abandoned his cigarette and reached for a down branch. It wasn't much, but it was something he could bring down on whoever dared to sneak up on him.

Just then, a rabbit darted into the open, its little furry nose twitching. Cecil breathed a sigh and settled back against the tree. That was enough excitement for one day. He needed to get over to the county house he'd refused to live in for so long. But first he'd stake out Moss's and see if that greasy fella showed up.

Cecil sat in his car outside Moss's for some time, the odd car and truck coming and going. None of them were the man he'd seen with the boy's clothes. His stomach growled, urging him to move on. He could always come back the next day. Then he chided himself. For all he knew the boy was out there hungry too. So he waited several more hours before going into the store, getting a case of Miller Highlife, a few cans of hash, and a half a dozen eggs.

The whole time he was in the store he kept his chin held high. Daring one of them old fools to say something to him. He wasn't the sort of man to go looking for a fight, but he certainly wasn't the kind of man who kept his eyes to the ground when he had nothing to be ashamed of.

He had to keep reminding himself of that as he paid for his things.

The man behind the counter, Moss, didn't even bother to look him in the eye. The old coot looked down his nose, sniffing in disapproval as he rang him up. Cecil took his items and walked out the door, his face burning red.

As soon as the door swung shut, one of the men inside yelled, "You better watch yourself, Cecil!"

Cecil ignored them. Cowards couldn't even say it when he was in the store. They weren't worth the shit on his shoes.

The drive to the county house only took about ten minutes, but his nerves were frayed, and the muscles in his arms and shoulders ached. When he finally pulled into the driveway, he sat a minute staring at the white, clapboard house. It was a plain little thing with a wide porch. Nothing about it spoke of home.

It was just a box.

He had never wanted to live in a big ol' house alone. Not that it would be that much different from the last few decades, but Millie had always been his home, and the place didn't matter. Cecil shook his head and got out. Scooping up his bags in hand, he trudged up the steps and went inside.

He dropped the groceries onto the kitchen table and looked around. He didn't like it. It was empty, lifeless, and it reminded him of the morgue at the funeral home. But it would do until, until what? He didn't have it in him to rebuild the shed. He was tired.

Tired of waking up every damn day. Some days, when he woke, he'd cuss, wishing death had taken him. But so far, death wasn't ready for him yet.

A blessing some would say, but to him, it was a curse. Every day alive meant another without Millie, and he didn't know how many more of those he could take.

Cecil shook his head, unable to stay in the house any longer, and headed out to the local diner. His hash could wait.

Chapter Seventeen

140 Hours Missing

In a corner booth at Diner 64, Krosby slumped down with his uniform shirt wrinkled and stubble covering his jaw. He was bone tired, all the dead-end leads blurring days into one long defeat. Even this late, the missing kid's face haunted behind closed eyes.

The new waitress, whom he had since learned was named Becky, handed him a chipped mug of burned sludge passing for coffee. She didn't greet him, just snapped her gum while waiting for him to order. As Krosby opened his mouth to order, the doors jangled open and a sudden silence fell over the place.

Cecil stood awkwardly in the entrance, cap twisted in gnarled hands. His tentative steps met steely glares on all sides as he approached the counter to order.

Becky bristled, knuckles whitening around her pen in her hand. In a stage whisper, she called to John, who was cooking in the back, "I ain't serving this pervert."

Krosby watched Cecil's shoulders slump, and he turned to leave. Anger surged in his gut. He was on his feet quickly, waving the caretaker over.

"Cecil, why don't you sit a spell and have supper with me? My treat for your cooperation earlier."

Cecil eyed him warily but shuffled over as Krosby shot Becky a pointed stare. "I do believe my friend here wants meatloaf. And a slice of pie too, if Diana has any back there."

Becky looked disgusted but snapped her gum and headed toward the kitchen. Krosby nodded for Cecil to take the seat across from him. If he could provide nothing else today, at least Cecil wouldn't face this ordeal alone.

Cecil lowered slowly into the bench opposite him, the way he had that morning in Krosby's office. Maybe it was arthritis more than worry. Krosby's own body was moving slower and slower these days, and most mornings he felt like his joints needed a good greasing.

"I hear you gave Deputy Hayes the slip," Krosby said, raising the coffee to his lips but deciding not to drink it when the smell of pencil shavings found his nose.

The ghost of smile curled on Cecil's wrinkled face. "I know you mean well. I appreciate your care, but that officer could have been out looking for the boy, not tailing me."

Krosby smiled, touched. If only the rest of the town could see this side of Cecil. "Is that where you got off to then?"

He nodded, threading his fingers together and resting his hands on the table. "No luck though. Then I went down into one of Waller's fields, looking for the man I seen hiding the clothes at my place, but I didn't see him."

"Good move. I was trying to get out there myself today. I think it's noble what you're doing, but you really should stay home." He scratched his jaw and lowered his voice. "Don't you have a county house near downtown? I'd feel better if you held up there until tensions in town calm down. Between you and me, the TBI is sending agents to take over. I don't want you doing anything that's gonna make them think you're up to no good."

There were whispers going around town that a rally would be held at the courthouse tonight. Krosby worried it would turn violent. He couldn't make Cecil do a damn thing, but he wished the man would just lay low for a bit.

Becky returned looking sour, roughly dropping off their food without a word before stomping off again. Neither man uttered more than muttered thanks before tucking messily into the piled-high meatloaf platters and generous slices of Diana's famous blueberry cobbler.

Silence lingered between them, but it held understanding rather than judgment. They finished their meal, and Krosby took care of the bill and left two pennies on the table.

Krosby had the pleasure of catching Becky's shocked and enraged expression through the window. Serves her right, he thought as he bid Cecil good night and climbed into his car.

He followed Cecil downtown and was pleased to see him turn off toward the house the county provided for the groundskeeper.

With one less thing to worry about, Krosby zipped to the station.

He sank into his office chair, the old springs groaning under his weight. He loosened his tie with one hand and reached for the whiskey bottle in his bottom drawer with the other.

The state agents would arrive by days' end tomorrow, and their "help" was the last thing Krosby needed. Their detectives would stroll in, noses high, and make a straight line for Cecil just to put a bow on this media nightmare with an arrest.

An arrest Krosby was certain would be unjustified. God forgive him, but he was starting to hope the boy would turn up dead or alive just so this whole mess would be over. Obviously, he wanted the boy alive, but Krosby was hard-pressed to believe that if the boy was still alive, that he was having a good time.

The town was going mad about to implode in on itself, or at least on Cecil. If he had more officers, he would have fired Hawkins for what he let happen at the cemetery.

He was a coward in Krosby's eyes.

Between fighting the media storm and dealing with angry locals, Krosby had not gotten a chance to question Mr. Waller. He rubbed his face, first thing tomorrow. Krosby threw back the whiskey, savoring its slow burn. He stared absently, regretting that he had not gotten more done today.

Grabbing his hat, Krosby headed out to the rally he got wind of earlier that day. They didn't need more trouble, but he guessed trouble would come.

Krosby steered the Blazer into town, his brow furrowing at the sight of Main Street clogged with beat-up pickups and clots of agitated people. He double parked and approached the swelling crowd warily.

In front of the courthouse steps, a makeshift podium had been set up with crude "Find Mike" signs duct taped around the edges. As Krosby edged closer, he spotted Steve Franklin ranting, "That kid snatching pervert practically turned himself in, but that bumbling idiot Krosby let him go."

The crowd jeered in agreement; it was an ugly mood. On the fringe, Krosby noted some of his deputies trying to maintain order and wrangle inflammatory shouts about Cecil being allowed to roam free. He caught Hayes's eye, both men realizing this powder keg could erupt any second.

"Today it's my brother, but tomorrow, it could be your son, daughter, cousin . . ." Steve bellowed suddenly. "Who knows what else he'll do if somebody don't stop him!"

The mob roared, the name "Cecil!" echoing along with calls for action.

"I say we get justice for Mike tonight! Grab Cecil and make him talk. Who's with me?"

Krosby hastily mounted the courthouse steps, grim faced as a wave of violence loomed before law and reason fled this hysteria entirely. If he couldn't control it, blood would surely spill next.

"That's enough!" Krosby roared, inserting himself between Steve and the crowd. He held up both hands as angry shouts washed over him.

"Steve, I know your family is hurting something fierce." He kept his voice steady, placating. "But I can't have you folks taking matters into your own hands. That won't help find your brother. While all y'all whine about Cecil, the real perpetrator is out there. He could be here tonight, among all of y'all. I bet he's laughing at what fools you are. How easy you made it for him. But I won't give him the satisfaction." He smacked the wood of the podium, the crack silencing the crowd.

The boy's eyes blazed with fury. He jabbed a finger at Krosby's chest. A bold move, but not bold enough to actually touch him. "Don't you preach at me! My father is locked up while you let that sick bastard Cecil walk free!"

The crowd bellowed agreement. Krosby signaled his deputies closer as the swarm of red, frustrated faces and shaking fists pressed tighter around the podium. He raised his voice urgently.

"Now I'm only gonna say this once! Cecil is under surveillance pending investigation. And the state boys will be here tomorrow to move things along." He paused, letting the weight of his next words sink in. "Anyone—and I mean ANYONE—caught trespassing at Cecil's place or trying to confront him will be arrested for obstructing justice. Am I clear?"

Resentful murmurs rippled through the mob. Most continued casting blame and insults Cecil's way. But slowly, people began dispersing in twos and threes once the immediate promise of violence receded.

Krosby kept silent watch until only the core troublemakers

remained. Relief washed over him, and he prayed the short fuse on this powder keg lasted for at least another night.

***

152 Hours Missing

Krosby pulled up at the tree house as first light filtered through the woods. Shafts of gold sliced through lingering shadows where Mike had gone missing. The tree house had since been worked on. Much of the materials which had been scattered around the base were gone, and the once-rickety structure looked a bit more sound. He didn't like to think of Kevin and his buddy hanging out here where they could get taken, but he was glad that at least for the time, they were able to just be a couple of boys, even if only for a few hours.

Walking the area afresh, Krosby recalled his very first night searching— lights he'd seen in the distance the first night he'd gone out there. Something about it nagged at him. During their search of the woods, they hadn't come across anything out there. But maybe they hadn't gone deep enough.

He scanned the woods in a fifty-foot radius of the tree house before getting back in his Blazer and heading over toward the Waller's farm. He caught sight of the overall-clad owner Jerry Waller working on a John Deere picker. From the way he was dressed and his weathered skin, you'd never know he was one of the wealthiest men in the county.

"Morning, Sheriff," Waller said as he groaned with the exertion of turning a wrench. He dropped the tool with a metallic clatter before wiping oil from his hands with a rag. "I'm guessing you're here on business, not pleasure."

Krosby let out a mirthless laugh. "Afraid it's all business until that boy is found." Krosby explained about the man Cecil had spotted, asking if any workers matched that description. Waller simply shrugged. "I've got too many hands to know for sure. These stupid machines are supposed to make it so I can save money by hiring less men, but the damn things break down so much. Not to mention everything it leaves behind."

He shook his head, seeming more concerned about the tractor than Mike Franklin.

"Would you mind rounding up all your men later this evening to see if we can get our witness to identify the man he saw?"

Waller shrugged. "Sure, but no way I can know for sure that all of them will be there or not."

Krosby repressed his growing irritation. "That's fine. Just do the best you can."

Waller nodded, but before he could say more, Krosby spoke. "I've been seeing some odd lights back in the woods out there. That's your property too, right?" Krosby pressed, hooking a thumb over his shoulder in the direction he guessed them to be from there. "Or know anyone camping there?"

Waller lifted his faded cap and scratched his balding head, gazing toward the distant tree line. "Lights? Can't says I recall any. Could be some boys blowing off steam back there I reckon. I'll take a walk out and have a look-see soon for ya. It's my property all the way out to the banks of the river."

Krosby nodded, sensing he was finally grasping something important. As his mind turned over everything about the case, he almost had it. He was turning to head toward those woods when Jones's voice crackled unexpectedly.

"Sheriff, there's been a development over at Cecil's county house. Over."

His blood chilled and he spun, muttering a quick goodbye and thanks before tearing back toward his vehicle.

"Copy that, Jones. I'm on my way from Waller's. What kind of disturbance? Over"

The line crackled open for a moment before Jones said, sounding suddenly serious. "A child was scene banging on the dormer window. Some passersby broke in and rescued the child. Hawkins and Triplett are on the scene. Over."

"Where's Cecil? Over."

The blazer roared and Krobsy put the petal to the metal. He peeled out of the dirt drive, heart racing as a hundred horrible possibilities filled his head.

"He's not on sight. Hayes and Grayson are out looking for him. Over."

"I want him brought in unharmed. You hear me? Over."

"Loud and clear. Over."

"I'll be there in fifteen. Over and out."

Krosby's thoughts raced. Surely he hadn't been wrong about Cecil all this time? But then again, everyone was capable of just about anything.

If this was true, and Cecil was their man, how the hell had he missed the signs?

When he arrived, there were several cars parked outside the old brick county house. The front door was wide open. The white paint around the door handle cracked, the wood freshly broken. Krosby hurried inside to the living room, finding a handful of neighbors huddled around a small girl with messy pigtails.

Hawkins and Triplett sidled up to him, and the threesome stepped out onto the porch.

"What's going on?" Krosby demanded. He didn't like that Hawkins was here.

Triplett answered. "Mrs. Deborah Jenkins reported her charge, Mary Alice Whitmore, was missing. About fifteen minutes later, Hawkins reported they found her in Cecil's place."

"Uh-huh," Krosby said, his suspicion mounting.

"And were you on scene when they broke down the door?"

Hawkins cleared his throat. "No, sir. Door was busted down. I happened to see it on my way to interview Mrs. Jenkins."

"Why wasn't Jones on his way to speak with Mrs. Jenkins?"

"I volunteered since Mrs. Jenkins is my aunt."

Triplett gave Krobsy a look that silently said, "Do you smell what I'm smelling?"

Krobsy did.

Without another word he went back inside. The little girl was dressed in a yellow rain slicker and matching rain boots, though there wasn't a cloud in the sky. Her tiny fingers clenched tightly around the arm of a well-dressed older woman.

Her large blue eyes were filled with tears. She looked scared to death.

Krosby crouched in front of the child, keeping a safe distance. His heart sank when he realized she wasn't the missing Franklin boy.

"It's okay, sweetie. No one's gonna hurt you." He offered his best calming smile. "Can you tell me what's your name? I'm Sheriff Krosby."

The girl sniffed, lip quivering as her eyes darted around the room. She inched closer to the lady holding her hand. She looked to the older woman, who gave her a go-on-now look.

The child blinked. "My name's Mary Alice."

Krosby smiled and nodded, pulling out his badge and showing her. "Nice to meet you, Mary Alice. I'm sure glad you're OK and back home. Would you mind telling me why you're here and what happened?"

She glanced at the woman again. "Mrs. Jenkins says that I was crying and banging on a window, and she came to save me."

The woman, Mrs. Jenkins, stood and cleared her throat. "That's right—" But Krosby cut her off.

"Mrs. Jenkins said you were? But what do you say?"

The little girl shrugged. "Mrs. Jenkins watches me sometimes when my mama works."

"That's nice, Mary Alice. And how did you end up in here?"

"I don't know."

"Yes, you do, Mary Alice. Cecil took you," Mrs. Jenkins said chidingly.

"Cecil took me."

Krosby had had enough. "Did Mrs. Jenkins tell you to say that, or did it really happen? I'm a police officer, and it's important that you tell the truth. You won't be in trouble if you tell the truth."

Her big blue eyes watered, and she spilled the beans.

"Mrs. Jenkins said I had to tell you that so you'd arrest the man that took the boy. I didn't want to lie. Mama says never to tell lies, but Mrs. Jenkins said it would be okay this one time because it meant we would be helping that little boy and, and no other babies would go missing." The little girl sniffed but no tears came.

"Thank you, Mary Alice. It was very brave of you to tell the truth. You did the right thing."

"Ow," the little girl said, yanking her hand away from Mrs. Jenkins, who was red face with fury in her eyes.

"Mrs. Jenkins, you know I could have you and," he waved a finger around the others in the room, "arrested for this little stunt. Try something like this again, and I won't hesitate to see you in jail. Now, I want all of y'all to go home, and stay out of my way." He walked toward the door and gripped it, his anger boiling as he looked at the unnecessarily broken door.

"Hawkins this door better be fixed by the end of today, and then I don't want to hear that anyone in this town so much as breathed wrong in the direction of Cecil."

He stormed out before he completely lost his temper. The state agents would arrive any time now, and he had a boy to find.

Hawkins was as good as fired.

Chapter Eighteen

158 Hours Missing

He yanked his worn cap low over bloodshot eyes, already feeling the promise of a headache in the glaring sunlight. Endless rows of cotton wavered ahead under a cloudless sky—too damn bright and cheerful for his mood today.

If the trailer had a damn phone, he would have called out. For a few minutes that morning, he considered just not showing up, dealing with the boy, and skipping town. But he was enjoying the turmoil in town a bit too much.

Since that old geezer laid eyes on him, he'd made efforts to change his appearance in whatever way he could. He shaved his hair, swapped his old cap for a slightly older one in gray instead of green. Today he opted for long sleeves instead of cut offs, which he regretted the moment he stepped out of the door.

The damp heat had his clothes sticking to his skin, and sweat pooled down his back. He could risk begging off sick or at least a bit hung-over, but that would draw more attention than not. So he sucked it up and did what was expected.

The backbreaking days bled together in endless sameness once cotton bolls ripened for harvest. Most days he rode one of the older John Deere tractors doing a first pass. Other times like today, the fields were infested with bowed shapes moving slowly down uneven rows as small burdens filled sacks to ease. Maybe in the next town he'd find some indoor work. A factory or some shit on a line.

One more day, and he'd abandon this backwater and he'd disappear.

Never again would he be this impulsive. Next time, he'd plan, do things right. This is what happened when he didn't plan, he thought bitterly.

He should have gotten rid of the kid immediately.

The last field he'd picked was only half-done. At this pace, he'd barely make his quota. He wiped his brow with a dirt-caked sleeve and squinted against the blinding glare. The boss's truck was pulling up, but he wasn't alone. The sheriff's Blazer pulled up in Waller's dust.

He could do two things, run or play it cool. Without conspicuously moving, he went about his work scanning for an easy way out, but it was all field, and if he hotfooted it, he'd as good as give himself away.

Instinct told him he should play this out. See what the old sheriff had come sniffing around for. The truck's brakes squeaked, and a few seconds later, Waller's voice cut through the din of cicadas and birds.

He whistled, waving them in like dogs. "Hey, boys. Sheriff wants to ask some questions, so take five and gather 'round."

"I'm sorry for the interruption, fellas. But I just need a word with you. I know you're all busy, and the crop's not going to pick itself."

The men nodded, and Waller's gaze settled on him, making his pulse race. But he remained still, his expression blank as Krosby addressed the group.

"Sheriff here needs all of y'all to get in line."

They all lined up, grumbling as the sheriff eyed each one of them, a man in a suit next to him scribbling in a pad.

"I'm looking for a man about my height, long, greasy, blond hair, sunken eyes, last seen wearing dirty jeans, a stained white shirt."

Heads swiveled around, accusatory eyes passing from one worker to another. He joined in, playing the part.

The sheriff paused, looking at a notepad in his hand, then backed up. "Y'all will pass through single file, then you can go on about your business."

With any luck, and he felt he had plenty of luck left, his changes would see him safe. They filed through, one by one, like a chain gang headed back to the clink. Sheriff shook his head, turning to Waller, likely to get names. But he guessed Waller didn't know half of their names.

At least ten other men here looked like they could be related to him.

They all had the same, gaunt, overworked, over-drank figures.

When it was his turn, he masked his disdain, pretending to look into the eyes of the sheriff, but really he stared at the brim of his hat. A trick he learned in the army. They were all just animals at the end of the day, and direct eye contact meant a challenge.

Out of the corner of his eye, Krosby's jaw hardened, his eyes searching his. There was a moment where time slowed, and he almost ran. He could make it. The sheriff was an old man and looked like the kind of guy who was used to sitting behind a desk. But again his instincts told him not to run.

The moment passed, the tension easing out of him. The sheriff nodded curtly, gestured with the pad, and moved on to the next. It took more work to not grin at that foolish fucker than it had to remain calm.

As he returned to work, a sense of calm overtook him. His mind cleared, and his movements slowed. A plan was forming in his head. A way to finish this without any loose ends.

When the sun started sinking in the sky, he headed back to the house.

There was no longer the need to wait until after dark. He had all the tools and supplies. It was the perfect time to do what needed done.

As he headed out the gates of the farm, he passed the sheriff and waved, a cigarette lit on his lips.

It had been almost four full days, and the kid was still alive. The kid wasn't dead, and the cops were getting closer. He knew this and could feel the walls closing in on him.

The last loose end left saw him sent to prison, and he'd die before he went back. Cecil needed to die, then the boy. Two for the price of one.

His cackle of laughter shocked him.

He turned onto the road leading to the old cabin. Once he turned off the main road, there were no houses to pass. He liked the isolation; he felt more are ease with it. At the end of the road, the trees were thick, and he could barely see through the brush. The car bumped and jerked along the uneven path, and he was sure that if he kept using the shortcut, he'd be scraping the bottom of the car.

It wasn't too bad when there was some light, but in the pitch-black, it was hard to see. The tires screeched to a halt, and he cut the lights. In front of him, the road was washed out, and the trees had fallen over. He'd throw the kid some food, don't want him dying before he had a chance to kill him.

The cabin was small, only a one-room shack. The boy was a little fuck, and he was lucky that the plan had changed.

The boy whimpered on the floor when he stepped. "Dinner bell."

He tossed a pack of crackers at the boy. He didn't know what the hell the kid was crying about. He was still breathing, wasn't he?

The kid opened the wrapper, shoving a cracker into his mouth.

"That's right, don't stop. You might not have the chance to eat again."

The boy choked, dropping the food.

He let out a cackle. "I'll be back for you."

He locked the door and set the chain, then grabbed his bag and the gas can. The night was quiet, no noise other than the sounds of insects chirping in the woods, and soon he'd kill a man.

***

163 Hours Missing

A few hours later, he nursed a flat Schlitz, his eyes crawling around the cramped hole-in-the-wall searching for any loose lips worth eavesdropping on. The wood of the table baked in the heat, smelling of stale booze and beer.

Factory workers occupied most of the lopsided stools, heads bent, complaining about work or taxes. Nothing reached his bored ears worth a good goddamn.

Where was the outrage about Cecil now? No way that lousy sheriff quieted up the good ol' boys that fast. He'd seen his little speech outside the courthouse steps while that kid called for the blood of an innocent man. All big and bad until Krosby showed up.

His grip around the beer bottle tightened.

A loud thump followed by a slurred groan drew his focus to the far end of the bar, where one beefy redhead had knocked over an empty glass. His wingman signaled the pot-bellied barkeep for a rag while the clumsy oaf wiped up the spilled drops with his flannel sleeve.

"Hell, ain't my fault Sheriff Ass-by can't find his ass with both hands. Too busy sniffing that killer Cecil's crack, I hear." The bartender handed the man a fresh glass of beer, the foam slopping over his knotted knuckles. "Taxpayers rewarding that freak with some downtown manor house instead of a shallow ditch . . ."

Ears pricking, he eased up to the bar, lifting a finger for the barman's attention and placing wrinkled bills on the counter.

"Whiskey, neat."

The man slid him a tumbler filled with amber liquid.

"Freak," the drunk mumbled before knocking back the foam.

He raised the glass in a mock toast. "Amen, brother. Ain't right, them keeping a child killer in a house."

The man's bleary eyes found his, a smirk spreading over his face. "You got that right. I got half a mind to go over to that county house and show that pervert what's what."

He clinked their glasses, grinning.

"Now you're talking my language."

"I'm not sure I know which one it is," he said, staring off to seem less interested in the answer than he really was.

"It's just off Main," said with a hiccup. "Green Victorian-looking thing. Used to be the old Mayor house 'fore they built the new one."

He swallowed down the rest of his drink, setting the empty glass on the counter. He tipped the bartender and made his way toward the door. He didn't bother with a goodbye or thank you to the two men who had just sealed Cecil's fate.

The county house sat dark as he drove by, but the windows were open. It was hot enough that even the breeze off the river couldn't keep the night from being humid.

He parked the car a few streets over for good measure. There were no cops parked where he could see. As usual, the universe was on his side. Walking up onto the porch, he tested the lock, which looked new.

Unlocked.

He stepped into the dark room, the creaking groaning underfoot. Electricity jolted through his heart, and he froze, fearing that he'd given himself away. Just inside there was a small foyer with a flight of stairs leading up, a hall leading to a door, which presumably led to the backyard and a living room to the left. The light from a TV flickered, but only static played in a low rush. No one was in there.

Floorboards creaked under his weight as he crept through the first floor, peeking in each closet and corner. He moved with care, making no unnecessary noises. He held his breath as he ascended the stairs, the treads groaning underfoot. The stairs curved up, a hallway extending out to his right and a wall to his left.

The door at the end of the hall was ajar. He slipped in and closed the door behind him, not wanting any unexpected visitors. The room was small, not much more than a twin bed, nightstand, and a dresser. A single window looked out over the street.

A perfect place for an ambush.

He opened the dresser, looking through the drawers, not sure what he was looking for. There wasn't anything interesting or suspicious in them. Clothes and a few old newspapers, nothing useful.

He searched the rest of the room and came up with nothing. He had no idea how long he'd been searching. His skin prickled. The silence was oppressive and made him nervous.

He was sure he'd heard footsteps in the hall. He'd heard a door open or shut. Was someone here? But there was no one.

Cursing under his breath, he sagged against the exposed lathing, adrenaline leaching away in a nauseous wash. He was so goddamned close. But never mind that now. He couldn't have everything.

Tomorrow the boy became top priority— with or without killing Cecil. He'd tarried overlong allowing indulgences. Now he needed to slash and dash, before this town became his own personal graveyard.

***

169 Hours Missing

Mike awoke again in darkness to the now familiar rotting smells and unyielding silence. His raw throat burned for water. Since his near escape, the man had not brought him food or water as often. The man seemed more and more distant the few times he'd come, like his hold on reality was slipping.

The vastness of the cabin made Mike feel oddly exposed, and he found himself missing the confines of the shed. Who knew he could miss such a place?

He shifted to relieve bound limbs, wincing as scabs cracked open. There was no comfort found anymore against the splintered floor. Each raspy breath was laden with dust. Part of him just wanted to let go, find a way to make his body stop living. But he couldn't, not yet.

Something scuttled suddenly across Mike's purpled instep, but he didn't flinch or bother shaking off the vermin. Instead he closed his eyes, willing more sleep.

A violent spasm jolted Mike from a fitful half-sleep. He panted into the darkness, momentarily disoriented by screaming nerves and concrete numbness. He tensed, listening for the heavy footsteps of his captor returning. But no creak of the door followed . . . must have dozed off and dreamed it. Or maybe a tree limb broke outside.

Mike shifted gingerly, his whole body screaming in pain. How long had it been now? He had lost track of days passing in this unchanging nightmare. Eyes burning with hopeless tears, he wiped away with grimy sleeves.

A quiet scuff made him glance up hopefully for the thousandth time, expecting to still find only an empty wall and padlocked door. Instead, Mike tilted his head—heart pounding, he leaned forward squinting into the shadows.

"K-Kevin . . . ?" The name cracked painfully past bloodied lips. Mike couldn't breathe.

But the slim figure stepped forward, and Mike gasped. Familiar smiling eyes met his.

"I can't believe you're really here! You have to get me out. Please!"

The figure was close enough now for Mike to reach, but the boy stayed just out of reach. Mike sobbed, his shivering fingers almost able to grasp his brother's, but Kevin stepped back, a sad smile on his lips.

"Why are you waiting? Please, Kevin, I can't take this anymore. We have to get out of here before he comes back."

"We will. You just have to stay calm." Kevin knelt down and took his hand. It felt cold and lifeless, and it scared Mike.

"What are you talking about? Stay calm? We have to get out of here. He's going to kill me soon, I know it."

Kevin's smile faded, replaced by a look of concern and sadness. "I can't, Mike."

"Why not?"

"You know why."

Mike's small body shook violently as things the man had done to him came back to him. He raised pleading eyes full of fresh tears. "You're not real, are you?"

Mike closed his eyes, shook his head, and sobbed until Kevin disappeared.

Chapter Nineteen

169 Hours Missing

Krosby nearly missed the slender form hurrying to catch the closing door behind him as he left the station. He turned sharply, tired eyes widening in surprise as Ms. Greco smiled brightly and offered a perfunctory wave.

"Heading home, Sheriff? Any chance we could chat a few minutes first about today's events?"

Krosby hesitated, bone-tired but also realizing here was a valuable opportunity. Jill's columns held significant sway over locals. If she took up Cecil's cause in the press, it could ease tensions and give Krosby more latitude pursuing this his way.

The state agents had yet to show their faces, so Krosby figured he had a few more cards to play.

"Let's talk in my office." He led her past the empty reception desk.

All of his men were out, and Mrs. Goodson had gone home for the day.

"Thank you for your time, Sheriff. I promise I won't keep you long. This case is a tragedy, and I hope to be able to bring a little justice and comfort to the community with a piece on the Franklins and how we can support the search efforts."

"I can't say I'm not surprised by your interest. You were pretty quick to condemn Mr. Jordan last week."

Ms. Greco shrugged, her cheeks pinking slightly. "Like I said, it was a bit premature. Besides, I tried to redeem myself after what those fools did out at the cemetery." She shook her head, jaw clenched. "You're right, and it's only going to get worse unless we can change how people see him."

He sat heavily behind his desk, rubbing a hand down his face. "Listen, the boy is our first priority. But I'm wasting so much damn time trying to keep the town from killing an innocent man that I can't get anywhere on the damn case."

"What can I do to help?" Her pretty eyes sparkled so genuinely; he felt bad for all the times he'd been gruff with her.

"Well, I thought, if you could dig up something about Cecil's past. He seems like a man who's no stranger to tragedy. Write a story about who he really is, and maybe folks will leave him alone."

"Or I learn there's a string of child murders in his wake."

Krosby laughed, surprised by her callous humor. "Hey, I'll take any leads I can get."

"So you don't think he did it?"

"No, and honestly, it'd be damn easier on me if he had. But easy and right ain't the same thing."

She nodded. "I'll do it. I can't say Hank will let me run it. But I'll try."

"Don't you worry about Hank. I'll make him see right."

Now it was her turn to laugh. "Well, I better get digging." She stood and offered her hand. He shook it and smiled.

"Good luck and thanks, Ms. Greco."

"Please, call me Jill."

He nodded and saw her out.

***

181 Hours Missing

Krosby sank into his desk chair clutching fresh-brewed coffee, going over his mental checklist, when Jones entered paper in hand.

"Sheriff, I've got an update from the State Police and a tip that might not be shit."

Krosby sighed, reaching for the paper. "Give it here."

"Due to budget restraints, the TBI is unable to assist in the ongoing missing persons case."

Krosby threw the paper. "Damnit. Why do we even have a Bureau if they won't help?"

"Well, technically speaking, they did help?"

"How so?"

He quirked his brow and shrugged. "You noticed how the press disappeared. TBI sent someone over to deal with the mess. It was a miracle the news didn't get a hold of that shit. Folks think enough bad about towns like this, even though my home town of Chicago is way worse. Country people get a bad rap."

"You're right." Krosby chuckled. "You'd think Hank would want to cash in on the story though."

"And what about the tip?"

"Could be nothing but sounds more legitimate than what we've been getting. Last night, an anonymous male suggested we look into John Franklin's finances. The caller claimed Franklin had substantial gambling debts. Allegedly, John hadn't paid up timely lately—perhaps the boy was taken as collateral."

Something about the message didn't sit right.

"I guess you're right; it beats a blank. Do you want to chase it or should one of the others?"

"I've got everyone pretty much spread out. We're still canvasing, exploring a few other tips, although I doubt they'll go anywhere."

"Who's on Cecil?"

"No one right now."

"Goddamn it. I want you to get on him and stay on him; don't leave him unless someone else takes your place."

"Sure thing, boss. So you'll follow up with Franklin?"

"Yeah, I'll do that before heading out to check out Waller's men."

Jones gave him a funny look.

"What?"

"You look like shit."

"Yeah well, not sleeping will do that to a person."

"If you say so. Anyway, I'll check in with the others and then get on Cecil."

"Good man."

Krosby grabbed his keys and headed for the door. His instincts bristled, although pragmatism argued for exhausting all plausible leads lest he be accused of negligence. Best to clarify facts discreetly before leaping down dead-end rabbit holes.

A loud buzzer preceded gates clanging open down the hall. Krosby watched curiously as a surprisingly kempt John Franklin emerged shuffling toward their partitioned meeting spot in regulation slippers and coveralls. His dark-blond hair stood neatly combed for once, and the perpetual booze bloat had already eased some in his cheeks and complexion after just a week eating regular meals and forced sobriety of incarceration.

If he didn't know better, Krosby might have guessed this was

John's quieter twin brother. He realized with a guilty start that he couldn't recall ever seeing Mike's father without him smelling like stale whiskey or having bloodshot eyes that gazed into a vacant stare. No wonder John aged a decade plus beyond his actual mid-forties.

"To what do I owe this pleasure, Sheriff?" John's sneer exposed yellowed teeth as he spat the honorific.

Ignoring the jab, Krosby dove in. "Let's play a little game I like to call, Truth or Bullshit."

John laughed but it held no mirth, and he nodded for Krosby to continue. "Got an anonymous report suggesting you owe substantial cash to some unknown thug. Truth or bullshit?"

John's bloodshot eyes narrowed. "The hell you implying with that tone? You think someone took my boy over some bets?"

"Just confirming the facts. How much money are we talking about?"

"I lost some money lately." John's nose twitched angrily like a cornered rodent. "But what the hell is it to you?"

"To who?"

"Grant Alderson, if you must know." John shifted in his seat, puffing out his chest like he was gearing up for a fight.

"Grant's not exactly an upstanding citizen, John. Now I'm going to ask you again, how much?"

"I don't know, $500 or so. Look, you're wasting time here. I doubt

Grant has anything to do with it."

"I doubt it. But I had to follow up. Look, I'm gonna be straight with you, John, because I think for once you'll actually hear me. We've got little to no evidence. I know everyone wants to string Cecil up, but right now, his eyewitness account is the first solid lead we have. Now, I'm gonna go out to Waller's farm today and see if I can pick out some possible matches to Cecil's account, and we'll go from there."

John's eyes were cold and angry, and Krosby had a hard time reading his expression.

"Okay, then. When do you think I can get out of here? I suspect I lost my job and my family—" he paused, his voice choking, "or what's left of it won't make it without me working."

"I'll work on getting those charges dismissed. But take a good look at yourself, John. You need to lay off the bottle and get your temper in check."

"I don't have a drinking problem," John snarled, fists balling.

"Whatever you say. I'll let you know if I have any further updates."

He rose, signaling the end of their chat. John stood, and the guard led him away. Krosby watched until the men disappeared through the door.

John's reaction seemed genuine. And Grant was a piece of shit. But still, something gnawed at his gut. Krosby made a mental note to have a little chat with Grant. He felt like it was a waste of time, but when there were few clues to run with, best to leave no stone unturned.

He grabbed his keys and headed for his car.

Krosby stepped from the relative chill of the jail into another blast furnace afternoon, squinting against the glare off parked cars. Deputy Pritchard waited beside the idling cruiser looking restless.

"Get anything useful from Franklin?" he asked hopefully, yanking at his collar as they pulled onto simmering asphalt.

"Alibis and excuses. Same as everyone else so far." Krosby sighed. "Let's verify his debts at least and rule it fully out."

He cast a backward glance at the shrinking prison façade. Somewhere John stared at similar walls cradling misplaced rage and guilt. The oppression seemed to seep from concrete pores filling their vehicle too.

Desperate for forward momentum, Krosby straightened determinedly. "Firstly though, let's see what Waller's bunch can tell us. Should be wrapping the packing shift soon."

Pritchard nodded, consulting scribbled notes. "Who are we eyeballing out there again?"

"Anyone who buys Schlitz for starters." Krosby smacked the wheel as the trees parted suddenly, Waller's equipment sheds shimmering ahead through restless heat devils on the blacktop. "And any squirrely behavior we see. We need to shake something loose out there yet."

He ignored his own skepticism echoing mockingly. They had to break the damned case soon before the wilderness consumed every promising thread . . . along with two lost souls wandering separate woods.

Krosby marched from Waller's sweltering hay field toward the distant tree line and meager shade. He fished out the handset to call Deputy Jones handling surveillance on their "witness of interest" Cecil.

"Where's our eccentric groundskeeper hiding out today?" Krosby inquired, swiping sweat from his eyes with a grubby shirtsleeve. "Any luck convincing him to view our potential suspects?"

He heard Jones clear his throat uncomfortably. "Still working on that small detail, Sheriff. Ain't pinned his location down since first light."

Krosby halted mid-stride. "Come again? Thought you had a tail on the man?"

"I did. But Cecil musta caught wind somehow in the night. Gave Hayes the slip 'fore dawn." Irritation colored Jones's admission of failure.

Krosby blinked toward an uncaring sun. The heat suddenly magnified threefold, pressing down. "Great. Well keep at it, dammit! Can't have our sole witness off grid with this powder keg still smoldering . . ."

He severed the connection harsher than intended. Glancing down, he realized one boot now rested halfway into a fresh mound from some mole or rabbit. The sinkhole held far too many local echoes lately. Krosby extracted himself with effort. . . . Cecil was surely out combing the land he so loved. And soon they would need his urgent help to continue doing the same.

***

185 Hours Missing

Waller had mentioned seeing Cecil on his rounds, but Krosby had yet to track him down.

"Hey, Sheriff!" Krosby turned at the sound of his name, squinting toward the sun and raising a hand to shield his eyes. "Waller." He nodded curtly.

"Any luck finding your culprit?"

"Nothing worth noting." Krosby grunted, tucking his notebook away.

"That's a damn shame. Well, I won't keep you."

Krosby turned to leave, but paused. "If you had to pick one of 'em. Which one would it be?"

Waller's brows shot up. "Now, how the hell am I supposed to answer that? What the hell kind of question is that?"

"Look, you know these guys. I just need a hunch. Maybe someone you think might've seen or heard something. Anything that makes them capable of it?"

Waller's jaw ticked, and his eyes grew distant, lips twisting in thought.

He finally answered, "I wish I could help. I'd like to think that I would recognize the kinda man that could take someone else's child. But I just can't tell."

Krosby nodded. He felt the same. There wasn't a single man that looked like a predator.

And that was the scary part.

"All right, thanks anyway. I'll see you later."

Waller tipped his hat and strode off whistling as he went.

Krosby watched him go, then headed toward his cruiser.

He opened the door, the heat rolling out in a wave. Krosby cranked the AC, not caring how long it would take to cool the interior. It was too damned hot. He sat, staring out the windshield, watching the men work, the sun sinking low in the sky.

The day had been a waste. He'd talked to most of the men and nothing had come of it.

He glanced down at his notebook and the names. Nothing stood out to him. No one name was repeated on more than one page.

The day had been a waste. Krosby talked to most of Waller's crew, but nothing substantial surfaced. He glanced down at his notebook, scribbled names failing to stand out. No repeats across interview pages. Only dead ends staring up mockingly.

Exhaling frustration, he grabbed the cruiser's crackling handset. "Jones? You copy?"

Static processed, then, "Jones here, Sheriff. What's the situation?"

Krosby pressed the transmit button again. "Wondering your status—any luck tracking him down yet?"

"That's negative, sir. No sightings still." Irritation coloring Jones's distorted voice. "It's like he vanished out there."

Krosby's gut tightened. "Ten-four. Keep the search active. We're gonna need Cecil's testimony if we locate this guy. . . ." Static drowned the rest.

Chapter Twenty

169 Hours Missing

"Come on, Cecil, what are you hiding?" Jill murmured to herself, pushing aside a coffee mug ringed with stains that told the tale of too many late nights spent at this very desk. Since leaving Krosby that morning, she'd paid the library and the county records a visit to see what she might be able to dig up on the old man. Fingers stained with ink and dust, Jill rifled through a mountain of archives piled high on her desk. Shadows shrouded her small office, the bulb in her desk lamp buzzing and flickering often enough to be annoying without the decency of burning out completely.

With each rustle of paper, dust motes danced in the air, disturbed from their resting places atop stacks of yellowed newspapers. Cecil's secrets were there, she was sure of it, hidden within the print of days past. She stared relentlessly, searching for any hint, any clue that could solve the mystery or at least absolve the man who had become the town's pariah.

An old article caught her attention, its headline now faded, but the words "Local Hero" were still legible. Her heart raced as she smoothed out the crinkled edges, eyes scanning the text for any reference to Cecil. But the piece was about someone else, another fleeting moment of past glory that had no connection to him.

The clock on the wall ticked away, indifferent to her urgency, as she plowed deeper into the papers. The boy was still missing, and if Krosby was to be believed, Cecil was innocent and misunderstood. It felt good to know her methodical process honed from years of chasing stories in the city hadn't disappeared in her idol years spent in Everrett—scan, assess, set aside, repeat. But tonight, Cecil's story was proving as elusive as the perpetrator in Mike's disappearance himself.

Voices chattered somewhere outside of her office. Was it really that late? The hum and clack of the printing press firing up answered her question.

Just at the point where she was about to give up, she told herself one more. One more page from the cascade of forgotten lives taking over her desk. Her eyes, burning from exhaustion or dust she couldn't tell. At random, she grabbed a paper police report from years ago published in the *Herald*, but it wasn't about Bush County. The paper, stained yellowed, nearly cracked as she unfolded it. It detailed a car accident, the stark words on the page painting a picture of tragedy.

She leaned in closer, the name Jordan jumping out of the fine print, but the name attached to it was not Cecil's.

Willow Creek, Tenn., May. 15, 1939 —In a somber turn of events, Millie Jordan, 21, a beloved schoolteacher, was fatally struck by an unknown motorist in a hit-and-run incident that occurred in the early hours of Thursday morning. The young Mrs. Jordan was en route to the schoolhouse where she dutifully taught when the tragedy unfolded.

Local authorities are urging any citizens who might have witnessed suspicious activity at the intersection of Johnson St. and Main, between the hours of 7 a.m. and 8 a.m., to come forward with any information that could aid in apprehending the culprit behind this senseless act.

The Willow Creek Police Department extends its deepest sympathies to Mr. Cecil Jordan, 22, who now bears the heavy burden of widowhood at such a tender age. The community joins in mourning the loss of a vibrant young woman and a dedicated educator, taken from us all too soon.

As the town grapples with this heartbreaking event, we ask that you keep Mr. Jordan in your thoughts and prayers during this difficult time. May the memory of Millie Jordan's kindness and devotion to her students serve as a shining light in the face of this dark moment.

Oh Cecil. Jill's heart tightened, and she clasped the gold cross around her neck out of habit. The story of Millie Jordan's untimely death and the shattered life of her young husband, Cecil, painted a picture of grief and loss that echoed through the decades.

As she gently set the clipping back on her desk, Jill found herself seeing Cecil in a new light. The reclusive old man, whose secrets she had been so determined to uncover, now appeared to her as a figure shaped by tragedy, a man who had carried the weight of his lost love through a lifetime.

Jill's journalistic instincts, once fueled by a relentless curiosity, softened into a profound sense of empathy. She realized that Cecil's solitary existence, his reluctance to engage with the world around him, might well be rooted in the unimaginable pain of losing his wife so young, so suddenly.

The image of a twenty-two-year-old Cecil, left alone to navigate the depths of grief, tugged at Jill's heartstrings. She couldn't help but wonder about the life he and Millie had dreamed of building together, the hopes and plans that had been shattered on that fateful morning.

As she sat back in her chair, the newsroom bustling around her, Jill felt a renewed sense of purpose. No longer was her goal to simply uncover the secrets of Cecil's past; now she wanted to tell his story with the sensitivity and compassion it deserved. She wanted to honor the memory of Millie Jordan and the love that had been lost, to paint a portrait of a man not defined by his mysteries but by his resilience in the face of unimaginable heartbreak.

Willow Creek was just an hour's drive away these days with the new highway. She glanced at the clock, mentally calculating the hours until dawn. Tomorrow, she would make the drive and see what else she could find.

Leaving the mess behind, she left armed with the newspaper and her notebook. Sleep was restless, her mind turning over imaginary stones desperate to find the missing boy, while worrying about Cecil and the part she'd inadvertently played turning the town against him.

Damn her mouth.

As the first light of morning crept over the horizon, Jill was already on the road, the miles disappearing beneath her tires as she headed toward Willow Creek. The town, with its quaint main street and sprawling farmlands, seemed an unlikely setting for the tragedy that had unfolded years ago.

Jill's first stop was the local diner, a place where she hoped gossip flowed as freely as the coffee. She settled into a booth, ordered a cup of joe, and struck up a conversation with the waitress, a woman who looked to be in her seventies at least, heavy wrinkles framing her kind eyes and smile.

"You're not from around here," the woman said as she poured the coffee with a shaky hand. Jill almost offered to help her but didn't want to come across as rude. The question, to Jill, who had just moved out of Memphis, would have thought the statement to be rude and unwelcoming, but Jill had lived in Everrett long enough to know that it wasn't meant to be unkind but more as a polite statement of fact.

Jill smiled. "No, I'm not. I live over in Everett. I'm a reporter actually."

The woman's faded blue-gray eyes lit up as if Jill had proclaimed to be a close personal friend of Elvis Presley.

"My, my, a reporter. And what's Willow Creek done to draw you here? Nothing ever happens here. We don't even have a paper no more."

Jill nodded, knowing all too well that small prints were getting harder and harder to keep going with larger companies snuffing them out.

"Nothing that happened recently. I'm looking into a car accident that happened here years ago, back in '39," Jill said, her voice low and conspiratorial. "A woman named Millie Jordan passed away; she was married to a man named Cecil."

The waitress's eyes widened, a flicker of recognition passing over her face. "Oh, honey," she said, her voice heavy with sympathy. "That was a terrible thing. Poor Cecil, he was never the same after that."

Jill leaned in, her reporter's instinct kicking into high gear. "What do you remember about the accident?"

"Not much. No one knew what happened. Not too many folks 'round had cars back then. Plenty of folks still used horses and wagons. Whoever done it might not even been from around here. A sad business."

"Did you know them well? Cecil or Millie?"

The old woman nodded. "Sure did. Millie was a dear cousin of mine. And everybody knew Cecil. I think that's why he left. Couldn't stand being somewhere that everyone knew what happened to him. A fresh start. I always wondered what happened to him. So many men left not long after the war started and within a few years, most of the men from around here were gone."

"Cecil's still alive. I don't know if he served in the war. But he's living over in Everett. He's the caretaker of our cemetery."

The woman clutched her heart. "Oh goodness me. That's a lovely word to have today. Tell him Esther Milton says hello. I'm a McNeil these days, but he'd know me by my unmarried name."

"I will. Would you happen to know if anyone else might have any information about him? I'm writing a piece about him. I want to tell his story and do it right."

She scrunched her lips, putting a hand on her ample hip as she thought. "Not that I know of. Most of the men he worked with on the railroad are gone now. We're a dying breed. Happens at this age. Everyone around you starts dying, and you wonder, Who's next? Will it be me?" Esther gave a laugh that seemed more nerves than mirth.

"I understand. But you seem to know a lot. I'm sure you've got more work to do, but I'd love to hear anything you've got."

Esther fanned a hand in the air and set the coffee carafe on the table, untied her apron, and plopped it on the table before sliding in the booth across from Jill.

"Trevor, I'm on break," she called to some unseen man who yelled back. "OK."

Then she turned to Jill and smiled. "What do you want to know?"

Esther launched into a detailed overview of the town, Cecil, Millie, herself and several people Jill had not cared to hear about, but she listened attentively, grateful for the woman's time and insight.

After way too much coffee and a mediocre BLT and fries, Jill thanked Esther and drove around Willow Creek, then made the drive back home.

In the miles between Willow Creek and Everett, Jill murmured to herself. Mentally writing the story. When she got back to her office, she slammed the door shut, daring any fool to bother her at their own peril. The words flowed from her, aching with the rawness of his loss and the story of an ordinary man.

By late afternoon, Jill leaned back in her chair. The story lay complete before her. She knew that her words had the power to alter perceptions, to challenge, to console. This was less of an exposé; it was more of an explanation and an appeal for people to show this man, who had experienced enough pain, some compassion.

Jill stood up from her desk, the wooden chair creaking as she pushed it back. She gathered the pages of her carefully crafted article, the words she had poured her heart into now etched in ink on paper. With a deep breath, she navigated the narrow hallways of the newspaper office, dodging stacks of old editions and whatever other detritus had been left here.

She approached Hank's office, the door slightly ajar, and knocked gently. "Hank? You got a minute?"

Hank looked up from his own pile of papers, his eyes narrowing as he took in Jill's determined expression. "This better be good, Jill. I'm up to my eyeballs in classifieds and ads for the county fair."

Jill stepped inside, holding out her article like an offering. "It's the piece on Cecil Jordan. I think you'll want to read it."

Hank leaned back in his chair, the old leather creaking under his weight. He took the pages from Jill, his skepticism evident in the set of his jaw. As he began to read, Jill watched his expression shift, the hard lines of his face softening with each passing paragraph.

Minutes ticked by, marked only by the rustling of paper and the distant chatter of the secretary fielding phone calls. When Hank finally looked up, there was a newfound respect in his eyes.

"Damn, Jill," he said, his voice gruff but tinged with a bit of strained emotion. "This is . . . this is something else. I had no idea about Cecil's past, about the tragedy he's been carrying all these years."

Jill nodded, a lump forming in her throat. "Neither did I, Hank. But it's a story that needs to be told. Sheriff Krosby asked me to do this. I think he's right; we owe it to Cecil. The people in this town have been treating this missing boy like a witch hunt. Any excuse to lash out at Cecil."

Hank ran a hand over his face, his fingers rasping against the stubble on his chin. "You're right." He stood up, the decision made. "Front page, Jill. This story deserves the spotlight. We'll print it tonight."

Chapter Twenty-One

195 Hours Missing

Krosby's grip on the steering wheel tightened as he navigated the narrow, winding streets of Everett. Home, this place had been home to him his entire life and now, he hardly recognized it. It wasn't the changing buildings, the businesses opening and closing. It was the people, the way the town turned into a hungry mob without a second thought.

He shook his head as his eyes reflexively scanned the streets around him. No one was outside, not even kids. Though he reckoned it was about dinner time and most folks would be sitting down together, saying grace and digging in.

Not him though.

The hum of his truck wasn't loud enough to drown out the whispers and accusations that seemed to seep from every corner, every crack in the sidewalk, every rustle of leaves, and worst of all from the smiling photo of Mike now burned into his memory. The collective demand for justice hung heavy in the air. The townspeople were hungry for answers, for someone to blame, and they had set their sights on Cecil. Something needed to be done, not only for the boy's sake, but for the town's.

The county house that had stood untouched for damn near a decade was now battered. Since he had been here the other day, shutters were damaged, windows broken, and CREEP had been hastily painted across the side of the house, near the front door. Krosby shook his head, unable to fathom the pettiness of it all. A glance in the rearview mirror revealed a frown creasing his weathered face, lines etched deeper, and for the umpteenth time on the case he wondered if this one would be his last. But he couldn't think on that now. Right now, he had a boy to find, suspect to catch, and a community teetering on the edge of chaos in need of soothing.

Krosby killed the engine and sat for a moment, surveying the scene before him. As he stepped out of the car, he couldn't shake the feeling that something wasn't quite right. The house seemed too still, too silent, as if holding its breath in anticipation of his arrival.

He walked up the path to the front door, his footsteps echoing loudly in the empty street. The porch creaked under his weight as he reached out to knock, the sound reverberating through the house like a mournful plea. He waited, his hand resting on the butt of his holstered gun, but no answer came.

Frowning, Krosby tried the handle. To his surprise, the door swung open easily, revealing a dimly lit living room. He stepped inside cautiously, his senses on high alert. The quality of the silence all but guaranteed that no one was in there, but he had to be sure.

"Cecil?" he called out, his voice sounding unnaturally loud in the stillness. "It's Sheriff Krosby. I need to ask you a few questions."

No answer. Krosby moved further into the house, his eyes scanning the room for any signs of life. The furniture was sparse and pristine from years of idleness, the walls bare save for a few faded paintings, likely artifacts from former occupants. It was a nice place; why hadn't Cecil wanted to live here? Krosby shrugged the question off almost as quickly as it came to his mind. People had their reasons and it usually only made sense to them. But more than that, it was really none of his business.

As he turned the corner into the kitchen, Krosby's gaze fell on a collection of empty beer bottles neatly lined up on the counter. He picked one up, examining the label, "Miller Highlife," he muttered under his breath, cataloging the detail in his mental ledger. It wasn't much to go on, but in the barren landscape of leads, it was something—a small piece of the personality behind the man he was hunting. Cecil's preference in beer might have been inconsequential to most, but it might just be the thing Krosby needed to not only absolve Cecil but the key to finding Mike.

A quick tour upstairs left him satisfied that no one was there. The stillness returned as he stepped outside, leaving the empty bottles to continue their silent vigil.

He took one last look at the scattering of glass on the porch and the graffiti, then turned back toward his car. As he walked, he reached into his pocket, pulled out a small notebook. Flipping it open, he scribbled a quick note about the beer bottles. There was Miller Highlife here at Cecil's, and there was Schlitz tied to the scene where the boy had gone missing. It was little to go on, and he knew it, but sometimes shit was better than nothing.

Krosby pulled away from of Cecil's house, his mind still turning over the discovery of the empty beer bottles. It wasn't much, but it was a start.

He drove through the quiet streets of downtown, his destination clear in his mind. Moss's Stop and Grab. If Cecil had been buying beer, chances were he'd been buying it there. Krosby pushed open the door, the tinkling of the bell above his head announcing his arrival.

Moss looked up as Krosby approached, his eyes sharp and knowing.

"Sherrif," he said, his voice a gravelly rumble. "What brings you out here?"

Krosby leaned on the counter, his gaze direct and unwavering. "I'm looking for information on Cecil. Specifically, if he bought his beer here?"

Moss nodded, his expression thoughtful. "Cecil? Yeah every week like clockwork, always buys the same thing. Miller Highlife, a case at a time."

Krosby felt a flicker of satisfaction. The beer bottles at Cecil's house, the confirmation from Mr. Moss—it was all starting to add up.

"What about Schlitz?" he asked, his tone casual but his eyes intent. "Cecil ever buy that? Or any other regulars who buy that?"

Mr. Moss frowned, his brow furrowing as he thought. "Schlitz? Cecil never bought no Schlitz from me. I got a few regulars who do. Mostly old-timers, set in their ways. But there's one guy, comes in every few days. Always the same, Schlitz, canned meat. Bachelor stuff, you know."

"What's he like? Do you know him well?"

Moss shook his head. "Younger fella, keeps to himself. Barely talks about the weather."

Krosby leaned forward, trying not to get his hopes up but praying this would be the lead that broke this whole case wide open. "Can you describe him? Got a name?"

"I think he goes by Seth. Not that he ever told me, but a man came in here and said hello to him by that name," Mr. Moss said, his eyes distant as he recalled the details. "Tall, skinny, with this greasy blond hair that's always hanging in his face. Quiet sort, never says much aside from thanks or what cigarettes he wants."

Krosby's heart skipped a beat. The description matched Cecil's account of the man who dumped Mike's clothes. And he drank Schlitz and smoked. It'd gotta be him.

Finally, a real lead, a thread to follow.

"You know anything else about him?" he asked, trying to keep the urgency from his voice. "Where he works, where he lives?"

Mr. Moss shrugged, his expression apologetic. "Not much. He works at the Waller farm, but I can't say for sure. I just assumed. He mentioned once while buying candy and Cokes that it was to treat the other field workers. But like I said, he's not much for conversation."

Krosby nodded, his mind already racing ahead. He straightened up, tipping his hat. "I appreciate the information, Mr. Moss. You've been a big help."

The greasy blond-haired man, the Waller farm. The pieces were starting to come together, the picture beginning to take shape. The man likely had opportunity, if he was working in the field. Maybe he stumbled upon the boy by accident.

Then he was gone, the bell above the door tinkling in his wake as he strode back to his car. As he reached for the Blazer's handle, he glimpsed tiny shreds of paper, just like the ones near the tree house. The day he'd paid Cecil a visit, he had been to Moss's first. The whole damn reason he'd gone to Cecil's was because of Moss's insistence of the oddity of Cecil's purchase, but it sounded like someone else had an abnormal purchase, and Krosby's gut said it was the same man who had stripped this cigarette.

There was no time to lose, considering the pitfalls of the case. If there was any hope for Mike, it rested on Waller now. The momentum built inside him, the thrill of the hunt coursing through his veins.

He started the engine, the car roaring to life beneath him, and peeled out, a trail of dust behind him.

The game was on, and he was determined to win. For the missing boy, for Cecil, for the town that looked to him for answers. He wouldn't rest until he had uncovered the truth, no matter how dark or dangerous the path might be.

Krosby turned onto the dirt road leading to the Waller farm, his mind still reeling from the information he'd gleaned at Moss's Stop and Grab. The sun was setting now, the sky more orange than blue. As he pulled up to the farmhouse, Krosby saw Mr. Waller emerging from the barn. He raised a hand in greeting as Krosby stepped out of the car, his expression curious. "Krosby," he said, his voice rough but not unkind. "What brings you back out here? Any news on the boy?"

Krosby nodded, his eyes scanning the property for any signs of the blond-haired man. "I'm following up on a lead. I heard you might have a worker who fits a certain description—tall, skinny, with greasy blond hair. Goes by the name of Seth."

Mr. Waller frowned, his brow furrowing as he thought. "Seth? Yeah, I know him. Hired him a few months back, good worker usually. Keeps to himself mostly, lives out in the woods in a trailer I sold him."

Krosby's heart skipped a beat, his mind flashing back to the mysterious lights he'd seen in the woods during his search for the missing boy. The lights he'd asked Waller about, the ones Waller had claimed to know nothing about.

"A trailer in the woods," he said, his voice tight with barely controlled anger. "And you didn't think to mention this when I asked you about those lights? When I was out there searching for a missing child?"

Waller had the decency to look ashamed, his eyes dropping to the ground. "I'm sorry, Sherrif. I didn't think about . . . I mean, Seth's a quiet guy, but he's never given me any reason to suspect . . ."

Krosby cut him off with a wave of his hand, his jaw clenched tight.

"Save it. Just tell me where to find this trailer."

Waller nodded, his hand shaking slightly as he pointed towards the woods. "About a mile in, there's a small clearing. Can't miss it."

Krosby was already moving, his long strides eating up the ground as he headed toward his car. His mind was racing, the pieces falling into place with sickening clarity. The lights in the woods, the trailer, the greasy blond-haired man—it all made sense now. There were no shadowy figures now, he had a name, a place, and he was going to get justice.

He cursed himself for not seeing it sooner, for not pushing harder when Waller had been uncertain about the lights. But, like everybody else, he had been so focused on Cecil that he'd missed the real threat in plain sight.

But now he knew, and he wasn't going to let this opportunity slip through his fingers. He was going to find Seth, going to get the answers he needed, no matter what it took.

As he slid behind the wheel of his car, Krosby's hand went to his holster, checking the reassuring weight of his gun. He had a feeling he was going to need it, a feeling that this case was about to take a dark and dangerous turn.

Backup though, he'd need backup. But he was ready, his mind sharp and his resolve unshakable. He would find the missing boy, would bring him home safe and sound. And he would make sure that whoever was responsible paid the price for their crimes.

With a final glance at the Waller farm receding in his rearview mirror, Krosby pointed his car toward the woods and the secrets that awaited him there. The hunt was on, and he was ready for whatever lay ahead.

No more games, no more half-truths and evasions. It was time for the truth to come out, time for justice to be served. And Krosby, his eyes hard and his heart pounding, was going to make damn sure that it was.

Chapter Twenty-Two

197 Hours Missing

Cecil's mind raced as he crouched behind the weathered fence, his heart pounding against his ribs like a caged bird desperate for release. He'd been staking out Moss's store for hours, his eyes fixed on the comings and goings of folks, searching for any sign of the man who'd disposed of the missing boy's clothes in the remains of his shack.

He'd almost given up hope, his patience wearing thin as the sun passed noon. Cecil had considered what other options he had for finding this guy, but just as his hand gripped the key to start his car, a white rust bucket crept into the lot. The greasy-haired man clad in a faded baseball cap and a sweat-stained shirt emerged from the car and slinked toward the store.

Cecil's breath caught in his throat, and he sunk down into his seat, hoping the man would not see him. The man disappeared inside without a backward glance. Less than ten minutes later, the man emerged with a sack tucked beneath his arms, eyes downcast, as he mumbled to himself. He seemed preoccupied to say the least, miserable at best. The man whipped out of the lot kicking up a cloud of dust in his wake. Without a second thought, Cecil started his car, counted to sixty, and then pulled out in a slow pursuit.

His heartbeat so hard in that moment, he worried the old ticker would pick now, of all times, to give out. But as he breathed deeply, the drumming eased.

At a discreet distance, his knuckles white on the steering wheel, he followed the car as it bounced and swayed, even though the road was as flat as they get. Abruptly, the man turned onto the rutted dirt road down a long, tree-lined drive that led to the heart of Waller's farm.

Cecil guessed the car's suspension was shot from driving down roads like that. Even though he feared losing sight of the man, Cecil waited, pulling off the side of the road, not wanting to turn in immediately and give himself away. That road, like so many in this part of the country, only went one way.

After twenty minutes of waiting, baking in the sun, Cecil pulled down the road until he got to the grassy lane where several battered cars and trucks were parked. The farmhands, he reckoned.

Turning around, Cecil continued down Vildo road and turned off down the lane where Kevin and Danny's tree house sat, still unfinished. Cecil parked his car, leaving the keys in the ignition, and hotfooted it through the woods to look for the man.

Sweating like a sinner in church, Cecil tried to quiet his heavy breathing as he crouched behind the weathered fence, peering through the slats bordering the Waller's farm. The scent of freshly turned earth and the distant whistle of a whippoorwill rang out as workers ambled about the field. It didn't take long for Cecil to spot him among the other workers, unaware that the man with greasy hair trailing down his neck, wearing a faded baseball cap, was a monster.

Cecil's gaze bore into him so hard; he half feared the man would feel it. The cap he wore today was a different color than when him first saw him, a sun-bleached navy, but that was no matter, the same wrongness emanated from him.

A monster once seen can't hide.

The man lifted a wheelbarrow loaded down with rocks, the muscles in his forearms straining under the weight. For as scrawny and lanky as the man appeared, he was laden with lean muscle. If it came to a match of brawn, Cecil knew he couldn't compete. But should it come to that, he'd give his best.

A cold shiver danced down Cecil's spine, chased by the hot flush of realization that the boy could be close by or dead, but he didn't want to think about that. He had to cling to hope.

With a glance back toward the town, his thoughts shifted to Sheriff Krosby. Cecil could go to him, lay it all out, but doubt gnawed at him. The sheriff he thought more friend than foe might not believe him. Or worse, what if the guy slipped away while Cecil was on some wild goose chase to tell Krosby?

No, Cecil didn't think the missing boy could afford to waste time on skepticism and red tape. Each moment wasted could mean another moment the boy wasn't safe. Cecil's jaw clenched, the resolve hardening within him like steel tempered in fire. This was his chance to save the boy and prove them all wrong.

Cecil's hands trembled slightly, aching for a cigarette, but not wanting to draw attention to himself. So he ignored the call of the vice and kept to the tree line, his eyes never straying from the figure moving about with a deceptive normality among the crops and other workers.

At last the man went to his car, the beat-up old thing growling to life. Cecil ran toward him, his heartbeat a steady drumbeat in his ears. Adrenaline surged through his veins, heightening his senses. Cecil paused only to wipe the sweat from his brow, wishing he had a pistol or some other weapon, but he had nothing. The only thing on his side was the element of surprise. By the way the man acted, he had no idea that someone was onto him. And that was what Cecil was counting on.

He had to hope that would be enough.

The man rolled his car slowly down the road but didn't head back to Vildo. Instead, he cut out onto a lane, barely drivable. Cecil walked briskly but kept his distance. The car could stop at any time, and he didn't want to get too close. Eventually, the lane emerged onto Old River Road. The word road was a bit polite; it wasn't much more than a dirt path that used to lead down to the river, but it didn't look like many people still used it.

The car disappeared from his sight, but the lingering dust it kicked up provided a helpful trail. And this road only went one way. It had to dead-end before it got to the river. The woods seemed to close in on Cecil as he cut through the underbrush. The road continued to the left, but tire tracks veered off the trail toward a small clearing. Cecil crept closer. The trailer sat like a festering sore on the face of the otherwise untouched woodland. Its metal sides were rusted and dented, the once-white paint now a sickly yellow, peeling in places to reveal the rot beneath.

A single window, covered in grime and cobwebs, stared out from the front of the structure, offering no glimpse of the horrors that might lurk within. Beside the trailer, an old shed leaned precariously, its wooden walls warped and weathered by the elements. The door hung from a single hinge, creaking softly in the breeze like a whispered warning. Cecil's eyes were drawn to the shed, a flicker of hope and dread mingling in his chest.

Could the boy be inside, hidden away from the world, waiting for someone to find him?

But before he could act on the thought, the man emerged from the trailer, a worn duffel bag slung over his shoulder. He paused for a moment, his head cocked as if listening for something, and then set off into the woods, his steps purposeful and sure.

Cecil hesitated, torn between investigating the shed and following the man. The seconds ticked by, each one a lifetime of uncertainty and fear. But in the end, he knew he couldn't risk losing sight of his target. The man was the key to finding the boy, and Cecil couldn't afford to let him slip away.

With a last, lingering glance at the shed, Cecil set off after the man, his footsteps muffled by the carpet of dead leaves and twigs. The woods closed in around him, a labyrinth of shadows which until now had never seemed ominous. This man's very presence could contaminate everything, even the purity of nature. The air was heavy with the scent of decaying wood and something else, maybe an animal. God, he hoped it was an animal. Don't let it be the boy.

For a moment, Cecil felt as though he were walking into a different world entirely. But he pushed the feeling aside, his focus narrowing to the figure ahead of him. The man moved with a swift, purposeful stride, his bag bouncing against his back with each step. Cecil matched his pace, staying far enough behind to avoid detection but close enough to keep the man in sight.

As they walked, the woods seemed to grow darker, the trees pressing in on all sides like silent watchers. The only sounds were the crunch of leaves underfoot and the distant cry of a bird, a mournful sound that echoed through the stillness.

Cecil's mind raced as he followed, trying to anticipate the man's destination. Was he leading him to the boy? Or was this all some sort of twisted game, a cat-and-mouse chase through the wilderness?

But then the cabin emerged from the woods like a malevolent specter. The woods were full of abandoned shacks like these. Used by hunters and fisherman, long neglected by their children. The man ascended the steps, unlocked a shiny padlock, and the door swung open with a creak that sent pecking birds fluttering through the trees.

Anticipation and dread swirled inside of him. This was it. *Millie, if you're watching, you might wanna look away.*

Through the window, the cold glint of the blade caught the last rays of the dying sun. Cecil ran to the steps as the raspy voice said, "Time to say goodbye, Mike." His whisper held a melody of perverse excitement.

The musk of old wood and damp filled Cecil's nose as he reached the threshold, the wooden planks creaking under the weight of his decision. Hand steady, he flung the door open, its hinges protesting with a haunting screech that seemed to pierce the stillness that had fallen over the forest beyond.

He surged forward, bursting inside with a force that seemed to shake the very foundations of the cabin. The man whipped around from where Mike was whimpering, lying face down with hands bound at his captor's feet. The man bore his rat-like teeth and lunged without a second thought toward Cecil. Instinct took over, and Cecil sidestepped, but he was not quick enough. Their bodies collided, and they tumbled to the floor. Cecil kicked at the man, squirming backward, trying to put distance between them.

The man gripped the knife and got to his feet. "You shouldn't have come here," he growled, "but on second thought, I don't like leaving loose ends, so you made my job a helluva lot easier."

He stepped closer, and Mike whispered, "Run, Mr. Cecil."

Cecil shook his head. "I didn't come here to make your life easier. I came to help the boy, and others are coming. It's only a matter of time."

"You're lying!" the man hissed sounding suddenly boyish. Then he screeched like a banshee, "Liar!"

And then they were on each other, a tangle of limbs and rage. Cecil focused on keeping the knife-wielding hand at bay. Fists flew, connecting with flesh and bone. The air was filled with the sounds of their struggle—grunts of pain, the thud of bodies against floor, the sharp crack of splintering wood.

Rage, white-hot and blinding, surged through Cecil's veins. Still on the floor, he slammed the man against the floor, his forearm pressing against his throat. But the man was strong, his own survival instinct lending him a feral ferocity. A fist slammed into Cecil's ribs, driving the air from his lungs. He tasted blood in his mouth, felt the world tilting dangerously around him. He lost control of the knifed hand as the man's fingers closed around Cecil's throat, squeezing with a strength born of madness. "You should have minded your own business," he snarled, his face twisted with hatred. "You should have stayed away." The man locked eyes with him as he plunged the knife into Cecil's gut.

Black spots danced at the edges of Cecil's vision, the world narrowing to a pinpoint. But then, through the haze of pain and oxygen deprivation, he heard it—the distant baying of dogs, the shouts of men. He had no idea if that was help or not, but sometimes it was better to believe the lie.

The man eased his grip on Cecil's throat as hot blood silently poured from around the knife still in his belly. "It's over," Cecil rasped, his chest heaving. "You're finished, you hear me? You're done!"

The man cast a wild glance around the cabin, as if seeing it for the first time, and then he was gone, fleeing into the woods like the coward he was. Cecil slumped against the wall, his body screaming with pain. He could feel the warm wetness spreading across him, knew that the man's blade had found its mark.

But none of that mattered now. All that mattered was Mike. He inched along the floor, the pain unimaginable, his hands shaking as he fumbled with the boy's chains. He couldn't free him; he just had to hope someone else was coming. Mike's face was streaked with tears, his eyes wide with a fear that no child should ever know.

"I've got you," Cecil whispered, patting the boy on the arms. "I've got you, buddy. You're safe now." Tears broke free, cascading down Mike's cheeks as Cecil fought against the darkness clawing at the edge of his vision. Each word he spoke was laced with gritty determination, despite the agony that threatened to overwhelm him.

"Listen to me," Cecil continued, mustering every bit of strength left in him. "You're strong. You're brave. And you're going to get out of here." His fingers trembled as they wiped away the boy's tears, leaving behind streaks of crimson.

"Help . . . help is coming," he gasped, a thin line of blood trailing from the corner of his mouth. It was a lie. Cecil had no idea if anyone would find them, but the boy would need something to cling to in the terrifying silence that would follow after Cecil's own life was extinguished.

It wouldn't be long; he pulled the knife from his belly and handed it to the boy. His head heavy, chin resting against his chest as his body succumbed. And then Millie was there, in the room or in his mind, he couldn't tell. Life without her had come to an end.

Chapter Twenty-Three

204 Hours Missing

Cecil's hand slipped from Mike's, leaving the blood-sticky knife in his hand. Tears streamed down Mike's face unchecked, burning a trail through the grime that had settled on his cheeks. The room was silent now, save for the ragged hitch of his own breathing.

"Mr. Cecil," he whimpered, but he knew there would be no response.

Mike's breath hitched in his throat as the sound of hurried footsteps faded into the dense forest outside, leaving behind a silence that was suffocating. With wide, tear-glazed eyes, he scanned the dim interior. The shackles around his wrists felt heavier now. The coppery smell overwhelmed him, but he was too weak to throw up. Too weak to hope.

Outside, branches rustled in the wind, a cruel imitation of someone walking to save him. Mike had long since given up on hoping there would be someone out there other than the man that brought him here. But inside, the feeling of being alone with Cecil's body beside him felt worse than when no one had been there at all.

Still, no panic clawed at his chest; hopelessness was all he had left. But Cecil had promised help was on the way. But what if they too met Cecil's fate? There was no telling if or when the man would be back. Then what?

At least he had the knife now.

In the middle of his spiraling fear, a glimmer of something else took root. "I am strong. I am brave." His voice was unrecognizable to his own ears. Raspy and fragile. But it didn't matter. He said it over and over again. "I am strong; I am brave."

The chains rattled as he shifted, rocking and muttering words to himself. The metal bit into his skin. He winced but didn't stop, "Help is coming." This would all end. It was only a matter of time. He hardened his focus on the window where threads of pale evening light dared to pierce the gloom.

Then he clutched the knife between his bound hands and set to working at the point where the chain was secured to the metal hook in the ground for the hatch to the dug cellar. If he could get the plate up that held the ring, he could escape. With every twist and pull he made, the metal fought back. Mike's already raw fingers were all but shredded as they trembled, refusing to relent, scraping against the unforgiving wood and iron in a frantic dance of desperation. His breaths came out in ragged gasps. "Come on, come on," he urged, his voice barely forming the words.

Outside, the rustle of leaves again called his heart to hope that someone was nearby. Could it be the sheriff or someone else, some hero? But his exhausted heart didn't dare leap at the sound. He couldn't let hope cloud his focus. He had to act, and act now.

With a surge of adrenaline, Mike twisted his wrist in a new angle, a painful contortion born from pure instinct. There was a grating sound, an almost imperceptible shift in the chain's grip. His eyes widened as the shackle loosened ever so slightly.

"Almost . . . there . . ." he panted, the words pulsing in his head.

The cabin door creaked on its hinges and Mike froze. Footsteps approached, deliberate and unhurried. His pulse throbbed in his ears; each beat a drum of dread. The man returning? Or someone else?

A shadow fell across the splintered floorboards, eating up the width of the cabin until it reached the far wall. The boy held his breath, trapped between the hope of rescue and the terror of what might walk through that door.

Chapter Twenty-Four

204 Hours Missing

"Open up, it's Sheriff Krosby; I just need a word with ya." Krobsy kept his voice level, despite the anticipation and fear welling inside him. A car was parked near the trailer, but there was no sign of its driver. "Seth, I'm going to come in," he called after minutes passed and no one answered.

Krosby's hand trembled slightly as it hovered over the doorknob of the decrepit trailer, a bead of sweat trickling down his spine despite the cool evening breeze. He had put out the call for backup, requesting the aid of men with their hunting dogs in case this guy got to running, but the gut-wrenching urgency of the situation had propelled him to charge ahead alone. Every second wasted was another second the boy remained in the clutches of a monster.

With a deep breath, Krosby twisted the knob, the door screeching open like nails on a chalkboard. The fetid stench that assaulted his nostrils nearly made him gag, a miasma of stale sweat, rancid food, and something far more sinister that he couldn't quite place. Stepping inside, his eyes struggled to adjust to the dim interior, the air thick with a palpable sense of wrongness that seemed to seep into his very pores.

As his gaze swept over the walls, Krosby's stomach churned, bile rising in his throat. Every surface was plastered with crude drawings, the lines jagged and frenzied, as if scratched out by a hand possessed. The images were explicit, vile, a window into a mind so twisted and depraved that it defied comprehension. They seemed to leer at him from the shadows, taunting him with their depravity. Images of things done to men, women, and children. He seemed to have no immediate preference.

Amidst the chaos of perverse sketches, Krosby's attention was drawn to the magazines scattered across a battered coffee table, their glossy covers boasting acts of unspeakable brutality and degradation. The lurid headlines screamed at him, a cacophony of depravity that made his skin crawl. These types of magazines were illegal. Sure, most stores, even Moss's, carried periodicals that needed to be sold in a paper wrapping, but what was depicted on these pages was violent.

Seth was no mere deviant—he was a predator of the worst kind, his desires so vile and inhuman that they threatened to shatter the very foundations of decency.

Rage and revulsion warred within Krosby as he tore his eyes away from the sickening display, his fists clenching so tightly that his nails bit into his palms. The evidence was damning, a testament to the depths of Seth's wickedness. But it wasn't enough. He needed more— needed to find the boy.

Staggering out of the trailer, Krosby gulped in lungfuls of fresh air, desperate to purge the stench from his body. But there was no respite to be found, not when he knew that every moment he delayed was another moment that Mike suffered unimaginable horrors.

With a sense of dread coiling in his gut, Krosby approached the neighboring shed, the door hanging drunkenly off its hinges like a broken tooth. As he stepped inside, the stench intensified tenfold, a miasma of decay and human misery that made his gorge rise. With shaking hands, he clicked on his flashlight, the beam slicing through the darkness to illuminate a scene straight out of a nightmare.

There, in the center of the shed, was a stained and tattered mattress, the fabric bearing the unmistakable marks of violence and depravity. And at its foot, gleaming dully in the flashlight's glow, was a chain—a rusted length of metal that spoke of unspeakable cruelty, its links encrusted with the dried blood of innocence lost.

Krosby's heart pounded in his ears, his breath coming in ragged gasps as he followed the trail of crimson spatters, his mind reeling with the implications. This was no longer mere speculation—this was the undeniable proof of a crime so vile, so heinous, that it defied all notions of humanity.

As he swept the beam of his flashlight across the shed floor, Krosby's eyes fell upon a scattering of crushed Coke bottles, their bright red color a jarring contrast to the gloom. There was a hole in the wall, and Krosby wondered if the boy had managed to escape. But if he had, where was he now?

The weight of the discovery crashed down upon Krosby like a physical blow, a leaden mass that threatened to crush his very soul. But he pushed through the horror and the despair, his resolve hardening into a white-hot blade of righteous fury. He had a job to do, a child to save or a body to recover, and he would not rest until Mike was found and his tormenter brought to justice.

Stepping out of the shed, Krosby blinked against the dying light, his eyes adjusting from the dim interior to the twilight of the woods. The distant baying of hounds told him that his backup had arrived, but their presence was a mere footnote in the face of the task at hand. His mind was consumed by a single, overriding imperative—to find Mike, to bring him home, to make this right. If Seth wasn't home and he wasn't in the shed, then he had to be somewhere nearby.

Krosby picked the line through the woods that most closely resembled a path. His steps were slow, pausing to listen as he walked deeper into the woods. There was a rustle, a disturbance in the underbrush that snagged his attention. He turned sharply, drawing his pistol, just in time to see a figure darting away—the very man he'd been hunting, unmistakable now in his hurried flight toward the trailer.

Krosby's instincts roared to life, any lingering horror from the shed's contents supplanted by a surge of determination. This was it—the moment of truth. The chase was on.

"Hey!" he bellowed, voice thundering through the stillness as he launched himself after the fleeing suspect. The man glanced back, a flicker of panic crossing his face before he picked up speed.

Krosby pounded across the leaf-strewn ground, his boots kicking up debris. He could feel his heart slamming against his ribcage, adrenaline flooding his system, sharpening his senses. Muscle memory from years on the force propelled him forward, every fiber in his body converging on one goal: capture.

The woods became a blur of green and brown as he navigated the terrain, ducking low-hanging branches and leaping over gnarled roots snaking across the forest floor. The setting sun cast an amber glow through the canopy, long shadows reaching out like spectral fingers, grasping at the edges of his vision.

He could see the man now, a desperate silhouette clawing its way toward escape, casting frantic looks over his shoulder. Krosby knew the terrain was working against the suspect; the dense foliage, the uneven ground—they were allies in his relentless pursuit.

"Stop! Police!" he shouted again, though he knew the command would go unheeded. Krosby fired a few shots, but none went where he needed.

The suspect reached his car, fumbling with keys, but Krosby was closing the gap, every stride bringing him closer. But he wasn't fast enough. The spinning of tires sounded as the car screeched in reverse, smashing into the driver's side of the Blazer and then speeding off. Krosby pushed harder, muscles burning, the image of the missing boy propelling him forward. The Blazer was undrivable now.

Krosby watched, chest heaving, fists clenched, as Seth got away, fishtailing, kicking up a cloud of dust and leaves in his wake.

"Damn it!" His voice was a harsh whisper torn from his throat, the words dissipating into the cool evening air.

His eyes tracked the fading dust cloud as it settled back onto the unpaved road. Krosby's jaw set, a silent vow etching itself across his features. This wasn't the end—it was another beginning.

As the final glimmers of sunlight receded, giving way to twilight, Krosby radioed, "This is Sheriff Krosby," he began, his voice steady despite the adrenaline that still surged through his veins. "Suspect fled in a rusted out white sedan, heading east on Old River Road. I need units in pursuit, now. Over."

The radio crackled back to life with affirmations, the sound mingling with the chorus of evening crickets. Somewhere out there, a little boy awaited rescue, and a kidnapper thought himself free. But Krosby knew better. The game had changed, but it was far from over.

Chapter Twenty-Five

204 Hours Missing

"Help!" Mike's voice tore through the stillness, ragged and raw. He screamed until his throat felt like sandpaper, his words desperate echoes in the cavernous space around him. "Somebody, please!"

The person, or thing, if it had been real, never come through the door. A trick of the dying light or the wind, Mike didn't know, but what he did know is that he was all he had left.

"Help me! I'm here!" His voice cracked under the strain, becoming a hoarse whisper battling against the oppressive silence. The sharp scent of his own filth mingled with the musty dampness of the room and the metallic odor of Cecil's blood.

Mike slumped against the cool floor, his energy seeping away like water through cupped hands. The hope that had temporarily fueled his shouts was now replaced by an all-consuming fatigue. Muscles quivered from exertion, and his mind swam in a sea of exhaustion, barely able to hold onto the thoughts that screamed for survival.

"Please. . . ." It was no more than a breath, a feeble plea lost amidst the remnants of his spent cries. His head lolled forward, chin resting on his chest as he gasped for air, each inhaling a labored effort. In the dimness, Mike's eyes fluttered closed, his body teetering on the brink of collapse. But even as darkness threatened to claim him, he knew he couldn't surrender—not yet.

Mike's mind was a battlefield, every thought a clash between hope and despair. His pulse hammered in his ears, a relentless drumbeat that seemed and it filled him with dread. He wondered if anyone would ever find him before it was too late, before he was dead on the floor like Cecil.

The idea clawed at him, each doubt a vulture pecking relentlessly at the remains of his resolve. Mike squeezed his eyes shut, trying to banish the images that haunted him: the faces of loved ones fading, the life he knew slipping away like grains of sand through an hourglass.

He forced himself to inhale, a ragged attempt to steady his racing thoughts. Exhaling slowly, Mike tried to anchor himself to the present, but the terror of eternity in this void gripped him tighter, like a vice around his chest.

Then came the silence—a deafening, absolute hush that descended upon the room like a heavy shroud. Mike's breaths were shallow gasps now, the only disturbance in an otherwise soundless expanse. Each second dragged, elongating into an eternity as the quiet bore down on him, oppressive and thick. It was as if the world had stopped spinning, holding its breath along with him, waiting for a sign—for anything.

The stillness magnified every fear, every shred of panic. In the silence, time lost all meaning, and Mike felt the weight of a thousand unseen eyes upon him, watching, judging his struggle to cling to hope in a place where light seemed forever banished.

His heart, once pounding with the urgency of survival, now throbbed with the ache of uncertainty. The creak of the door hinge shattered the silence like a hammer through glass, and a ghostly beam of yellow light spilled into the room, casting long shadows across the dusty floor. Mike squinted against the sudden brightness, his eyes stinging with relief as much as they did from the intrusion of light.

"Mike!" The voice was authoritative yet laced with concern—a familiar sound that yanked at his memory. Through bleary eyes, he saw the figure of Sheriff Krosby emerge from behind the brightness, like a ghost stepping out of a dream. The sheriff's weathered face was set in taut lines, his silver hair a stark contrast to the deep creases marking his brow. The star badge on his chest gleamed dully, catching the light as he moved closer.

"In here," Mike croaked, his voice barely a whisper. He tried to lift a hand, but his muscles screamed in protest, fatigue chaining him down.

"We've been looking for you."

Krosby knelt beside him, his expression softening for a moment before snapping back into focus. "Hold tight, son. We're gonna get you out of this mess." His hands, steady and sure, checked for injuries, fingers probing with practiced care.

As Krosby surveyed the scene, his steely blue eyes took in the disarray—the overturned furniture, the scattered remnants of a struggle.

His jaw clenched at the sight of dried blood on the floorboards, the light lingering on the dead body of the man who'd given his life to try and save Mike.

"Hang in there, Mike," he said, a calm command in his voice.

"Can't you get it off?" Mike's question was half plea, half gasp, as each word came out laced with pain.

Krosby shook his head; his lips formed a tight line. "It's no use without the right tools." He looked around the desolate space, and Mike could almost see his mind ticking through possible solutions.

"Help is on the way," Krosby reassured him. Krosby reached for the radio clipped to his belt.

"This is Krosby. Mike has been located. I need a rescue crew at the cabin that belonged to Waller's father. It's east of the river, I'd say quarter mile past the trailer off Old River Road. Bring bolt cutters—large ones. Over."

He paused, his mouth turned down as a series of "Copy that, Sheriff" crackled in reply, breaking the heavy silence that had settled over them.

"And someone notify the coroner. We've got a deceased civilian. Over."

"Yes, sir," came quickly, and if more came with questions, Mike wouldn't hear them because Krosby held his mic button, silencing the line for a moment before saying, "What's the rescue team's ETA?"

"Ten minutes, Sheriff."

"Make it five. Over and out," Krosby shot back, urgency sharpening his words. He clipped the radio back onto his belt and turned his attention back to Mike, whose breaths came in short, ragged pulls.

"Five minutes, Mike. Just hold on for five more minutes." Krosby's voice was the solid thing in the shifting sands of Mike's consciousness, a lifeline thrown across the perilous expanse of pain and fear. Mike nodded weakly, his eyes closing against the wait that stretched before him like an eternity.

Sheriff Krosby's eyes, usually sharp and assessing, softened as he turned away from Mike. He moved toward the still figure of Cecil, lying awkwardly on the floor. Krosby crossed the room and grabbed a blanket and shook it out, then he crouched down, his movements gentle, almost reverent, as he draped an old, moth-eaten blanket over Cecil's lifeless form. His hands lingered for a moment, smoothing the fabric across the contours that no longer held life.

"Rest easy, old man," he murmured under his breath.

Mike watched from where he lay trapped, his gaze fixed on Krosby's back. The sight of Cecil covered up brought an odd surge of relief, sparing him the constant reminder of death just a few feet away. Yet, it did little to stem the tide of images that crashed through his mind. A cocktail of emotions churned within him—relief at the prospect of rescue clashing with the raw edges of things he knew he could never unsee.

He swallowed hard against the lump forming in his throat. "I . . . I never thought . . ." His voice cracked, betraying the turmoil within.

"Hey, look at me, Mike." Krosby's voice was firm yet carried an undercurrent of warmth. "You're going to get through this. You hear me?"

Mike managed a nod, blinking back the hot tears that threatened to spill over. He wanted to believe Krosby, wanted to cling to the promise of safety that the sheriff's presence offered. But the darkness that had taken root in his mind, the shadows that had haunted his every waking moment in this hellish place, they weren't so easily banished.

He watched as Krosby moved about the room, his eyes never straying far from the door, as if expecting the monster who had put Mike here to come bursting through at any moment. The sheriff's hand rested on his gun, a silent reminder of the danger that still lurked, the evil that had yet to be vanquished.

Mike's throat felt tight, his tongue heavy and clumsy in his mouth. He wanted to ask about his parents, about his brothers, but the words wouldn't come. It was as if the very act of speaking, of giving voice to his fears, would make them all too real, too impossible to bear.

So he lay there, silent and still, his eyes fixed on the ceiling as he listened to the sound of Krosby's footsteps, the crackle of the radio, the distant wail of sirens growing ever closer. Each second seemed to stretch into an eternity, a lifetime of waiting condensed into the space between one breath and the next.

And then, just when Mike thought he couldn't stand it a moment longer, the room was suddenly filled with light and noise, a cacophony of shouts and footsteps and the clatter of equipment. He blinked, his eyes watering against the sudden brightness as a sea of uniforms surrounded him, their faces a blur of concern and determination.

"We've got you, buddy," one of them said, his voice gentle as he knelt beside Mike. "You're safe now."

Mike felt hands on him, careful and sure, as they worked to free him from the chains that had held him captive for so long. He heard the snap of bolt cutters, the clank of metal on metal, and then, miraculously, the pressure on his wrists and ankles was gone, replaced by a blessed lightness that made him feel like he might float away.

"Easy there, kid," another voice said, strong arms lifting him onto a stretcher. "We're gonna get you out of here, get you back to your folks."

Mike's heart leapt at the mention of his family, a sudden, desperate longing washing over him. He wanted his mom, wanted to feel her arms around him, to breathe in the familiar scent of her perfume and know that everything was going to be okay.

But even as they carried him out of the cabin, even as the fresh air hit his face and the sun warmed his skin, Mike couldn't shake the feeling that nothing would ever be okay again. He had seen too much, had endured too much, to ever be the same carefree child he had once been.

As they loaded him into the waiting ambulance, Mike's eyes sought out Krosby, the man who had been his lifeline, his beacon of hope in the darkest of hours. The sheriff stood watching, his face lined with a weariness that seemed to go bone-deep.

"Thank you," Mike whispered, his voice hoarse and trembling. "For finding me. For . . . for saving me. Mr. Cecil told me I was brave, and help was coming."

Krosby's eyes softened, a sad smile tugging at the corners of his mouth. "You're a brave kid, Mike. Braver than most grown men I know. You just focus on getting better now, you hear? Let us worry about the rest."

Mike nodded, a single tear escaping to trail down his cheek. He knew there would be questions, knew there would be nightmares and flashbacks and a long road to recovery ahead. But for now, in this moment, he let himself feel the overwhelming relief, the sheer, staggering gratitude for the simple fact that he was alive.

As the ambulance doors closed, as the siren began to wail and the vehicle lurched into motion, Mike closed his eyes, his hand seeking out the reassuring grip of the paramedic beside him. He held on tight, anchoring himself to the certainty that this was real and, when he opened his eyes, he wouldn't be back in the cabin or the shed.

He tested it several times. Opening and closing his lids, just to be certain his escape was real. And so far, it was.

Chapter Twenty-Six

Found

The phone's shrill ring cut through the quiet like a knife, making Kevin's heart jump into his throat before anyone even said a word. His mom's hand shook as she picked up the receiver, her "Hello" so soft he could barely hear it. Kevin watched, holding his breath, as the worry lines on her face started to melt away, replaced by something that looked a lot like a miracle. And then she was sobbing, her whole body shaking with it.

"He's safe," she managed to get out, her voice barely louder than a whisper, but it hit Kevin like a shout. "Mike's safe."

Dad shot up from his recliner like it was on fire, the newspaper falling to the floor in a crumpled heap. Those two words were like a lifeline, yanking them out of the ocean of fear they'd been drowning in for days.

"Where? How?" Kevin's voice cracked as he tried to get more info, but Mom was already herding them toward the door, her words tumbling out in a rush. "The hospital. We have to go—now!"

They all piled into the car, and Dad took off, the mailboxes turning into a blur as he flew down the roads. Mike was coming home. They found him. Everything could go back to normal. Kevin wished he could tell Danny the good news. Maybe he could borrow a phone at the hospital.

The county hospital loomed up ahead, its lights glaring in the darkness. Kevin spotted a bunch of police cars in the parking lot, but he didn't see Sheriff Krosby's ride. They ran inside, Mom leading the way, bursting through the doors where a nurse in a crisp white uniform showed them to a room.

And there was Mike, propped up in bed, covered in bruises and bandages that made Kevin's stomach twist. He froze in the doorway, his feet glued to the floor. Guilt chewed at his insides, the memory of the last time he'd seen his brother playing over and over in his head.

After Mom and Dad had hugged Mike and cried all over him, he finally looked over at Kevin and Steve. Steve, in his typical too-cool-for-school way, just said, "Welcome back." Kevin rolled his eyes.

"Mike," he managed to get out, his voice raspy as he walked up to the bed.

Mike turned his head slowly, his eyes meeting Kevin's. There was no anger there, no blame, just a flicker of recognition and relief. It was too much for Kevin to handle. The floodgates opened, and tears started pouring down his cheeks, leaving clean tracks through the dirt and grime.

"I'm so sorry, Mike," Kevin sobbed, reaching for his brother's hand. "I should've been there for you. I—I left you alone."

In the quiet of the hospital room, with the steady beeping of the heart monitor filling the silence, Kevin felt the first glimmer of hope. Mike's hand, surprisingly strong for how pale and weak he looked, closed around Kevin's shaking fingers. He gave a small smile that seemed to chase away some of the shadows on his bruised face.

"Kev," he started, his voice raspy but filled with reassurance, "it's okay. We're together now. That's all that matters."

Kevin blinked away the last of his tears, his chest tight with a mixture of relief and leftover guilt. Mike's forgiveness was like a Band-Aid on his raw emotions.

"I'll do better," he promised, his voice rough and shaky. "I'll be the best big brother ever from now on."

Mike's smile grew a little wider, a hint of his old self shining through. "I know you will, Kev. I know you will."

As Kevin basked in the warmth of Mike's smile, a nurse bustled into the room, her face pulled back in a polite smile, but her eyes were all professional concern. "I'm sorry to interrupt," she said softly, her eyes scanning the monitors beside Mike's bed, "but he really needs his rest now. One person can stay overnight, but the rest of you should head home, or you can stay in the waiting room."

Mom immediately volunteered to stay; her hand still clasped tightly around Mike's. Dad and Steve nodded, their eyes heavy with a weariness that seemed to go beyond just physical exhaustion. Kevin hesitated, not wanting to leave his brother's side, but a nudge from Dad propelled him toward the door.

The waiting room was completely different from Mike's room, with bright fluorescent lights and a strong antiseptic smell. Kevin slumped into a chair, his body suddenly feeling like it was made of lead. Dad and Steve settled in nearby, their faces drawn and pale.

As Kevin's eyes drifted around the room, they landed on a sight that made his blood run cold. There, in the far corner, was a gurney with a sheet-covered body, the outline of a human form clearly visible beneath the stark white fabric. And standing next to it, deep in conversation with a man in tan scrubs, was Sheriff Krosby.

Kevin watched, his heart in his throat, as the man, maybe a doctor, nodded solemnly and wheeled the gurney away, disappearing through a set of double doors. Krosby turned, his shoulders slumping as if a great weight had settled upon them. When he caught sight of Kevin and his family, he made his way over, his face drawn with grief and exhaustion. He removed his cap, and before he could say a word, Kevin cut in, "Who was that?" his voice sounding small and frightened to his own ears. "Under the sheet, I mean."

Krosby sighed, running a hand over his face. "That was Cecil Jordan," he said quietly, his eyes filled with a sadness that seemed to go beyond words. "He saved Mike. Cecil found him and fought off the man right as he was going after Mike. His last words were encouraging Mike to stay brave."

Kevin felt like he'd been punched in the gut, the air rushing out of his lungs in a whoosh. Cecil, was gone. It made about as much sense as the idea that Mike had gone missing. It just couldn't be true.

Kevin's heart seemed to beat in a jagged rhythm. He looked over at Dad and Steve, saw the shame and regret etched across their faces. They had been horrible to Cecil, had said such nasty things about him in front of the whole town. And now, faced with the truth of the man's bravery and selflessness, they couldn't even meet Krosby's eyes.

But Kevin had almost always believed in Cecil, had always known that there was more to him than the rumors and the gossip. He felt a surge of anger toward his dad and brother, toward everyone who had ever treated Cecil like he was less than human.

"He was a hero," Kevin said fiercely, his eyes burning with unshed tears. "He saved Mike's life, and nobody ever gave him a chance."

Krosby nodded, a glimmer of respect in his eyes. "You're right, son. Cecil was a good man, a brave man. This town ought to all be ashamed of how they treated him." He turned to Dad, his expression growing serious. "John, I need to talk to you for a moment. About the man who did this."

Dad's head snapped up, his eyes wide and frightened. "You know who it was?"

Krosby nodded grimly. "His name is Seth Harris. He worked at Waller's farm, kept to himself mostly. We're still in pursuit, got every available unit out there looking for him. I don't believe that he's a threat to your family at this time. I think taking Mike was about opportunity, not a target."

Dad's face went white, his hands clenching into fists at his sides.

"But he's still out there?"

Krosby nodded as if he was ashamed to admit it. "We won't rest until we find him. Until we make him pay for what he's done."

Kevin sat there, his mind reeling with the revelation. Seth Harris. The name meant nothing to him, but it filled him with a dread that settled like a stone in the pit of his stomach. This man, this monster, had taken his brother, had hurt him in ways Kevin couldn't even imagine. And he was still out there, still a threat to everyone and everything Kevin held dear.

He looked over at Steve, saw the same fear and anger reflected in his brother's eyes. They were just kids, just a couple of scared, confused kids who had wanted their little brother back, who wanted their family to be whole again.

But as Kevin sat there, listening to the murmur of voices and the beep of machines, he knew that nothing would ever be the same.

Chapter Twenty-Seven

Mike

6 Months Later

Mike walked through the front door, his hand shaking a little as it touched the cold metal. The normal smells of home and the soft hum of the fridge felt weird and wrong compared to the crazy thoughts still screaming in his head. He felt like a ghost walking around in his own life, going through rooms that looked the same but felt totally different. Like any second the dream would end, his eyes would open, and he'd be back in that cabin, trapped with Cecil's body.

Even after a whole year, nothing felt right. Going outside was scary and full of things that could hurt him. Staying inside felt suffocating, like being back in that shed and cabin. In the morning, right when he woke up, there was a tiny second without the pain and fear of his memories. Then, like always, they'd come crashing back in, hitting him like a big hammer.

He could see him—the man that took him—in every little shadow or creak of the floor. A shape behind the shower curtain, a face looking through the window, a dark figure standing just out of sight. Mike knew it wasn't real, that these were just ghosts from his messed-up nerves, or at least that's what his mom told him over and over again. But knowing that didn't make the fear go away. It was like the man had left a piece of himself behind, a whispering ghost that followed Mike, breathing down his neck with every step.

There was no way back to who he was before that man told him to get in his car. There was no map to help him through this thick fog of fear that stuck to him like a second skin.

Crowds were the worst. Walking down the street was like swimming in a pool of paranoia, every person he passed a possible danger. Mike's heart would race when he saw the back of someone's head with hair or clothes that looked kind of like the bad man's. In the middle of the day, they would turn into monsters with just a trick of the light. He would flinch at sudden movements, his eyes darting around, always looking for the danger he was sure was there. School had been impossible, so his mom had given him the year off, half teaching him at home, half just letting him stay in bed.

Trying to sleep was either the only thing he could do, or he couldn't sleep at all. Some nights, he was so tired that he'd sleep for what felt like days. Other times, the walls would close in on him, and the man was there, yelling and screaming about all the awful things he planned to do.

Mike sat at the kitchen table, his spoon stirring the cereal without him really thinking about it, making little ripples in the milk. The sharp click of the deadbolt locking into place broke the quiet of the morning as his mother checked the front door for the third time since they started eating. Her eyes flicked to the window, looking out at the quiet street before coming back to her son with a worry she didn't say out loud.

"Mom," Mike started, but the words got stuck on his tongue, heavy and useless.

She turned to look at him, her hand still on the lock—a real-life picture of the fear that now controlled their lives. "I know, honey," she said softly, even though he hadn't actually said anything.

His dad came into the room, a newspaper under his arm. He stopped to ruffle Mike's hair—a simple thing, but one that felt like an anchor in these stormy seas. There was a new clearness in his dad's eyes, a soberness that hadn't been there in months. He wasn't exactly sober; when Mike had first gone home, he claimed he'd never drink again, but that didn't last long. Now he just drank less, and Mike thought that was good enough.

"The county dropped the charges, claiming unusual circumstances," his dad said, sounding relieved but also a little guilty. "The lawyer called first thing this morning."

Mike's mother gave a small nod, her lips pressed together in a tight line. She moved to the coffee maker, her movements stiff and controlled. The news should have made things feel a little more normal, but the word "normal" didn't mean anything anymore. The charges weren't something Mike knew a lot about. Just that his dad had gotten in a spot of trouble when Mike was missing and a bunch of men in town had gotten in trouble too.

"Good," was all she said, pouring herself a cup with hands that didn't shake, even though everyone knew they wanted to.

"Hey, champ," his dad said, leaning against the counter, his eyes on Mike, looking for signs of the boy who used to start each day with a smile instead of a frown. "What do you say about a game of catch?"

Mike just shrugged, his eyes dropping to the mushy cereal. "Maybe," he mumbled, not really promising anything.

John nodded, understanding—or at least pretending to—that the road back to normal was going to be long and bumpy. He took a sip of his black coffee. "Okay then, maybe it is," Dad said with a smile that didn't quite make it to his eyes. He looked over at Mom, who was holding her coffee mug so tight it was like she thought it could keep any of them from getting lost ever again.

Mike sat at the kitchen table, the silence broken only by the ticking of the clock and the sound of his own breathing. His mom and dad were there too, looking at him with worried eyes that made his stomach twist. They kept trying to talk to him, to find the right words to make everything okay again, but nothing seemed to work.

"Mike, we could . . ." his mom started, her hands twisting a dishtowel into knots.

"Could what?" Mike snapped, instantly feeling bad when he saw his mom flinch. He didn't mean to be angry, but everything just felt so mixed up inside him.

His dad cleared his throat, trying to be the calm one. "We just want to help, son."

But all their "help" felt like being trapped. The double-checked doors, the windows that wouldn't open, the constant check-ins if he was out of their sight for more than a minute. It was like he couldn't breathe.

"Help feels a lot like prison," Mike mumbled, pushing away from the table, the chair scraping loudly against the floor. He wasn't even really upset about the locks; in some ways he liked it. What he hated is the fact that it wasn't normal. Is shouldn't be like this.

His dad didn't get mad. Instead, he nodded like he understood, even though Mike was sure no one could really get what was going on inside his head. "We're just scared, Mike. We can't lose you again."

Mike looked down at his shaking hands, a reminder that he was still fighting a battle no one else could see. He should be happy to be home, to be safe, but happiness felt like a foreign language he couldn't speak anymore.

"I don't know how to be happy anymore," he whispered, the words hanging heavy in the air.

His parents looked at each other, having one of those silent conversations that grown-ups do when they don't want kids to know what they're thinking.

"Mike, happiness isn't something you find overnight," his mom said softly, reaching across the table to try and close the distance between them. "It's okay to not be okay."

"Is it?" Mike asked, his voice barely louder than a whisper. How could they understand? They hadn't been the ones taken, their world shattered into a million scary pieces.

"Son, we're here for you," his dad added, his voice strong but also unsure, like he was trying to figure out how to be the dad Mike needed now.

Mike nodded, but it was more of a robot nod than a real one. He felt so far away from who he used to be, and he didn't know how to find his way back. As his parents watched him, Kevin slipped outside, almost unnoticed. But Mike wouldn't say anything. He envied how easily Kevin seemed to go back to normal.

A few moments later, Mike heard the familiar sounds of Kevin and Danny working on their bikes, their voices carrying through the open kitchen window. Their laughter, once so comforting and inviting, now felt like a reminder of everything he had lost, of the carefree joy that seemed so out of reach.

Suddenly, the house felt too small, too suffocating. The walls seemed to close in around him, the air thick with the weight of his parents' concern and his own swirling thoughts. Before he could second-guess himself, Mike stood up, his chair scraping against the floor.

"I'm going outside," he said, his voice sounding strange to his own ears. "Just . . . just for a bit."

His parents exchanged a look, a silent conversation passing between them. "Okay, honey," his mom said, her smile a little too bright, a little too forced. "Just stay where we can see you, alright?"

Mike nodded, already moving toward the door. He stepped out into the sunlight, blinking against the brightness that seemed to mock his inner darkness. The sounds of Kevin and Danny grew louder as he approached, their chatter a familiar backdrop to the summer day.

"Hey, Mike!" Danny called, waving a grease-stained hand. "Wanna help? We're almost done, and then we're gonna ride out to the tree house!"

Mike shook his head, even though he knew the tree house used to be one of the places he longed to be invited to. The thought of being out there, in the middle of nowhere, made his heart pound and his palms sweat.

He wandered over to the old oak tree, the one with the tire swing that used to make him feel like he was flying. Now, as he sat on the worn rubber, his feet barely brushing the ground, he felt like he was sinking.

The breeze rustled the leaves above him, but instead of a comforting whisper, it sounded like the hiss of a voice he couldn't forget. The shadow of a branch looked like the outline of a man, and Mike found himself holding his breath, waiting for it to move.

"Mike? You okay?" Kevin's voice broke through the haze of fear, and Mike realized his brother was standing right in front of him.

"Yeah, I'm . . . I'm fine," he lied, forcing a smile that felt like it might crack his face. "Just didn't feel like working on bikes today."

Kevin frowned, his face scrunched up with concern. "You sure? Mom said when you're not feeling good, you should go inside and rest."

Mike shook his head a little too quickly. "No, no, I'm okay. I just . . . I think I'll sit out here for a bit."

Kevin looked like he wanted to argue, but Danny called his name from across the yard, and he turned away with a shrug. "Okay, but if you change your mind, we'll be here."

Mike watched his brother and Danny walk away, their backs straight and their steps sure. They moved through the world like they belonged in it, like nothing could touch them. He envied that, envied the ease with which they laughed and played and lived.

He sat on the swing until the sun started to dip behind the trees, until the shadows grew long and the air turned cool. His mom called his name from the porch, her voice tight with a worry she tried to hide.

"Mike? Honey, it's getting late. Come inside and wash up for dinner."

He stood up, his legs stiff and his heart heavy. The walk back to the house felt like a mile, each step a reminder of how far he had to go to get back to where he used to be.

At dinner, his parents watched him, their eyes full of questions they didn't ask. Mike pushed his food around his plate, his appetite lost somewhere between the green beans and the mashed potatoes. They talked about the weather, about the new factory that was going to be built on the Johnson's farm, about anything but the empty chair at the table where fear now sat.

Later, in his room, Mike stared at the ceiling, his mind racing with thoughts he couldn't outrun. The memory of that place, of those days, played on a loop behind his eyes, a horror movie he couldn't turn off.

He could hear his parents talking down the hall, their voices muffled by the floorboards but still clear enough to make out the words.

"He's not getting better, John," his mother said, her voice thick with tears. "It's been months, and he's still . . . he's still not our Mike."

"He will be," his father said, but there was a hollow note to his words, like he was trying to convince himself more than her. "We just have to give him time, Jess. He's been through hell, and it's gonna take more than a few months to come back from that."

Mike rolled over, burying his face in his pillow to block out the sound of their worry. He knew they loved him, knew they were trying their best, but sometimes their love felt like a weight, like an expectation he couldn't meet.

As he drifted off to sleep, his mind played tricks on him, turning the creak of the house into the sound of footsteps, the rustle of the curtains into the whisper of a threat. He tossed and turned, his dreams a tangled web of memory and imagination, until he woke with a start, his heart racing and his skin damp with sweat.

The old Mike, the one who used to sleep through the night and wake with a smile, felt further away than ever. But as he lay there, staring into the darkness, he made a promise to himself.

"I'll find you," he whispered, his voice small but determined. "I'll find a way back to you, no matter how long it takes."

It was a promise he knew he might not be able to keep, but it was all he had, all he could cling to in the face of a future that felt like a question mark. And so, with the weight of that promise on his shoulders, Mike closed his eyes and tried to will himself back to sleep, back to a place where the nightmares couldn't find him, if only for a little while.

Chapter Twenty-Eight

Krosby

6 Months Later

The cardboard box seemed to groan under the weight of Krosby's career as he slid one last manila folder into its depths. His office stood barren, the walls stripped of his flags, commendations, and the shelves emptied. He lingered over the faded labels on his personal case notes.

"Mike," he whispered, fingering the edge of a particularly worn file. The missing boy case that had gnawed at the edges of his sanity, leaving an indelible mark on his soul. Mike's wide-eyed innocence stared back at him from a photograph paper-clipped to the inside. He remembered the relentless search, the false leads, the nights spent questioning if more could have been done. With a heavy sigh, he closed the file for what he hoped would be the last time, tucking it away with the others.

"The time went fast, old friend," murmured Jones from the doorway.

"Yes, it did," Krosby replied, sealing the box with a strip of tape—a final punctuation on his life's work.

"Want me to walk you out?"

Krosby arched his brow, "I think I know the way."

Jones put his hands up. "Alright, well, you better invite me on your fishing trips. Who knows, maybe I'll be the next one to retire."

Krosby smiled and nodded. "You bet."

Jone's patted the doorway and walked off.

Krosby hefted the box under his arm, the weight of his decisions, his sacrifices, and his few regrets pressing down on him like the gravity of the badge he'd worn faithfully. It was a slow procession through the precinct, his footsteps muffled on the carpeted floor. They had held a send-off party the day before, a gathering of colleagues and friends who had come to pay their respects to *the man who had given so much to the town*. There had been speeches and toasts, words of gratitude and admiration that should have warmed Krosby's heart. But as he stood there, a forced smile plastered on his face, he couldn't shake the feeling that it was all a sham, a hollow celebration of a job left unfinished.

The weight of the unsolved case hung over the proceedings like a dark cloud, a reminder of the failure that had haunted Krosby's final year on the force. He had chased leads and hunches, had poured every ounce of himself into the pursuit of justice, but in the end, it hadn't been enough. Seth Harris had slipped through his grasp, disappearing into the shadows like a ghost.

It was a bitter pill to swallow, the realization that sometimes, no matter how hard you tried, the bad guys got away. Krosby had always believed in the power of the badge, in the ability of good men to triumph over evil. But even as the doubt crept in, Krosby knew that it was time to step aside, to pass the torch to a younger generation. He had fought the good fight, had given everything he had to the pursuit of justice. And now, with his body aching and his mind weary, he knew that it was time for a new sheriff to take up the mantle, to bring fresh eyes and fresh energy to the hunt.

It wasn't an easy decision, and the thought of walking away from the only life he had ever known was a daunting one. But Krosby was a realist, a man who understood the harsh truths of the world. He knew that sometimes, the only way to move forward was to let go, to trust in the strength and the wisdom of those who would come after.

Now, the afternoon sunlight hit him like a spotlight as he stepped outside, his eyes squinting against the glare. He placed the box in the trunk of his new Crown Victoria with ceremonial care, feeling the finality of the act in every fiber of his being. Slipping behind the wheel, he paused, hands resting on the steering wheel as he took one long, lingering look at the brick-and-mortar guardian of justice that had been his second home.

With the turn of the key, the engine rolled over with a purr. He still missed the Blazer, just another damn thing Seth Harris had ruined. Krosby pulled out of the parking lot, the rearview mirror framing the police station as it grew smaller in the distance. A mix of relief, at the thought of no longer carrying the burdens of others, melded with a twinge of sadness for the identity he was leaving behind.

The road stretched before him, an open question that mirrored the uncertainty in his heart. What lay ahead for a retired sheriff? Who knew for certain?

Right now—fishing.

Krosby's car rattled and crunched over the stones as he pulled up near the riverbank. Stepping out, he squinted against the glare of the sun bouncing off the water. A soft breeze played along the riverside, mixing with the gentle gurgle of the flowing water. Krosby stood for a moment, his eyes following the winding path of the river as it carved its way through the land, always moving, always going somewhere.

The smell of damp earth and wildflowers filled his nose, grounding him in the here and now. This peaceful spot was his sanctuary, a place where life's tangles straightened out into the simple back-and-forth of nature. He took a deep breath, letting the warmth of the sun ease the tension from his shoulders. Here, by this river, thoughts that once churned like a storm could settle into a calm pool of reflection. *A man could get used to this.*

With careful, practiced moves, Krosby got his fishing gear from the back of the car. Each piece—a rod, reel, and a small box of lures—was like an old friend, keeping him company through countless hours of solitude. His movements were slow and steady, matching the pace of the life he was easing into. As he threaded the line through the guides of the rod, the delicate task demanded a focus that quieted the noise of memories.

Krosby snapped the reel into place, the sharp click cutting through the afternoon quiet. It reminded him of locking a perp in cuffs—that satisfying click that meant the job was done. 'Cept the job was never really done, was it? There was always another dirtbag waiting in the wings.

He thought about Cecil as he tied on a lure. Poor bastard. Gave his life to save that kid, and what did he get for it? A pauper's grave and a town full of hypocrites shedding crocodile tears. Where were they when he was alive, huh? When he was busting his ass to keep their cemetery looking nice, mowing the grass and pulling weeds in the blistering heat?

Krosby gave the line a hard tug, checking the knot. Trying to push aside the cascade of regrets that came to mind every time he thought about poor old Cecil. But who knows, maybe wherever he ended up, he's happy. Happier than he was when he was on this side of the dirt.

Krosby knew he wasn't just here to fish. He was here to forget, to find some kind of peace after the hell he'd been through. Fat chance of that, though. The river might wash away a lot of things, but it couldn't wash away the blood on his hands, the weight of the lives he couldn't save.

He thought about Mike, about the haunted look in that boy's eyes. That was a look that would never go away, not really. Kid might learn to smile again, might even learn to laugh, but deep down? He'd always be screaming. Krosby knew that feeling all too well. It was the price you paid for staring evil in the face, for seeing the ugliness that men were capable of.

Krosby cast his line, watched the lure arc through the air and land with a satisfying plop. Felt good to be out here, away from the bullshit and the politics. Just him and the river and the fish. Simple. Uncomplicated.

But even here, he couldn't escape the ghosts. They followed him like his own shadow, whispering in his ear, reminding him of his failures. And the biggest failure of all? Letting that son of a bitch Harris slip through his fingers. That was a mistake that would haunt him for the rest of his days. He'd had that bastard in his sights, and he'd let him get away. And Cecil had paid the price.

Krosby reeled in his line, the lure skipping across the water like a stone. The memory dulling around the edges as a soft breeze teased the edges of Krosby's mind, nudging him gently back to the present. The line remained still and untouched in the water. The line jerked tight, breaking the glassy surface of the water—a sharp contrast to the stillness of Krosby's thoughts. His heart skipped in time with the sudden ripple, an echo of the adrenaline that had once pulsed through his veins during a hot pursuit. He shook off the bits of memory and instinctively gripped the rod, reeling in with a practiced hand. The reel's mechanical whir the only thing he could hear. A gleam broke the surface as he drew the fish closer, its body thrashing against the inevitability of its capture.

For a fleeting moment, surprise flushed Krosby's features into a boyish grin—untouched by years of furrowed brows and stoic frowns. It was a small victory, but it sparked a lightness in his chest he hadn't felt in years.

With quick, easy movements born from countless hours on this very riverbank, Krosby lifted the fish from the water. Its scales shimmered like liquid silver in the sunlight, a stark contrast to the dusky corners of his mind where shadows of the past lurked. The fish's gills flared in silent desperation, its eyes wild with the primal urge for survival. Krosby found himself staring into them, a silent exchange between hunter and hunted.

"Time to go back," he murmured, almost apologetically. In one fluid motion, he removed the hook, careful not to hurt the creature more. Then, cradling the fish in his weathered hands, he knelt by the water's edge. The cool rush kissed his skin as he lowered the fish, releasing it with a reverence that exceeded the act's simplicity.

It darted away, disappearing beneath the ripples, leaving Krosby with an empty hook and a full heart. This was more than a catch-and-release; it was an ending and a beginning. Retirement wasn't giving up—it was just a change in currents, a new path carved by the passage of time. And as much as the uncertainty of uncharted waters lay ahead, Krosby understood that life, like the river, flowed on, not caring about the wants of men.

Krosby sat on the damp earth of the riverbank, elbows on knees and gaze fixed on the slow dance of water weaving through the reeds. The sunlight flickered across his face as it filtered through the leaves above, casting a mosaic of light and shadow that played upon his furrowed brow. He was still now, the motion of casting and reeling replaced by a stillness that seemed almost foreign to his weathered frame.

"Beautiful day for fishing, ain't it, Sheriff?" The voice sliced through his thoughts, friendly and familiar.

Krosby looked up to find George Hemley, owner of the local bait shop, ambling down the path with a fishing pole slung over his shoulder.

"Sure is, George. Though I ain't the sheriff anymore," Krosby replied, the title feeling like a suit that no longer fit.

"Retired or not, you'll always be our sheriff," George said with a knowing smile, settling himself a respectful distance away on the bank. "You've done more for this town than anyone can say, Krosby. That business with the Franklin boy . . . we all felt it. But you brought him home. That's what matters."

"Thanks, George. It's hard to shake off though, you know? Feels like some part of me is still out there, searching, even if I'm sittin' right here." Krosby's voice trailed off, lost in the ripples of the current.

"Nobody expects you to forget, but remember this—you did good, real good. And now, maybe try and do some good for yourself, huh?" George tipped his cap in a salute.

"Maybe so," Krosby conceded, the corner of his mouth lifting in a half-smile.

Krosby's hands worked methodically, taking apart his rod with a care that betrayed years of practice. He paused, holding the reel in his palm, feeling its familiar weight. This river had been his refuge, a place where the roar of the world faded into the background, replaced by nature's calming symphony. The thought of leaving it behind squeezed at his chest, a physical ache for the peace he wasn't sure he could find beyond these banks. It was here, amongst the whispering reeds and the watchful eyes of perched kingfishers, that he'd found solace when the case files piled up and the leads turned to dust.

With the gear packed away, Krosby stood and shouldered his bag. His gaze swept across the water, over to the opposite bank where shadows played among the trees. He knew every twist and turn of the river, each spot where the fish liked to hide, and every nook that offered silent companionship when the ghosts of unsolved mysteries haunted him.

Taking a deep breath, he let the scent of the river fill his senses one last time. Then Krosby turned away slowly, each step heavy with reluctance. His feet came to a halt, and he looked back over his shoulder. The river flowed on, not caring about his leaving, yet it felt as if it whispered a farewell through the rustling leaves. He stood there, a figure carved against the setting sun, the fading light casting long shadows that stretched out like fingers trying to pull him back.

"Goodbye," he murmured, the word barely more than a breath lost in the wind.

And he walked back to his car knowing this was just the beginning.

Chapter Twenty-Nine

Kevin

Six Months Later

Kevin sat on the rough wooden planks of the perpetually unfinished tree house, his legs dangling over the edge as he gazed out at the sun-dappled forest. Beside him, Danny was busy hammering away, his brow furrowed in concentration as he worked to secure another board. The sound of the hammer striking wood echoed through the stillness of the summer afternoon.

"Do you think Mike will ever come out here?" Danny asked, pausing in his work to wipe the sweat from his forehead. "Once we get this thing finished, I mean."

Kevin shrugged, his eyes never leaving the horizon. "I don't know," he said, his voice flat and noncommittal. "Maybe."

But inside, Kevin's mind was churning with thoughts and emotions that he couldn't quite put into words. It had been almost a year since Mike had been taken, since that awful day when their lives had been forever changed. And while Mike had been rescued, had been brought back to them in body, Kevin couldn't shake the feeling that a part of his brother was still lost, still trapped in that dark place where the monster had held him.

He remembered the Mike of before, the boy who had been full of energy and life, always ready with a joke or a prank and, if he was being honest, sometimes a whiny brat. But that Mike was gone now, replaced by a skittish, withdrawn shell of a boy who flinched at loud noises and shied away from human contact.

Kevin would have given anything to have the old Mike back, to hear his laughter ringing out through the woods as they explored and adventured together. He would have gladly traded a thousand peaceful moments for just one of the little brat's infamous pranks, for the mischievous gleam in his eye that had always spelled trouble.

But that was a wish that could never be granted, a dream that had died in the darkness of a monster's lair. The Mike that had come back to them was a different person, a stranger wearing his brother's face. And while Kevin loved him just the same, while he would have moved heaven and earth to protect him, he couldn't help but mourn the loss of the boy he had once known.

"I miss him," Kevin said softly, his voice barely audible over the sound of the hammer. "The old Mike, I mean. The one who used to drive us crazy with his stupid jokes and his crazy schemes."

Danny nodded, his eyes sad and understanding. "I know," he said, setting down the hammer and scooting closer to his friend. "I miss him too. But he's still Mike, you know? He's still your brother, even if he's a little different now."

Kevin knew that Danny was right, knew that there was no changing the past. But it was hard, harder than he had ever imagined possible. Every time he looked at Mike, he saw the scars, both physical and emotional, that the monster had left behind. And he couldn't help but wonder if those scars would ever truly heal, if the old Mike would ever find his way back to them.

"I just wish I could fix it," Kevin said, his voice cracking with the weight of his emotions. "I wish I could make it all go away, make everything back to the way it was before. I know my parents want the same thing. They're trying so hard and everything's, just wrong."

Danny put a hand on his friend's shoulder. "I know," he said softly. "But we can't change what happened. All we can do is keep on living. I mean look at Cecil, he didn't get a chance to keep on living. So we've got to do it for him. Every one of us."

Kevin nodded, blinking back the tears that threatened to fall. He knew that Danny was right, and so, with a deep breath and a force of will, Kevin pushed aside his grief and his longing for the past. He turned to Danny, a small smile playing at the corners of his mouth. "Come on," he said, picking up a hammer of his own. "Let's get this thing finished. Mike's going to need a place to hang out, once he's ready."

Danny grinned, his eyes sparkling with renewed enthusiasm. "Damn right he is," he said, turning back to his work with a newfound sense of purpose.

And as the sound of hammers once again filled the summer air,

Kevin felt a flicker of hope, a sense that perhaps, in time, the wounds of the past would heal.

As Kevin hammered away at the tree house, his thoughts drifted to Cecil. It had been a shock to everyone in town when they learned of Cecil's fate, of the quiet bravery that had driven him to confront the monster who had taken Mike. No one knew how he did it, whether by blind luck or careful searching, but he'd given his life, and that was all that mattered.

He thought of the cemetery where Cecil now lay. Someone else was tending to the graves now, keeping the grass trimmed and the headstones clean. It seemed strange to think of anyone else in that role, anyone but the solitary figure who had been such a constant presence in the town's life.

***

The mayor, and he guessed the town, had put up a memorial in Cecil's honor in the town square, a simple plaque on a bench that spoke of his bravery and his sacrifice. It was a nice gesture, Kevin thought, a way of acknowledging the debt that they all owed to the old man. But at the same time, it annoyed him, made him feel a flicker of anger and resentment. Because where had that appreciation been when Cecil was alive? Where had the kind words and the gestures of friendship been when the old man was still walking among them?

Kevin couldn't help but wonder if things might have been different if the town had shown Cecil a little more kindness, a little more understanding. Maybe he would still be alive, still be there to tend to the graves and keep watch over the town's lost and lonely souls.

But then, a darker thought crept into Kevin's mind, a terrible realization that made his stomach churn and his heart ache. If Cecil hadn't been there, hadn't been willing to confront the monster, what would have happened to Mike? Would they have ever found him, ever brought him home safe and sound? Or would he have been lost forever?

The thought made Kevin feel sick, made him want to scream and cry and rage against the unfairness of it all. Because what kind of world was it where a child's life depended on the sacrifice of a lonely old man? What kind of universe allowed such cruelty, such senseless waste of life? Cecil's kindness had touched him when Mike went missing, and Kevin knew his life was changed for knowing the man.

All of these thoughts squirmed inside him, and he longed for a simpler time, for the days when his biggest worries had been homework and chores and the occasional prank gone wrong. He wanted to be a normal teenager again, to think about things like girls and cars and the latest hit songs on the radio. But that innocence was gone now.

Just then, a loud yelp pierced through Kevin's somber thoughts. He whirled around to see Danny hopping on one foot, his face scrunched up in a comical expression of pain and surprise.

"Damn it!" Danny exclaimed, rubbing his foot. "I dropped the hammer on my toe!"

Despite the heaviness in his heart, Kevin couldn't help but chuckle at the sight of his friend's exaggerated antics. It was such a Danny thing to do.

"Don't laugh, asshole," Danny said, picking up a small rock and chucking it at Kevin.

"Hey! Don't start something you can't finish."

Danny just smirked and picked up another rock and hurled it at him.

"That's it!" Kevin called, scrabbling down from the tree for ammo, and the pair launched into a full-out rock battle. No wonder the tree house wasn't finished yet. But Kevin didn't care. For a moment, he felt a flicker of hope, a sense that maybe, just maybe, things would get better with time. Because if Danny could still find a way to make him laugh, to bring a smile to his face even in the middle of such a difficult time, then perhaps things would get better.

Chapter Thirty

Unknown

Six Months Later

The dusty ribbon of highway stretched before him, unwinding under the relentless Texas sun like an invitation to oblivion. He walked with a purposeful gait, his shadow long on the cracked asphalt, a worn-out hat casting a veil over his sharp features. A backpack, weathered and nondescript, hugged his shoulders, its contents as unremarkable as the man who bore it. The landscape rolled by—a vast expanse of ochres and tans, dotted with the occasional stubborn cactus or tumbleweed that skittered across his path. Each step took him further from his past, a litany of whispered sins left to be carried away by the dry wind.

Freedom, raw and intoxicating, surged within him. It was not the freedom of innocence but that of escape, the exhilarating anonymity granted by wide-open spaces. The horizon promised no judgments, no prying eyes—only the chance to dissolve into a new identity, to become a ghost in the machine of the world.

A cloud of dust heralded the approach of an old pickup truck, its bed filled with the quiet chatter of migrants. They were men and women of the earth, their hands hardened by toil and faces etched with the hope of better tomorrows. He stuck out his thumb, the universal signal of the road, and the vehicle slowed to a merciful stop beside him.

"Headed to the Henderson farm," called out the driver, a man whose skin bore the patina of long days under the sun.

"Perfect," he replied with a grin that didn't quite reach his cool-blue eyes, which remained hidden beneath the brim of his hat. "Name's Joe," he lied smoothly as he hoisted himself into the back with the others. His voice was amiable, the timbre of a man grateful for company, any company.

"Welcome, Joe," a woman said, her accent thick and her smile genuine. She made room for him, her own bag nestled between her feet like a trusty companion.

"Gracias," he said, injecting warmth into the word, though his heart knew nothing of gratitude. His gaze swept over his fellow travelers, a practiced eye noting details—a tattoo peeking from a sleeve, a locket around a neck, hands that spoke of labor in their every crease and callus. He mirrored their body language, adopting the slouch of the weary, the restless fidgets of the hopeful.

The truck rattled along, the hum of conversation ebbing and flowing around him. He contributed where expected, a laugh here, a nod there, all while his mind wandered to the future that lay ahead. The fields of Henderson farm would be a means to an end, another chapter in the book of "Joe," a tale spun from thin air and darker truths.

As the landscape shifted subtly, the sparse beauty of the desert giving way to the greener hues of farmland, he settled into his role. The killer within cloaked himself in the garb of the migrant, invisible and insidious, ready to reap a different kind of harvest.

The sun bore down on the killer like an unspoken challenge as he bent his back among rows of vibrant crops. His hands, though more accustomed to a different kind of labor, moved with practiced ease—plucking, sorting, depositing produce into containers. He was one with the rhythm of the fields, his motions synchronized with the workers around him.

"Joe," called out a stout man beside him, offering a water bottle. "Take a break, amigo."

"Thanks, Miguel," he replied, his voice rough from disuse in conversation that didn't involve preying or pleading. He took the bottle, their fingers brushing—a touch of humanity, perhaps, but he only felt the pulse of survival beneath skin worn by the sun.

As they rested briefly under the unforgiving Texas sky, camaraderie formed in light conversation, teasing, and the communal passing of food. They were a mosaic of stories and struggles, and he, a chameleon amongst them, drank deeply from the reservoir of their unwitting trust. Laughter erupted from a joke told in a blend of broken English and fluent Spanish; he echoed it with a smile that never reached his eyes.

"Hard work, huh?" said Miguel, slapping him on the back.

"Nothing I can't handle," he responded, the lie as smooth as the sweat that coated his brow.

Later, as the day waned and shadows began to stretch across the earth like creeping doubt, he made his way into town. The local barber's pole spun lazily in the afternoon heat, a beacon for transformation. He stepped inside, the bell above the door tinkling an announcement of his presence.

"Need a clean-up?" asked the barber, a grizzled man whose own hair betrayed years of standing behind that chair.

"Something short. Less trouble," he said, settling into the chair and draping the cape over himself like armor.

The snip of scissors became a meditative sound as locks of hair fell away, revealing a newer, starker version of "Joe." With each slice, he shed not just strands of his past but also the remnants of suspicion. As the barber worked, he gazed at his reflection, studying the contours of a face now sculpted by necessity. His eyes, however, remained the same—pools of dark intent that he masked with a grateful nod to the man who unknowingly abetted his disguise.

"Looks good, fresh, and honest," the barber declared, brushing off the stray hairs with a thick hand.

"Much better," he agreed, his voice steady while his mind whispered a litany of deceit. The mirror held the image of another soul joining the ranks of hardworking laborers, the illusion complete.

"Good luck out there," said the barber as he paid and stepped outside, the door closing softly behind him.

"Thanks. I'll need it," he murmured to no one, his face now the very picture of anonymity. Yet, beneath the façade of a simple migrant worker, the killer within bided his time, a predator in plain sight.

The thrift store door clanged with the chime of anonymity as *Joe* stepped inside, his eyes scanning the racks for the attire that would cement his new identity. The air was thick with the scent of mothballs and faded dreams, the perfect olfactory backdrop for a man looking to disappear. He'd let himself go in Everrett. A drunk hick, like the rest of him. He wouldn't be making that mistake again.

With methodical precision, he fingered through the clothes, each piece a potential camouflage. He needed shirts weathered by the sun but not threadbare, pants stained with toil but intact. His hands, callused from days in the field, betrayed his feigned familiarity with such labor, yet they selected garments with an innate understanding of the workers he now mirrored.

A plaid shirt with sleeves frayed just enough whispered of long days under the relentless Texas sun. Jeans, once a deep blue but now a soft sky hue, spoke of countless washes after backbreaking work. A belt, its leather cracked like the earth he tilled—each item was chosen not only for its appearance but for the story it told.

At the counter, he laid out his selections, offering a polite nod to the cashier whose interest in him didn't extend beyond the crumpled bills he handed over. She bagged the items, oblivious to the fact that she was dressing a wolf in worn denim.

"Stay cool out there," she said casually, the bell above the door tolling his departure.

"Will do," *Joe* replied, the midday heat embracing him as he walked away, his silhouette melting into the landscape of laborers and lost chances.

Back at the shack that passed for the room part of "room and board," *Joe* found his gaze drawn to a flickering television in the corner of the communal area. On the screen, a face he recognized materialized, her expression solemn as she discussed the latest on the missing boy. Her words were a siren's call to the monster within him.

"Complete incompetence," Jill Greco lamented, her disappointment cutting through the crackle of the poor signal. "To think he could still be out there, somewhere. . . . It's terrifying."

As her image flickered, the killer felt a stab of anger, hot and raw. Her condemnation felt like a personal affront, a challenge to his perceived failure. No, he hadn't failed; he had simply been . . . interrupted. And here she was, casting aspersions, unraveling the threads of control he had woven so meticulously around himself.

His jaw clenched involuntarily; the muscles tight as he fought to maintain the façade of indifference. Around him, the others that shared the little shack were engrossed in their own conversations, paying no mind to the news or the quiet fury of the man among them. To them, he was just another face, another pair of hands toiling for meager wages, while inside him, a tempest of rage and vulnerability threatened to breach the levee of his calm exterior.

"God help us if he strikes again," Jill's voice broke through, a final nail driving into his conscience.

"God help you indeed," *Joe* whispered to himself, the TV's glow reflecting in his eyes—a dark mirror of the storm within.

From the corner of his eye, he watched the distant sway of the trees of a park built for the families who worked the land. He could feel it again—the itch, that insatiable hunger that clawed at his insides like a caged beast pining for release. It wasn't just an urge; it was an imperative, a demand from the darkest recesses of his mind. He clenched his fists until his knuckles turned white, the grime from the fields ingraining itself into the lines of his skin.

"Keep it together," he muttered to ward off the demons. But they lurked there still, nestled deep within, whispering sweet promises of power and dominance. The fear of capture buzzed in his head like a mosquito he couldn't swat away, a constant reminder that his freedom hung by a thread—one wrong move away from unraveling.

Joe stepped outside to get a better look but forced himself to focus on the mundane—the clatter of a soda can rolling across the pavement, the hum of a distant tractor, the rhythmic thwack of a ball hitting concrete. He couldn't be too obvious. But then he saw him. A boy, no more than ten, was dribbling a basketball on the court, alone. His laughter floated over, piercing *Joe* like a needle through fabric, pulling the thread of his restraint tighter, threatening to snap it.

The boy's innocence was a beacon of temptation, shining oblivious to the shadows that hungered just beyond its reach. As the child maneuvered the ball with youthful exuberance, *Joe* felt the familiar surge of adrenaline, the primal satisfaction of knowing he could snuff out that light in an instant.

"Look away," he urged himself, but his gaze remained locked on the boy, his muscles tensing with the effort to resist the gravity of his own desires. Every bounce of the ball echoed in *Joe's* chest, a countdown to the moment when the predator might break free and pounce. But he couldn't just take him the way he'd done the last one. This time, he'd do it right.

Joe swallowed the bile rising in his throat, tasting the bitter tang of his own self-loathing. For a fleeting second, he saw himself through the boy's eyes—a monster lurking in plain sight. He thought of that bitch on the TV, her words still searing in his memory, branding him as both a failure and a threat.

"God help you indeed," he repeated, the irony not lost on him. It was neither divine intervention nor luck that had kept him hidden in the open. It was his willpower alone fraying but holding.

Memories flickered through his mind like a broken film reel—faces contorted in terror, the significance of his actions carved into their final expressions. He understood what he was, what he would always be.

Joe drew in a deep, steadying breath, his eyes never wavering from the boy who now sat down in the grass, pulling his knees close to his chest as he gazed up at the sky. Was he watching the buzzards circling? *Joe* wondered, a twisted curiosity mingling with his darker thoughts.

"Can't risk it," he whispered to himself, the statement a double-edged sword that cut through both his desire to act and his instinct to preserve the life on the run he'd painstakingly crafted. The tension coiled within him, a spring wound too tight, ready to snap.

He took a half-step forward, his shadow stretching out toward the boy, a silent, spectral hand reaching out in longing. Then, as suddenly as the impulse came, he retracted it, the battle lines drawn once more within his fractured soul.

Joe turned away abruptly, distancing himself from the sight, the temptation too vivid, the risk too great. He shoved his hands into the pockets of his worn jeans, feeling the crumpled bills he'd earned that day, whistling like a—you've guessed it—*average Joe.*

"Another day," he whispered, a promise or a warning, he wasn't sure which. Today, he had to walk away, leaving the park and its lone occupant behind oblivious to the dangerous interest he'd sparked.

For now, he retreated into the shadows of the bunkhouse, the darkness a comforting embrace. Tomorrow was another day. Another opportunity for the monster to come out.

About the Author

Keith Russell is a husband and father living with his family in Williamsburg, VA. He has fond memories of growing up in rural Tennessee in the '70s and '80s. For many years, Keith has wanted to write a crime thriller that tells a story just a little different than most. *A Stranger in the Shadows* was written with a unique plot to keep readers on edge.